A WICKED REPUTATION

the Once Wicked series

A WICKED REPUTATION

the Once Wicked series

LIANA LEFEY

Entangled Publishing, LLC
2614 South Timberline Road
Suite 105, PMB 159
Fort Collins, CO 80525
rights@entangledpublishing.com

Amara is an imprint of Entangled Publishing, LLC.

Edited by Erin Molta
Cover design by EDH Graphics
Cover photography from Period Images, Deposit Photos, and 123rf

Manufactured in the United States of America

First Edition February 2019

For my wonderful husband, whose faith and patience are a testament to true love.

Chapter One

My life is over. Lady Diana's hand trembled as she handed the paper back to her furious uncle, Lord Bolingbroke. Her fiancé had disappeared last week and, according to this morning's *Gazette*, had yesterday returned from Gretna Green a married man. Lucille, her best friend—*former best*, she corrected herself—was now Lady Grenville.

Aunt Jane, her normally timid voice shrill, shattered the stifling silence. "I warned you what would happen if you lifted your skirts before his ring was on your finger!"

Diana's temper flared. "And I told you it's a lie! I never allowed—"

"Oh, stop it, girl!" snapped her aunt. "Everyone *thinks* you did, and that's what matters. That, and the fact that Grenville is now lost to us forever."

"I beg to differ," Diana shot back, folding her arms across her chest so they wouldn't see her shaking hands. "The facts matter a great deal. Aunt Jane, you've been with me to every ball, every party. When has there ever been an opportunity for me to behave in such a manner? You know it's not true! You can tell all those gossiping old—"

"Not every party," interjected her uncle. "Your aunt did not attend the Hancocks' party with you a fortnight ago. *I* did, and you were out of my sight for quite some time."

The insinuation elicited a pain in Diana's heart such as she'd not felt in years. She was accustomed to her uncle's hard ways, but this was too much. In spite of the rage and fear coursing through her, she kept her voice calm. "If you will remember, Uncle, you went to play cards in the library with the other gentlemen and I was not permitted to accompany you. But I remained in the ballroom the entire time, as you instructed. I did not even visit the powder—"

"It matters not where it happened," he said, cutting her off with a look of cool disdain. "Thanks to your imprudence, you've been painted in an ill light, and us along with you."

Her gasp was a sound halfway between laughter and horror. "*What* imprudence? I beg you tell me so I may know what lie dares threaten my good name."

"It is no lie," he replied, narrowing his eyes. "Grenville told everyone you invited him to take liberties with you, and I know it to be true. Your aunt told me you let him kiss you."

She let out an incredulous laugh. "I allowed him a chaste kiss the day I accepted his proposal. Nothing more! One simple kiss with one's fiancé surely cannot be equated with 'liberties'."

But his expression remained unmoving. "He intimated it was far more than 'one simple kiss,' which you should never have permitted in the first place. That…among other things."

Heat crept into Diana's cheeks, and her heart began to pound anew. "It was once, Uncle, and *only* once. He'd only just asked for my hand, and you specifically ordered me not to discourage his affection for fear of endangering the match with—how did you put it? Ah, yes: 'female frigidity'."

Bolingbroke's beefy face darkened to an ugly purple. "Insolent harlot! You dare cast my own words back at me?"

"I am no harlot!" Diana shouted, past caring. "And *you* were the one to speak them. Do you deny them now?" She braced herself as he took a step toward her.

Aunt Jane stepped in, her cheeks as pale as parchment, and laid a restraining hand on his sleeve. "Arthur, please—"

"Enough!" shouted Bolingbroke, shaking himself loose with a growl. "I will not tolerate defiance in my household. Not from her, and certainly not from you," he rasped, shoving a fat finger in his wife's face and causing her to flinch. "There is more to this than one kiss. Grenville said he'd heard tales concerning her lack of propriety on other occasions from several different men."

Shock coursed through Diana, swiftly followed by anger. "What men? Who has spoken such lies?"

But her uncle ignored her outraged inquiry. "Being a gentleman, he had refused to believe them—until he'd witnessed it himself. It is an embarrassment not to be borne!"

"But she claims to be innocent," pleaded Aunt Jane in a small voice. "Surely there must be some way to prove—"

His eyes widened until the whites showed all around his small brown irises, and Diana shook her head slightly, willing her aunt to be silent.

Bolingbroke's voice was as cold as a cheerless winter's dawn. "You dare persist in pleading this creature's case when the stain of her scandal threatens to taint us all? Think of your own children, woman. People will talk of this for years to come. No matter what 'proof' is offered, there will always be the question. Even *you* confessed doubts as to her virtue."

It was all Diana could do to conceal how deeply this revelation wounded her.

"But she is our niece, Arthur. We cannot—"

"She's none of *my* blood!" he snarled, his mouth thinning to a bitter line.

Dread filled Diana, along with icy calm. She knew what was coming. Aunt Jane had been kind after her parents' deaths and had loved her as best she could, but Bolingbroke had never warmed toward his wife's orphaned niece. He'd tolerated her, but after assuming the title of viscount last year he'd become insufferable, always reminding her she lived as befitted a lady only because of his charity and sufferance.

Puffing out his chest, he continued, relentless. "I have a responsibility to this family, to my own good name, and I refuse to shirk it. You are to leave this house at once."

"Arthur!" gasped Aunt Jane. "You cannot cast her out into the street! Think of—"

"Silence!" he thundered, sending flecks of spittle flying. "I will *not* be prevailed upon to house a wanton trull under my own roof!"

Rejecting the sudden impulse to crumple to the floor, Diana squared her shoulders and stood her tallest. She'd rather die than beg this man for mercy, if such a thing even existed in his cold, empty heart. "I vow before God I'm innocent of any immorality," she said with quiet dignity. "You accuse me wrongly and will only add to the undeserved slurs against me by refusing to deny them."

Beneath her withering gaze, he shrank a little. But it wasn't enough. "I have little choice but to renounce you—for the sake of my *own* daughters," he countered, but his tone was less strident than before. It weakened further as she continued to stare him down. "I do it for my family!"

Unbidden, a strangled chuckle rose up in Diana's throat. "I realize you feel no personal obligation where I'm concerned, Uncle," she said, placing deliberate emphasis on the familial title, "but despite your fervent wishes otherwise, I *am* a member of your family."

Vicious glee kindled in his eyes. "Not anymore."

Again, Aunt Jane risked censure to do what Diana couldn't. "Arthur, I beg you to be sensible about this. If she *is* innocent…" she trailed off, and for a moment Diana thought she'd fall silent rather than face his anger. But her aunt had more courage than she gave her credit for. "If that is not reason enough, think how others will view us. Remember that you are being considered for the Order of the Garter." This time when she rested a hand on his arm, Bolingbroke let it stay. "As such, it would be far better to be merciful and be looked upon as overly kind rather than cruel and unfeeling."

The silence stretched taut between them. Then: "Three days," he said at last. "I'll give her three days to settle herself elsewhere. Quietly." He turned to again address her. "You may take what came with you when you go, as well as your clothing. I want nothing of you to remain in this house."

"I assume that includes my dowry?" Diana heard herself ask mildly. It was almost as if someone else were forming the words with her lips. Satisfaction seeped into her, warming her as his face registered first surprise and then outrage. *That's right, you greedy bastard! I've not forgotten.* "My father's will made provision for seven thousand pounds for my dowry. You've held this in trust on my behalf. I am still unwed. As stipulated by the will, the moment you cease to be my guardian, it belongs to me."

The plum flush returned to his cheeks with alarming swiftness. "Ungrateful little bitch! I have put a roof over your head and food in your mouth for ten damned years!"

But his rage was no match for hers. Diana no longer felt any fear, for she had nothing to lose. What good were clothes and a few pieces of furniture when one had nowhere to put them and no means to feed oneself? "Perhaps I should seek an audience with the king? I'm certain His Majesty would see the daughter of his dear friend, the late Duke of Avondale," she reminded him. "Perhaps he would award you a fair portion to cover the expense of feeding and clothing a child for ten years—taking into account, of course, that the interest from my dower fund has been accumulating in your coffers for the entire duration—but I'm certain he would not ask me to forfeit the entire amount."

His lips went white, slowly followed by the rest of his face. Diana knew his accounts would not withstand close scrutiny by the Crown. Even so, the man quickly recovered his bluster. "Do you truly believe His Majesty would tolerate someone like you in his presence? You can be assured he will have heard of your downfall."

"Naturally, I shall request that the court physician examine me and attest to my innocence," she said lightly. "And once my name has been cleared of the slander that has besmirched it, I shall protest your undeservedly harsh treatment of me and beg His Majesty to make me a ward of the Crown."

"You would not dare!" he spluttered.

She smiled her sweetest smile. "In addition to reclaiming my *entire* dowry, the reinstatement of my good name would be well worth any embarrassment I might have to endure. You, on the other hand..."

"This is extortion!" he shouted. "I should have you—"

"*Arthur!*" hissed Aunt Jane, tugging on his arm hard enough to jerk his attention away. Braving his wrath, she leaned close, and Diana heard her whisper urgently: "If she petitions the Crown, His Majesty will hear her—her rank guarantees it. And she will have the right of it. You yourself said Avondale's will ensured her dowry was well protected. And what if she should somehow manage to prove herself innocent? It would look very bad on you." Her voice lowered further. "You would have had to part with the money when she married."

Diana watched him struggle, his greed and loathing for her battling against prudence. His jaw worked, and the vein at his temple bulged as he tried to think of a way to rob her of her inheritance with impunity. She knew he'd never rescind his eviction—not that she'd stay now, even if he got down on his knees and begged her. His pride had suffered too much injury by her refusal to succumb to his bullying. "Aunt Jane is right," she said quietly. "If you give me what is mine, I'll have no legitimate grounds to petition the Crown. Or indeed to ever disturb you again," she added for good measure.

He leveled his index finger at her, his fierce gaze belied by its trembling, his voice low and savage. "Three thousand, and not a penny more."

It was more than she'd hoped for five minutes ago. She nodded acceptance, sending a silent prayer of thanks to God that he hadn't called her bluff. In truth, she had no idea how to gain an audience with the king. Her father's name might have held sway at court once upon a time, but ten long years had passed since his death.

"And another thing," her uncle added, raking her with mean eyes. "After you leave, you are to have no communication with anyone in this household ever again. Is that understood? No visits and no letters. This family cannot risk further association with such as you."

Though it pained her, she nodded again. Little Bellatrisse and Rowena were away visiting their grandmother and would not be back for a week. *I won't even be allowed to say goodbye, even in a letter...* They were the closest things to sisters she'd ever had, and the thought of never seeing them again made her eyes smart. Steeling herself, she pushed her pain aside and focused on her outrage at his treatment of her.

"Well?" he demanded after a moment. "Will you not even thank me? I should think you'd be grateful for my generosity. A less kind man would have turned you out with nothing, regardless of your threats. I'd be well within my rights."

Diana bit her tongue so hard she tasted blood. *How dare he expect my gratitude for casting me out with only a portion of that which is mine to begin with?* Still, she could little afford to provoke him further. Lowering her eyes, she forced the bile back down enough to say in what she hoped sounded like a meek tone, "Thank you."

It seemed to mollify him somewhat. "That's better." He turned from her to face his wife. "A man ought to be more respected in his own household. I blame *you* for how this one turned out, Jane."

Aghast, Diana tore her gaze from the floor to stare at her white-faced aunt.

Bolingbroke continued to berate his wife. "Had you done a better job of teaching her the importance of propriety, this would not have happened. I shall expect you to look upon this incident as a lesson to be applied to our own daughters whereas it pertains to instilling a sense of proper decorum." He turned back to an infuriated Diana. "You've been bold here today, girl, but the world out there will teach you your place," he said, jerking a meaty thumb toward the window. "I suggest you make good use of the time I've granted you, for it won't be extended by so much as a minute."

Oh, how I hate him! How could he blame either of them for something that hadn't even happened? She wanted to rail at him, to claw at his eyes and tear the cruel smirk from his face. Instead, she stood in sullen silence, concentrating on the interminable ticking of the mantel clock, waiting to be dismissed.

"You may go," he finally grumbled.

Turning on her heel, Diana stalked out and mounted the stairs on trembling legs. Upon entering her room, she closed the door and leaned against it, willing herself not to cry.

There wasn't time to grieve. *Three days. I have just three days to find a place to live and a means of supporting myself.*

The money would be enough to rent rooms in a halfway decent part of Town and feed herself—if she were frugal—for a few years. *And what good will that do? Cast out, my reputation in shreds, who will receive me? What man will consider marrying me? Without connections, how am I to make my way in the world?*

Moving to the country was an alternative. The money would certainly last a lot longer there, but not indefinitely. *And then what?*

The question loomed before her like a great black cloud, obscuring all else. She could write and calculate sums, but neither of those skills would earn enough to support herself. No self-respecting mother would consider her for a governess once the tale of her "ruination" came to light. And none of the other feminine arts she'd learned at her aunt's knee would afford her a living beyond that of the meanest poverty.

Three days. What could she do in three days except pack her things and sink into despair? *I might as well leave now.* She cast about, looking at the familiar room and wishing it was anywhere but in Bolingbroke's house. Her newest ball gown hung on the wardrobe door, where her maid had left it to let out the wrinkles. She ran reverent fingers over the soft, petal-pink damask, noting how the diaphanous layer of fine gold silk covering the skirt panels made it look like a rose-tinted sunrise.

She was to have worn it to the Whitfield ball tonight.

Not anymore.

Her aunt would have no choice but to sequester herself until the "harlot" had been ejected from their house, thereby restoring her to her proper place amongst the moral majority.

Why not go without her?

The rebellious thought was so ridiculous she almost laughed. But at the same time it was so utterly appealing that she was tempted. Sorely tempted. She'd give just about anything to be out of this room, away from this place. She eyed the gown again.

Why not? The invitation still stood, after all. No one knew her aunt and uncle were about to disown her. She'd wait until everyone had gone to bed, which ought to be soon, considering her aunt had already complained of a headache. Her uncle would likely closet himself in his library, nursing his beloved brandy, until the wee hours. Her hair was already done. All she had to do was put on that gown and get out unnoticed. The servants' stair would work. She could hire a carriage to take her to the ball, which would not end until dawn.

It would be her last chance—her *only* chance—to ensnare a husband. No doubt that, like her uncle, many had read the papers and were even now drawing their conclusions, but she'd not yet been ostracized. There might still be a way out of this.

If I can somehow arrange to become truly compromised by a gentleman...

But hope's flame guttered after only the briefest flare. It would never work. No man would offer her marriage under the current circumstances, not even after having taken her maidenhead. Despite her innocence, he'd deny it to save himself from the scandal of marrying a woman of questionable virtue, and then she'd truly be branded a harlot. A strumpet. A—

Courtesan.

A prickly, unpleasant sensation crept across Diana's scalp and slowly marched down her back. Now *there* was an option that would provide a comfortable life, for all that it would be a life of sin. That she'd even think of taking such a course showed the depths to which she'd already sunk.

Yet some courtesans become mistresses, and some

mistresses eventually become wives. What *if* she agreed to become a gentleman's lover tonight? And what if he then fell in love with her? As for returning the tender sentiment, she had no intention of it. Her heart wouldn't be part of the bargain. Love was unreliable. People always broke your heart. Like her parents when they'd died. Like her aunt when she'd turned her back on her own kin. Like the fiancé who'd claimed to love her, only to betray her with her supposed-best friend.

Better to keep one's heart to oneself than let it be torn apart.

She looked at the rose gown again. It was an enormous risk. If her first mark did not fall hopelessly in love with her and marry her, she would indeed have to become a courtesan in truth.

Can I bring myself to do such a thing?

A gleam of gold and a spark of reflected light caught her eye as she turned away. Her mother's jewels lay on the vanity, ready for her to wear tonight. Bolingbroke might be willing to let her take furniture and clothing, but her jewels might be another matter entirely. Those, he could say, belonged to her mother's sister—his wife.

She shook her head to clear it. *Focus on the task at hand!* If Bolingbroke decided to take them, there would be nothing she could do about it. *Unless I wear them out tonight and never return.* If this worked, she would send for her other things and hope he failed to remember them. She picked up her mother's diamond necklace, feeling the cool weight of it in her palm.

Mama. Had she lived, none of this would have happened. She would've been presented two years ago and already be safely married.

As Diana clutched the jewels, a strange peace came over her, along with renewed resolve. Bolingbroke couldn't take them before she wore them one last time, at least. When she was done, provided all went according to the half-formed and completely mad plan taking shape in her mind, London's gossips would be telling another story entirely, one that would take the malicious lies that had ruined her and turn them on the very people who'd betrayed her.

Laying the necklace back down, she went and took the pink gown from the wardrobe and laid it across her bed. Next, she rummaged in her sewing basket and took out her embroidery scissors. With its lace-embellished bosom and a fichu, the pink gown was a very modest affair. Without those affects, however...

Her hands paused over the delicate lace, and she marked how they shook. *Can I really do this? Can I deliberately set my feet on such an unsavory path?* So much could go wrong. But the prospect of a slow decline into abject poverty loomed ahead if she didn't take this final opportunity. Never again would she be received on her own by Polite Society.

Taking a deep breath, she began to carefully take out the tiny stitches securing the lace to the neckline.

Anything was preferable to starvation.

Chapter Two

Lucas tossed his cards on the table and excused himself. Far more interesting than the game was the hushed confrontation going on between Lords Brampton and Harrow on the other side of the room. Rising, he went to the hearth under the pretense of fetching a rush to light his pipe. The men stood nearly nose to nose, anger clear in every taut line of their bodies. But where Brampton was red-faced and clearly enraged, Harrow appeared utterly unmoved by emotion.

"If that is your desire, then so be it," he heard Harrow say calmly. "Dawn?"

"Dawn," sneered the other man. "Better tell that pretty little whore of yours to prepare to find herself a new patron," he threw in as Harrow turned away. "Perhaps I'll take her myself and show her what it feels like to have a *real* man between her legs."

Harrow's back stiffened, and he turned back around, a hard, dangerous look in his dark eyes. "That is the second time you've referred to Lady Diana in a less than courteous manner. If you wish to live tomorrow, I would advise you to curb your tongue."

The other man let out an ugly laugh. "*Lady* Diana," he snorted. "I don't know many *ladies* willing to t—"

"I promised that *lady* I'd merely nick you," Harrow cut in so softly Lucas almost didn't hear him. "She was kind enough to ask me to spare your life for the sake of your wife and children. *Don't* make me disappoint her."

All the color drained from Brampton's face.

Harrow's mouth twitched up at one corner. "I'll see you at dawn."

All eyes followed as Harrow turned his back on the man and left the room. The silence was tangible, everyone waiting to see his opponent's reaction, but Brampton merely slumped down into a chair and sullenly called for more wine. Conversations resumed around the room, though at a more subdued level than before.

Lucas joined his friend, Westing, who'd also abandoned the card table. "What was that about?" he asked, keeping his voice low.

Westing chuckled. "By George, man. I thought everyone knew."

"I've been away," Lucas reminded him. "Or have you forgotten?"

A twinkle appeared in the other man's eye. "The circumstances of your departure don't encourage forgetfulness, I'm afraid. Lord Grafton is still quite wroth with you."

"His anger has cooled enough to make him sensible. Now, tell me," Lucas prompted, knowing his friend could no more resist the compulsion to spill the tea than he could the urge to gamble.

A grim smirk twisted Westing's mouth as he capitulated.

"Harrow is, as you've just observed, particularly fond of his mistress. Let a man speak ill of her, and Harrow will soon give him cause to regret it. He's already fought and won several duels on her account."

"Looks like he has another appointment in the morning," Lucas muttered. "She must possess incredible skill to elicit such devotion."

"Legendary," sighed Westing. "Or so I've been given to understand."

Lucas couldn't help laughing at his wistful tone. "If you're keen on having her, why not make her patron an offer? I've done it on occasion. As long as you have his blessing, her agreement, and make it profitable for them both..." He shrugged.

The look on Westing's face changed from one of regret to one of wariness. "That would be the height of foolishness, however tempting the prize. The man is exceedingly jealous of her favor. It's all but a certainty Lady Diana Haversham will become the next Lady Harrow the instant his current wife is in the ground."

"A man should never marry his mistress," Lucas drawled. "Or is he fool enough to have fallen in love with her?" *That* was an error he'd vowed never to make—with *any* woman.

"One can only surmise so," said Westing. "Heaven knows there is no romance between him and his wife. They live at separate residences. It's common knowledge she's not shared his bed since giving him his heir. Told everyone she'd fulfilled her obligation and that there would be 'no more nonsense'. That was several years ago."

"Not a love match, I gather?"

"Cradle arrangement, or so I heard," confirmed Westing, laughing a little. "When news of her husband's philandering reached her, it's rumored she told her friends she was quite pleased he'd finally taken a mistress upon whom to vent his bothersome lust."

Lucas snorted. "I imagine she might feel differently if she knew he was planning to eventually marry the wench."

A devilish grin spread across the other man's face. "In truth, the current Lady Harrow and the prospective one are quite friendly with each other. They take tea together every other Tuesday and have been seen together about Town on several occasions. It's one of London's biggest scandals."

Silence fell for several heartbeats before Lucas huffed out the breath he'd been holding and laughed. "You nearly had me, Westie. For a moment I thought you were serious." But the laughter died on his lips as Westing stared back at him soberly. "Good Lord, man. Surely you're joking?"

"Upon my honor, I swear it's the truth," said the other man. His voice lowered to a whisper. "The ladies' private tête-à-têtes have inspired some to speculate that the countess likes Lady Diana's company better than she does that of her husband—or indeed that of any man."

He felt his brows rise. "And how does Harrow feel about their...association?"

Impossibly, Westing's grin stretched even further. "Someone told me the man said he was glad his wife had finally found a confidante." He lowered his voice a bit more and winked. "Can you imagine having a mistress your wife loved equally as well as you did?"

"And here I thought I'd seen everything during my travels abroad," muttered Lucas, shaking his head.

"Yes, well you ought to see the three of them *together*," said Westing with relish. "Oh, yes. They can be seen every other week or so in Harrow's box at the Theatre Royale. The story goes that in the early days of their affair Harrow brought her to see a performance under the mistaken notion that his wife had decided not to attend that night. Naturally, everyone thought there would be a nasty confrontation, but instead of causing a scene and departing in a huff, Lady Harrow *invited them to stay*—and called for an additional chair to be brought for their 'guest'!" His chuckle was one of pure delight. "What a wife!"

Lucas realized his mouth was hanging open. "The woman's clearly an eccentric."

"I'd die to know the man's secret," said Westing as if he hadn't heard him.

Haversham... "Is this the same Lady Diana Haversham that was disgraced just before I left?"

"One and the same," confirmed his friend. "You met her once, remember? We both did. I was there with you that night."

The memory that had been nagging at him at last surfaced fully. It had been several Seasons ago. When they were introduced, the girl's voice had been hardly more than a whisper when she'd greeted him with bowed head and blushing cheeks, hands gripping her fan as if for dear life. She'd been red to the tips of her ears and had never even raised her eyes. In the throes of a torrid affair with Lady Atherby at the time, he'd been too preoccupied to give her more than a passing thought. She'd been a pretty little thing, but no more interesting than any of the other debutantes flocking him at every turn.

Now, however... "Thrown over, was she not?"

The other man nodded. "As I understand it, Grenville eloped with her closest friend. Harrow, sly devil that he is, wasted no time in snapping her up. Lucky bastard. I'd give my inheritance to have her for just one night."

Lucas laughed again. "I take it this paragon of moral abandon must be a veritable Helen of Troy."

"Having met her, I can attest to it." His friend's look turned wry. "I'd be willing to wager most of the married men attending tonight will go home with tired ears, if not sore cheeks, thanks to wifely rancor over her presence."

"What—she's here with him now?"

Alarm sparked in Westing's eyes. "Oh, no. No—bad idea, Blackthorn. If you so much as look at her the wrong way Harrow will run you through."

"I only want to have a peek," Lucas assured him, unable to quash his curiosity. The daughter of a duke become a man's mistress wasn't something one saw every day. "Any woman capable of seducing not only a man, but his wife along *with* him, is worth seeing."

"Oh, God," said Westing weakly. "The last time this happened, your father made you leave the bloody country. He'll disown you if you get yourself into another debacle."

In truth, his temporary banishment had been a convenient excuse to leave England's shores as a matter of service for the Foreign Office, but he could hardly say so. Lucas straightened his cuffs and grinned. "He cannot. I'm his only heir. And considering he's already cut off my allowance—to what end I know not, since we both know I have no need of it—I see no reason to deny myself the pleasure." And with that, he turned and headed for the door. He paused before exiting. "Are you coming?"

Grimacing, Westing followed. "If only to keep you out of trouble," he muttered as he passed.

"Excellent. You can point her out to me, and if she's not with him you might even reintroduce us." He wiggled his brows. "If I manage to seduce her between now and tomorrow, and Harrow challenges me, I shall need a second. You'll do."

"That's not funny, Blackthorn."

"It bloody well *is*," laughed Lucas, ignoring his friend's sour tone.

• • •

A sudden bout of nerves took Diana as she slipped through the crush in the ballroom. Harrow would've allowed her to accompany him had she pressed, but he'd requested that she not, lest she distract him. She hated being left on her own. Harrow was like a suit of armor, protecting her from the world's cruel caprice. Without him at her side, she felt naked and altogether too vulnerable.

She cast about, desperate for some sort of anchor. *Always have something in your hand*, she remembered him telling her.

Eyes flicked up to glance at her as she snagged a glass of champagne from a passing tray. Taking a sip, she began to drift among the partygoers, trying to project an aura of calm and sophistication. She was accustomed to people looking at her, to their speculative stares, and made sure to boldly meet them.

No shame. She couldn't afford it. Not anymore. She had a part to play and was being paid to play it well. The daring plan she'd conceived at her uncle's house had succeeded even better, in fact, than she'd hoped in her wildest imaginings. Harrow kept her in what could only be termed outrageous luxury. Her home was a small palace, her servants legion. Everything she possessed was of the very highest quality. The sapphires and diamonds she wore tonight were worthy of Queen Charlotte herself.

And it all belonged to her. Harrow had given it to her, along with a monthly allowance that was nothing short of astounding. In the time since he'd publicly set her up as his mistress, she'd accumulated quite a sum. By the time their arrangement came to an end, she'd be able to live the rest of her life in comfort and independence. She might even leave England, start afresh under a new name. The world was wide open to a woman with money.

Remembering how she'd worried herself to distraction

over how to make three thousand pounds provide a sustainable living, she allowed herself a small chuckle. Harrow was many things to many people, but to her he was both friend and savior. He'd raised her up from the ashes of ruination and taught her everything she'd needed to know to survive in a courtesan's world. But while he was kind and generous, and though she knew he cared for her a great deal, he couldn't give her that for which she truly longed.

The next few years will fly as if on wings, and then I'll be free. Until then, she would hold her head high and walk as if she owned the world.

Per her protector's instruction, her gown tonight was particularly provocative. Though swathed in yards of lavishly embroidered cerulean silk, she felt almost nude. Never before had she displayed so much décolletage. Glancing down at herself, she saw the very tops of her areolas peeking through the lace at the neckline.

Don't think about it! She looked away quickly, before a blush could steal into her cheeks and make anyone wonder at it. The reality of being left on her own for the first time since her shocking return to Society a year ago settled in, and with it, trepidation. Would anyone speak to her without Harrow at her side? If not, it was just as well. She didn't really feel like conversing at the moment. But if they did, she had to be ready to answer them.

A familiar head of red-blond hair caught her eye. In an instant, all desire to hide vanished. Taking an unladylike gulp of liquid fortitude, Diana made straight for the center of the ballroom. Coming up behind her mark, she stopped.

The pile of coppery curls before her ceased their bobbing as those in front of it began to whisper and peek around it with wide eyes. Slowly, the owner of the mountainous coiffure turned around.

Deliberately pitching her voice low and husky, Diana

greeted her as one would an old friend—entirely appropriate, as that was exactly what they'd been, once upon a time. "Lady Grenville, how pleased I am to see you again after your long absence." Lips that had before quivered with the effort to smile did so now with an insolence that required no effort whatsoever. "You look well," she said, eyeing the other woman. *Not bad for having given birth only a few months ago, but I wonder that she can breathe with her stays so tight?*

"Th-thank you," choked Lady Grenville—Lucille—before apparently remembering she was never supposed to speak to or even acknowledge a woman of Diana's ilk. Color flooded back into her face, chasing away the pallor of a moment ago.

Diana's smile broadened. *Too late now!* The door had been flung wide and an invitation issued. "And how is Lord Grenville? Also well, I hope?" she said, her tone belying the sentiment.

Her opponent answered as though it were being dragged out of her. "Y-yes. Quite well."

"How lovely for you both. Allow me to offer my felicitations on the arrival of your daughter." How disappointed Grenville must have been! The guarantee of male issue had been one of his main points when negotiating a match with her uncle.

"Thank you," repeated Lucille weakly, her eyes darting to those avidly drinking in the spectacle. She paled again and swayed slightly.

For a moment, Diana thought the traitorous wretch might actually faint. As she stared into her former friend's miserable, pleading eyes, she marked the violet shadows beneath them and the fine lines etched beside her once ever-smiling mouth. She'd thought to shame Lucille, but now she saw the woman was not only embarrassed to the soles of her feet, but absolutely terrified.

Suddenly, there was no more pleasure to be had in the

confrontation. Diana searched for the words to release them both, wanting—needing—to say something that would forever rid her of the pain of this woman's betrayal. *It's time to move on.* "I'm pleased for you, Lucille."

The use of her opponent's Christian name elicited faint noises of disapproval from their audience.

It was a good thing Diana didn't give a tinker's dam what they thought. "My mother once said sons are a necessity, but daughters are a mother's blessing and joy. For all that it's ephemeral, I wish you and your daughter good health and happiness. Good evening, Lady Grenville."

Brows shot up and gasps erupted as she dipped a small curtsy.

Too late, Diana remembered her décolletage.

The silently trembling Lucille appeared at a complete loss for words, so Diana did the merciful thing and turned without waiting for a response. Head high and heart in her toes, she walked away. That had brought her no satisfaction and no joy. Yes, Lucille had stolen her fiancé and caused her to become a pariah, but it appeared she'd been ill rewarded for her theft.

Truth be told, Diana counted herself fortunate she'd escaped Grenville. Married life rarely afforded women the sort of freedom she now enjoyed.

"Happy in your triumph, my dear?" whispered Harrow at her ear, making her turn in surprise.

"Quite pleased. Is it done?"

"It is. Are you ready?"

"I am," she lied, wanting nothing more than for him to take her home.

A group of men standing to one side caught her attention. Pressing closer to Harrow, she softly cleared her throat. When he looked down at her with questioning eyes, she flicked her gaze toward the men. Chuckling, he shifted his hand a little lower to rest on the small of her back and altered their path.

When Lord Bolingbroke's companions fell silent, he turned to follow the direction of their gazes. All at once, his cheeks took on the appearance of ripe pomegranates as he spied her.

Though she'd tweaked his nose many times since he'd cast her out, Diana still took immense satisfaction in it. His discomfiture was a sweet balm. She flashed the bastard an impudent grin, relishing the strangled noise he made as she brushed past.

A quarter of an hour later, Diana tossed her head and laughed as if delighted, although Lord Atworth's flattery was far from inspiring. "Such a high compliment, my lord. You'll make me blush," she said, bringing up her fan to hide cheeks that were, in fact, quite cool—all the while encouraging him with her eyes in a game she'd practiced until it had become second nature. Beside her, Harrow looked on with an approving eye.

She warmed beneath his silent praise. It was of utmost importance that she be as desirable as possible. The more his peers lusted after her, the better. As long as their comments remained favorable and admiring, he would remain well pleased.

"Harrow, I vow you're the luckiest man alive," said Atworth, licking his thick lips. He winked broadly, apparently unaware he'd just sloshed wine all down the front of his jacket. "I'd just about sell my soul to be in your place. If you ever decide to leave him, dear goddess, I beg you to consider my patronage. I would build you a temple, fill it with delights for your pleasure..." his voice lowered to a suggestive growl, "and worship at your delectable altar every night with utmost devotion."

Coupled with the leering expression on his fat face, it was just about the worst double entendre she'd ever heard.

One bad insinuation deserves another. "As tempting as that sounds, I'm afraid even your most devout worship would fall short of my lord's nightly offerings." Turning, she favored Harrow with a smoldering gaze and stroked his silk-clad forearm, giving it a light squeeze.

Atworth's eyes widened until she could see the whites all around. Then great guffaws began to erupt from his portly person. "Ho-ho! Harrow, I'll say it again: You're the luckiest fellow alive!"

"Indeed," murmured Harrow, taking up her wayward hand to kiss the tips of her fingers. "I can only count myself the most fortunate of men." He smiled down at her. "Shall we dance, my love?" Without bothering to excuse himself, he tucked her hand beneath his elbow and led her away.

"Better?" she murmured as they waited for the dance to begin.

"Brilliant, now we've extricated ourselves. It's time to provide further grist for the mill," he whispered, tilting her face up with a finger beneath her chin.

Letting her eyes drift halfway shut, Diana tipped her head back and favored him with the sultry smile she'd practiced. Her ears pricked at the faint gasps that sounded from a nearby group of ladies as her 'patron' dropped a kiss on her exposed throat, another on her jaw, and another by the corner of her mouth. She repressed a smirk.

Another face drew her attention. It caught her eye because it wore neither a look of disapproval nor one of outright lust, but rather one of amused interest. It was a handsome face, too. One raven brow cocked in acknowledgment of her attention.

She looked away, a rush of heat flooding her cheeks. "Who is that gentleman over there? The dark-haired one by the pillar?" she asked Harrow.

"That is Viscount Blackthorn, recently returned from abroad."

"He's staring at us."

"No, my dear, he's staring at you." He chuckled. "And well he should, for you are quite the loveliest woman here tonight. A man of his reputation would be remiss if he failed to notice you."

"His reputation?"

"*Mm.* It's very nearly as wicked as yours," murmured her protector, smiling. "Blackthorn was sent abroad by his father out of desperation to keep his heir atop the grass. He's been in numerous duels, most of them over some woman."

"You mean like the one you face tomorrow?" Diana said, not bothering to mask her displeasure.

"Just so," he answered easily. "You need not be concerned. My opponent lacks any skill with a sword or pistol. His ineptness is the stuff of legend."

"Accidents happen," she said darkly. "He could get lucky."

His answering smile was grim. "I don't allow for such things as luck."

She ducked her head. No, indeed he didn't. When Harrow aimed at a target—whether with bullet or blade—it fell. His deadly speed and precision were no surprise to Diana. The man practiced both sword and pistol several times a week with a master.

With monumental effort, she put the duel out of her mind. *I'll fret about it tomorrow morning.* Her eyes wandered back to where Lord Blackthorn was standing, still observing them. His steady stare was disconcerting. It felt as if he could see right through her disguise. As if he somehow knew she was a lie. "I hope that one causes us no trouble."

Following her gaze, Harrow let out a low laugh. "As do I, but for different reasons, I surmise."

She tore her eyes away, annoyed at her own transparency. "You know I would never—"

"I *do* know," he agreed, his manner placating. "But I also know this cannot last forever. And it should not. You are young and beautiful, Diana. And someday, you'll encounter a man who touches your heart. When that happens, it will be the end of our arrangement."

"I promised you five—"

"And I told you I would not hold you to that number. This arrangement is for our mutual benefit. As long as you are happy to remain with me, Diana, I'll continue to protect you. But whenever you deem it time to leave and make a new life for yourself, I shall allow you your freedom without any reservations." His dark eyes grew sad. "Knowing as I do what it is to love someone and have to keep it a secret, I would never impose such a condition on you."

She felt her own eyes filling and blinked to keep the tears at bay. Tears would be completely out of character and immediately questioned. A brazen mistress such as herself couldn't afford to display such sentimentality. "You are a good man, my lord. I wish—"

"I know," he interrupted softly. "But none of us can change the way things are, and so the truth must remain a secret—for all our sakes."

It was a stark reminder of exactly what was at stake. Nodding, she pasted on a bright smile for the benefit of those watching, including Blackthorn, and moved to the proper starting position for the dance.

Later that evening as their carriage wended its way toward her home, she reflected on her encounter with Lucille. The woman she'd seen tonight was a vastly different person than she remembered. Lucy, the friend of her childhood, had always been a cheerful little sprite of a thing, alive with mirth and constantly into mischief. Life with Grenville had taken its toll on her and had clearly changed her into someone else.

Life as a fallen woman has done much the same to me.

It was a sobering thought. For all that her external life was a facade, she, too, had changed. Her eyes had been opened, her reality transformed by knowledge. *The world is never as it seems on the surface. Secrets abound in every life.*

"When will René arrive?" she asked, keeping her voice low even though there was no danger of being overheard.

"One hour past. I presume all is ready?"

"Indeed," she confirmed. "However, I feel I ought to tell you the new maid you hired may be cause for some concern."

"Oh?"

She nodded. "She crossed herself when I told her you and another gentleman would be dining with us and were likely to stay until morning. I saw it in the mirror. I fear she won't last the night."

"Don't worry yourself overmuch." Harrow's face twisted into a wry grin. "As long as she labors under the intended assumption, any tales that leave with her will only work in our favor. And we'll take extra care to give her the right impression. Won't be too difficult—René loves to give a good performance. He would have been a great actor had he not been born with such a love of music."

"I believe it," she said soberly. "His disguises are both clever and complete. Even I failed to recognize him the last time. I just hope the girl doesn't run screaming from the house like that one we had a few months ago. I thought the neighbors were going to call out the guard—it's not the least bit amusing!" she scolded, frowning as he chuckled. "I have to live there, you know."

"Not for much longer," he said, catching her by surprise. "I've wanted to relocate you to somewhere closer to me for some time now. As fortune would have it, I've managed to quietly acquire Number Nine, Old Burlington Street. It belonged to Baron Uxton, who was having it renovated when he died. His widow decided to sell it. It's very nearly finished.

I shall, of course, leave the decorating to you."

The thought of living in one of London's most fashionable boroughs should have made her woman's heart beat faster, but it didn't. Still, she could hardly refuse. "What of my current residence?"

"Let it out, if you like, or sell it. It's sure to fetch a nice sum either way."

He said it just as they pulled to a stop in front of her townhouse. She looked up at her front door, already missing the cozy rooms behind it. "When?"

"A fortnight."

"So soon?"

He must have heard the reluctance in her voice. "If you truly wish to remain here, I won't force you to leave."

Guilt assaulted her. They might be good friends now, but she'd been hired to make it easier for him to live—and love—as he desired. "I'll be happy to go wherever you wish. I did not mean to sound ungrateful, it's just that since my parents died this is the first place I've truly thought of as home."

"I understand," he said gently. "And if you wish to retain it, I won't object. That said, the new residence is quite a bit larger, stands alone, and boasts a proper garden in the back."

Now *that* pricked her interest. Her current abode had only a small, glassed-in conservatory. She'd longed for a real garden for some time.

"Lord Fane lives to the north," he went on as a footman rushed up to assist them in disembarking. "Cork runs to the west immediately behind—all townhomes, there, with the exception of the two houses behind yours—and in the house to the east is Lord Mallowby," continued Harrow quietly as they walked up the steps. "I'll be only a few minutes away."

"I suppose living in Mayfair would be more convenient," she said, biting her lip.

"Yes, and much more private," he agreed. "We won't

have to worry about your neighbors hearing everything the way we do here."

And it would be a right rub in my uncle's face. Old Burlington Road lay just three streets west of Bolingbroke's residence in Golden Square. Far too close for his comfort, no doubt, and in a much more prestigious neighborhood. Looking up again at her front door, she bid it goodbye in her mind. "I shall make ready," she told Harrow.

"Excellent. I know you'll love it. Now let us prepare to once again scandalize London," he whispered with impish glee.

Chapter Three

Two days later

"Why could it not have been me?" moaned Westing, tossing aside the paper he'd been reading.

Lucas had already read it. The night of the ball, a young maid had fled Lady Diana's house after bearing witness to what she'd termed "utter depravity" within its confines. The girl claimed Lord Harrow had invited another male guest to join him for an evening with his mistress as hostess. According to the maidservant, they'd plied said guest with strong spirits and then *both* men had joined Lady Diana in her bedchamber to, as the girl had put it, "engage in such wickedness as warrants eternal Hellfire."

"You don't actually believe it, do you?" Lucas scoffed. "Was it not you who told me he's the jealous sort?"

"This is the second time I've heard of him allowing another to enjoy her charms," said Westing, ruefully shaking his head. "I did not believe the first such rumor."

"I suppose now you must consider it truth."

"And a bloody Frenchman, too!" exclaimed Westing with rancor. "Why not let a solid Englishman have a go? It's an insult, I tell you."

"You see?" Lucas laughed, settling himself by the fire. "Did I not tell you to make him an offer?"

"It was probably the result of him trying to keep up with that damnable Frenchie," groused his friend. "Brandy is like mother's milk to that lot, you know. I'll wager Harrow barely remembers that night."

"I have my doubts," Lucas told him. "The man had a duel the morning after, and I understand he bested his opponent."

A snort erupted from Westing. "A mewling infant is capable of besting Brampton. Even I, on my worst morning after a good night's drenching and wenching, could fell him with one shot."

"Perhaps, but what about with a blade?"

"Was it swords?" said the other man with a frown.

"The account I just read said it was," Lucas affirmed. "A crapulous man would have been at a severe disadvantage, even with a sluggard like Brampton. He most certainly would not have been able to disarm Brampton within seconds and then slap his broad backside with the flat of his blade as the old tosspot bent to retrieve his errant weapon."

"Bloody hell, did he really?"

Lucas laughed at his friend's wide-eyed incredulity. "Indeed. And then he bled the poor fellow. Thus, I expect this sordid tale of a threesome is just that—a fanciful exaggeration of far less licentious events." Through his work for the Foreign Office, he'd come to understand the papers regularly embellished their so-called "witness accounts" in order to feed London's appetite for gossip. "The wilder the tales, the better the sales" was their philosophy. He'd have to find the author of this piece and ask him how much truth there was to it. "I imagine the maid was paid quite handsomely to attest to such debauchery."

"Perhaps." A smile twitched at one corner of Westing's mouth. "You've got to admit, though—it *is* a hell of a tale. It would not surprise me if even Lady Harrow got her hackles up over it."

"From what you've said of the woman, she'll likely invite Lady Diana over for tea to discuss the details." Lucas sipped his sherry and stared into the fire. The truth was that he'd seen Lady Harrow recently, and the woman was, to put it plainly, plain. Lady Diana, however, was anything but plain. He'd only seen her at a distance, of course, but what he'd seen had made him want to weep: honey hair, light eyes, and a form that was lush enough to give a dead man a stiff-stander.

"…going to the Latham party next Wednesday?" Westing was asking.

Stirring himself from his musings, Lucas grimaced in distaste. "Not by choice, but yes." He sighed at the other man's askance look. "If I fail to be sociable and attend such events with minimal regularity—even if only for half an hour—my mother forces me to escort her to them. I'd much rather go on my own. Less risk of my neck getting caught in a marital noose."

"Lady Diana will be there," his friend murmured, giving him a sidelong look.

Despite his better instincts, Lucas bit. "How can you be certain?"

"I have it on good authority Harrow has accepted the invitation."

"I see. And what makes you think he'll bring *her* along?"

Westing looked smug. "Lords Harrow and Latham are longtime friends, but their wives are not—which all but guarantees Lady Harrow won't accompany her husband to the event. But Harrow never attends these things alone. Mark my words, she'll be with him."

"And you really think she'll show her face in public after..." Lucas nodded meaningfully at the discarded paper.

"Oh, she'll be there—if only to spite Bolingbroke. She positively loathes the man. To this day she maintains she was unjustly cast out and was unspoiled until meeting Harrow." He sniffed. "Grenville, of course, says otherwise. I suppose only the three of them will ever know the truth."

"Indeed," agreed Lucas, draining his glass. "Though I doubt it matters much, given the papers have now touted the lady as having participated in *ménage à trois*." He shifted and leveled a suspicious look at his friend. "Why did you tell me she'll be there?"

"Because I knew you'd been invited, and, knowing you as I do, I know you would discover her in attendance and be unable to resist. Now I know to be there, too, if only to stop you from doing anything extraordinarily foolish."

"Are you my keeper, then?" Lucas asked, unable to help laughing at the dour grimace that subsequently crossed Westing's face.

"If anyone requires one, old fellow, it's you."

As Wednesday approached, Lucas found himself increasingly preoccupied with thoughts of one Diana Haversham. The woman was an anomaly, to be sure. When faced with ruination or other similarly disastrous events, very few ladies of quality chose to become courtesans. Most went for the church or into service for a relative.

Not, apparently, Lady Diana. And that choice made her infinitely interesting.

Given what he'd seen of her thus far—her bold demeanor and seductive manner of dress—she'd made the transition with remarkable speed for a girl who'd only a short time ago been prim, proper, and boringly respectable. He positively burned with curiosity. What did her voice sound like? What was the color of her eyes? He couldn't remember either detail from their previous meeting.

From the confines of his carriage, he searched for Harrow's crest on the other conveyances clogging the drive to the Latham estate, but the increasingly inclement weather and general chaos made identification impossible. It began to rain in earnest, and the congestion grew so terrible that nothing moved for over a quarter of an hour.

"At this rate, it will be nightfall before I arrive," he muttered. Frustration at last prompted him to rap sharply on the roof. "I'll walk the rest of the way," he told his coachman through the portal. Grabbing his umbrella, Lucas climbed out and opened it, drawing stares from those who hurried past him, huddled beneath their sodden cloaks. Living abroad had taught him many useful things, including the benefit of keeping one of these contraptions in his carriage. Considering how much it rained in London, heaven only knew why his fellow Englishmen still declined to adopt the use of such a worthwhile device.

Twenty minutes later and dry, with the unfortunate exception of one damp shoe, he entered the ballroom and greeted his hosts while those coming in behind him went off to dry themselves. Circling, he looked for Harrow and, more importantly, his infamous mistress.

"I was beginning to wonder whether or not you'd make it," said Westing from behind. "Then I saw that bloody tent of yours coming up the walk. A right odd sight, it is."

"Perhaps, and yet here I stand warm and dry rather than wet and chilled. Is she here yet?"

"Who, may I ask, are you looking for, Lord Blackthorn?" asked Lady Latham, pausing beside them on her way across the ballroom.

Westing's mouth clamped shut.

Following the story of the alleged *ménage à trois*, any respectable hostess doubtless would dread hearing the name

"Lady Diana Haversham" in connection with her party, but Lucas had no compunction about saying it.

As anticipated, the woman's smile faltered and died. "She is with Lord Harrow, of course," she answered flatly, jerking her chin toward a point beyond his left shoulder. "Over by the terrace doors."

Lucas looked, and there she was, gowned in yellow with pale green ribbons, looking for all the world like a sweet—waiting to be gobbled up. When he turned back, all that remained of Lady Latham was the lingering scent of her overpowering perfume.

"You could have said you were looking for Harrow, you know," muttered Westing.

"Yes, but that would have been a lie," Lucas said cheerfully, ignoring his friend's black look.

"You're hopeless," sighed the other man. "Very well. Shall we?"

• • •

Diana tried not to let her anxiety show on the surface as she watched Lords Westing and Blackthorn approach. *Damn me for telling Harrow I'd be fine on my own!* He'd gone off with Lord Louden to discuss an investment proposal.

Though Blackthorn was conversing with his friend, she'd seen the way he'd stared at her and knew he was coming for her. *That man is trouble.* Turning just before they reached her, she tried to make a tactical retreat but wasn't quick enough to avoid being caught up.

"Lady Diana?"

Damn. She turned, a careful smile on her lips. Not unfriendly, but not overly encouraging, either. "Lord Westing, how delightful to see you again."

"Likewise," the gentleman replied, his face pinking

slightly. "Might I beg a moment of your time to introduce a friend of mine?"

Flicking a glance at his companion, she nodded. "Of course."

"Actually, we are already acquainted," said Blackthorn. To his credit, his gaze remained fixed above her décolletage. "It's been several years, madam, but your loveliness remains unchanged."

She barely refrained from snorting. Had they ever met, she would surely remember it. "Thank you, my lord."

Before she could gracefully extricate herself, he continued. "I understand your uncle, Lord Bolingbroke, has recently returned after retiring from his post this winter."

Despite her most valiant effort, Diana felt her face tighten. She kept her tone light. "I believe you'll find that, in truth, he was discharged from it," she corrected. *And may he never recover from the humiliation!*

Blackthorn's lips quirked almost as if he shared in her satisfaction at how badly things had gone for her former guardian. "My apologies. I'm still not yet caught up on the goings-on at court. I've been away, you see. In Germany."

Was that supposed to impress her? "A matter of the Crown or of pleasure?" Alarm bells pealed in her mind at her foolish choice of the word "pleasure."

"A matter of my father wanting me out of the way, I'm afraid."

"I see. And now you're back and once again looking for trouble?" She said it with a smile, but her warning would only be mistaken by a complete fool—and for all his brashness, Blackthorn didn't seem like a fool.

Now his gaze dropped to appraise her fully. "It would seem so."

Her face heated, and she had to take a deep breath to calm her traitorous pulse, which had leaped. *Damn, but he's a bold one!* "Those who seek trouble often find it less appealing than it first appears—and far more costly."

"Sometimes. But not always," he murmured, his rain-gray eyes twinkling. Clearly, he'd understood not only her words of warning, but her silent censure. "Of course, one's level of enjoyment depends greatly upon the kind of trouble one seeks. As for the cost, I'm always willing to pay the price for the right sort of trouble." He cocked a suggestive brow.

Indignant shock made her forget for a moment the role she played. Thankfully, before she could fling her fan at his head, the sound of a throat rather violently being cleared drew her gaze away to Westing.

"I think I see Marlborough over by the entrance," said he, fidgeting. "Blackthorn, did you not wish to speak to—"

"May I have the honor of a dance this evening?" Blackthorn asked her, ignoring his friend.

She blinked at his brashness. Normally, a gentleman spent a bit of time on compliments and pleasantries before making such a request. Of course, he probably didn't feel it necessary to put forth such effort with someone like her.

The thought rankled. She'd like to answer his request with a proper dressing-down but marked that others had now begun to take notice of their conversation. She couldn't afford to step out of character even for a moment, no matter how tempted. Casting her gaze down, she answered demurely and with all the polish he'd lacked, "My Lord Harrow has, of course, already claimed the first and last dances; however, I shall be pleased to grant you the second." Better to get it over with quickly.

"As you wish, of course." His smile was a devilish curl along one side of his mouth as he bowed and took up her hand to hover briefly over it. "Until then, my lady."

Hot lightning shot from where his fingers slid across hers, traveling straight up her arm and down to slam into her lungs and pool in her belly. She watched his eyes darken and felt a corresponding tug deep inside. Her breath released in an inelegant burst as he let her go, and she looked away, mortified.

To cover her slip, she focused on Blackthorn's companion. It went completely against all proper etiquette for a lady to ask a gentleman to dance, but she needed to let Blackthorn know where he stood—and besides, she wasn't exactly a "lady" anymore. "And shall I reserve the third for you, Lord Westing?"

Westing's eyes widened, and an altogether different sort of smile creased his face: the same a young boy might wear upon being taken into a sweet shop with a newly minted guinea and no restrictions. "Indeed, my lady," he answered eagerly. "I should be most honored."

Triumphant, Diana looked to Blackthorn to see his reaction. To her disappointment, his face remained impassive. "I must confess to being immensely flattered at having simultaneously earned the attentions of *two* such fine gentlemen."

It was a deliberate reference to the recent gossip. As expected, Westing's eyes took on a glazed, hungry look. Blackthorn's gaze, however, was more curious than lustful. Diana bit back a curse. Lust, she could handle. Curiosity was a far more dangerous beast—much harder to tame.

Fortunately, Lord Harrow chose that moment to resurface. "I see you've made some new friends," he said as he approached. His manner was cheery, but she knew him well enough to know he was concerned.

"Lords Westing and Blackthorn have each just engaged me for a dance this evening."

Harrow's smile would have melted any other woman's knees. "I'm glad you're enjoying yourself, my dear. Not that I thought for even a moment that you would languish for lack of company." He turned to the gentlemen in question. "After all, is she not the loveliest of women?"

The pink stain in Westing's cheeks became beet red, and even Blackthorn looked a bit chagrined.

Fortunately for them, Harrow's question was rhetorical. "Forgive me, but I cannot help being prideful," he continued, slowly lifting her hand to his lips. "That such perfection should deign to grant me her favor is a miracle."

The look on Blackthorn's face plainly stated his opinion of that "miracle."

That's right. Money can buy anything. The thought was a bitter stone in her heart. If he only knew the truth! Money could buy one many fine things, including status, but it couldn't buy back a reputation. It *could*, however, purchase a new name and a clean slate. *Just a few more years…*

"Come, my love," said Harrow, holding out his arm. "I wish to show you something extraordinary. Lady Latham is sponsoring a new artist and is currently displaying his latest work in her gallery." He turned to the men. "Gentlemen, if you will please excuse us?"

Diana shot a coy glance over her shoulder as she moved away. "Until later, gentlemen." She waited until they were out of earshot. "Thank you," she murmured. "I'm sorry, but I had no choice but to accept. I did not expect him to be so bold. That Westing fellow is harmless enough, but Blackthorn…" Her stomach still felt strange and fluttery, as if she hadn't eaten enough. She took a deep breath to steady it.

Harrow's glance was piercing. "You think he'll be a problem?"

"I expect that, like most of those inquiring after my favors thus far, he thinks to sample my charms and have done—if only to brag to his friends that he's achieved the impossible." She didn't bother to keep the resentment out of her tone. There was nothing she need hide from Harrow.

"I warned you this would happen, that there would be a few wolves amongst the sheep. I tried to prepare you as best I could."

"You did," she agreed. "And I ought to have handled him better, but I let him catch me off my guard." What was it about Blackthorn that set her so on edge? When she looked at other men, Westing for example, she felt nothing. When she looked at Blackthorn, however, she became all unbalanced and uncertain of herself as she had not been in years. "It's nothing."

"What's nothing?"

His inquiry startled her. *Did I say that aloud?* "It's nothing that cannot easily be remedied," she said briskly. "I shall, as promised, dance with them, and thereafter avoid him—them—as much as possible."

"Diana..."

Her face warmed, and she averted her eyes. "Yes?"

"If you don't wish to—"

"No," she said, shaking her head. "I accepted his request in front of witnesses. If I fail to follow through, everyone will wonder why. I think it better to leave no room for speculation, don't you?"

· · ·

Lucas cursed quietly as he watched her saunter away.

"Oh, nicely done," said Westing, clapping softly. "I think you extraordinarily fortunate to have made it through that without getting slapped—or worse, called out."

"Enough," Lucas muttered, though without any heat. His speech with her had indeed been blunt and graceless—offensive, even. His only excuse was that he'd been distracted by the incongruities she presented. The shy girl who'd been unable to look him in the face was now a blazing seductress.

Or is she?

He'd always had a knack for being able to tell when someone was lying or attempting to conceal something. It was what made him a good gambler, and the reason the Foreign Office had approached him just before he'd been shipped off to the Continent for his little mandatory hiatus. That sense was telling him something was "off" with Lady Diana.

The wariness in her sea-green eyes had been unmistakable, as had the outrage that had flashed in them when he'd all but asked her to name her price. For a moment, he'd thought for sure she *would* slap him—the reaction of a woman of moral fiber, not a courtesan. He'd seen the twitch in her eyelids, had marked the whitening of her knuckles and the trembling of her hand as she'd gripped her fan. And then he'd watched her masterfully hide her wrath behind a cool veil of cynical sensuality. He suspected her provocative words and daring manner were no more than masks. Lady Diana was more a mystery now than ever. One he was determined to fathom out.

As they disappeared into the crowd, Lucas turned and made for the stairs to the gallery.

"It's no use, you know," said Westing, alongside him. "Mark my words, you'll never get more than a dance with that one."

"I'd lay no wagers, if I were you," Lucas said absently, moving to the rail to continue to monitor from above.

Westing let out an exasperated sigh. "Don't even consider it, Blackthorn. He's put holes in men for far less. You're lucky he failed to overhear you earlier. Have your dance with her—if she does not renege—and be done with it. It's not worth it."

Lucas deliberately ignored him in favor of keeping his eyes on the couple below. Their manner together was easy and familiar, as it would be between two people entirely comfortable with each other. But their physical interactions lacked a certain warmth, a certain…intimacy. Clearly, she felt affection for her protector, but he detected nothing deeper. Something was missing.

Lust.

Lucas knew lust. It had been the constant companion of his youth. It had taken him twenty-nine years, several interesting scars, and finally a two-year sojourn abroad to learn not to let it lead him into trouble. Or so he'd thought, anyway. Being near Lady Diana put a definite strain on his self-discipline. Even now his breeches were uncomfortably tight. His reaction to touching her bare fingers had been instant and not a little alarming.

If anyone was worthy of a man's lust, it was that woman— and yet Harrow had looked at her as one might a sister. Lucas shook his head, dismissing the inane fancy. No man in his right mind would keep a woman like that around and not avail himself of her charms at every possible opportunity. If Harrow looked at her with anything less than raging desire, it was probably because his appetite was already well sated.

A hand suddenly passed before his face, startling him. "Bloody—!" Lucas hissed, turning to face Westing, who wore a grim, disapproving look.

"You're a damned fool, you *do* know that?"

"Are you my father now?" Lucas shot back, annoyed.

"Worse. I'm your friend. I know you better than your father, and I know *that* look," said Westing, narrowing his eyes. "Don't do it. I'm telling you, it's a mistake. Harrow will—"

"Not know a damned thing until it's too late," Lucas finished for him. "I want her." It was a flat statement that brooked no argument. Even so, he knew Westing wouldn't give up yet. He braced himself for an earful.

"George's balls, man! Are you serious? There are a thousand females out there just itching to sink their claws into you, yet you decide to pursue the *one* that is unattainable."

Lucas felt a grin spread across his lips. "You ought to know by now not to tell me something like that, Westie. No woman is unattainable."

"Fine. The one that will get you *killed*, then."

"I'm not going to be killed," Lucas replied with an irritated sigh. "He's not as in love with her as you seem to think—I can tell." He intercepted a passing tray of champagne and relieved it of a glass.

"It matters not whether he loves her, she belongs to him," reasoned Westing, helping himself to a glass as well.

"I saw no wedding ring on the lady's finger."

Westing snorted into his champagne. "Remind me again why you were sent abroad? Since when did a wedding ring ever keep you from pursuing a woman?"

Lucas ignored him in favor of moving back toward the stairs.

Doggedly, Westing followed. "My point is that it does not matter whether or not she's married, she is his. And what's more, he keeps her in complete luxury. If you think she's going to give that up for anything, you're out of your mind. He's a bloody marquess, and a wealthy one at that. You cannot buy the favor of a woman who wants for nothing."

"Oh, she wants for something," Lucas replied. "*Every* woman wants for something. If not money, then something else. I need only find the proper key, and the door will open."

Westing let out an incredulous bark of laughter. "You really *are* mad." He skipped down a few steps, getting ahead of him and bringing them to a halt before swinging around to face him again. "The only man capable of prying that woman away from her gold mine is the bloody Prince himself."

Now it was Lucas's turn to laugh. "Care to lay a wager on that? I can promise you that if such a thing ever happens, there will be a *very* long line of gentlemen sneaking into the lady's chambers. For all that he is a prince, a great lover His Royal Highness most certainly is not, despite his boasts to the contrary."

Westing's eyes went round. "Have a care, Blackthorn," he whispered, glancing nervously at the surrounding crush. "The state of things being as they are, what with Perceval's death, people are scrambling for position and putting heel marks on each other's backs at every turn, if not outright planting knives in them."

"I'd first have to become an actual presence at court in order for that to happen," Lucas whispered, winking. And that was unlikely, given the last thing the Crown wanted was an open association between them.

"I understood you were planning to assume your father's seat this year, which will require you to present yourself at the palace," said Westing. "Your father—"

"Is going to have to wait a bit longer before turning me into a replica of himself." Pushing past, Lucas left Westing behind and headed to the other side of the room. There she was, his Helen of Troy, hovering at her patron's side. Harrow was speaking with an exceedingly pleased-looking Liverpool. It was no wonder the normally taciturn man was smiling. Lord Perceval's recent assassination had resulted in his appointment to the position of Prime Minister.

Doubtless, Lady Diana would welcome a rescue. But upon moving closer, Lucas was surprised to see she appeared anything but bored. As unobtrusively as possible, he maneuvered to a position behind a pillar just close enough to overhear the conversation. The words "impending elections" and "gathering support" caught his attention.

"Do you really think he'll still try to sway the vote?" he heard Liverpool ask.

To Lucas's surprise, it was Lady Diana who answered. "His recent dismissal from his post as Lord Lieutenant all but assures his continued dissent."

Liverpool grunted. "I had hoped he would heed the warning and stand down. Instead, he has been more outspoken than ever and has earned the Prince's displeasure. I fail to see why he's so determined to stir the pot."

The lady replied, "With all due respect, my lord, his malcontent began years ago. In truth, his recent dismissal was but the latest in a long line of thwarted ambitions."

"Oh, indeed?"

"Yes," she answered. "It began many years ago when the title he'd long anticipated inheriting was instead granted to a cousin whose claim, it turned out, superseded his own. He contested that claim to no avail. Then he was further injured when Paget was appointed Lord Commissioner of the Treasury over him. There have been other perceived slights of less importance to him, but those two he believes grave injustices. If he is unsupportive of the current ministry, it's because he feels there is little to gain by it. At the same time, there are others promising rich rewards to any who advocate change. Unfortunately, a good many share my uncle's view. I would not discount his ability to influence others."

When Liverpool spoke, his tone smacked of indulgence. "And have you any speculation as to how he will contrive to do so when his standing at court is so greatly diminished?"

Again, she spoke with quiet confidence. "It is my belief he will attempt to leverage the recent dispute with the United States as a strong point of contention. Our forces are already engaged in the war against France. Many have no desire to become involved in another conflict."

Lucas felt his jaw go slack. The Foreign Office had many eyes and ears, himself among them, but he'd not heard of her being under their aegis.

"You must pardon my skepticism," said Liverpool, "but how can you know all of this when you are no longer a member of Bolingbroke's household?"

Silence followed for a long, tense moment before she spoke. "Suffice it to say that men don't often bother to quiet themselves in my presence. As such, I hear many things of interest." She chuckled, a low seductive sound that trailed heat through Lucas's vitals. "You may be assured, my lord, that the information I've given you is quite reliable."

"And I shall use it to see that he fails in his efforts to undermine our purpose," replied Liverpool, his voice grim. "Thank you, my lady. This has been a most enlightening conversation. If you will please excuse me, there are matters to which I must at once attend. Harrow, shall I assume we'll see you at this week's meeting?"

"Alas, I'm afraid I'm engaged that evening," replied Harrow. "Perhaps another time?"

"Of course. I'll send word to you well before our next one. You are, of course, invited to attend as well, my lady."

Lucas's brows inched higher as the niceties were observed, and the three broke company. *Well, well. Lady Diana. You're simply full of surprises.* He ventured a peek from around the pillar to see her gliding away alongside Harrow.

If there was one thing he'd learned over the years, it was that all women were dangerous to some degree. This one, it appeared, was no exception.

Chapter Four

Though good sense begged him to leave and forget his growing obsession with the woman, Lucas watched as Lady Diana paired with Harrow for the first dance. Her movements were sure and graceful. He'd expect no less from a gently raised female. Or a courtesan, for that matter.

Her eyes, however, were what interested him the most. They looked everywhere but at her partner's face. A woman in love ordinarily had eyes only for her lover. Even if she weren't in love with him, any courtesan worth her salt knew to attend her patron as if she were. Harrow was equally distracted, his gaze flicking back and forth over the crowd. And the two of them talked almost incessantly while they were dancing—a serious and decidedly unromantic discussion by the look of it.

He soon marked his scrutiny had not gone unnoticed, for at the dance's close the couple at once began to make their way directly over to where he stood.

"My lady," he said, bowing low before her.

"Lord Blackthorn," she said, inclining her head politely. "I believe you promised me this next dance?"

"Indeed," Lucas answered automatically. Half a heartbeat later, he caught himself—he'd asked *her* to dance.

"I trust my treasure is in good hands, Blackthorn," said Harrow, his stern tone belied by his amused expression. Turning to the lady, he smiled and took up her hand to kiss it. "Enjoy yourself, my love."

When Harrow had disappeared into the crush, Lucas turned to her. "Why did you do that?"

"To what are you referring?" she asked, all innocence.

He marked the appearance of a dimple in her cheek as her smile turned knowing and mischievous. "You deliberately made it seem as though you were the one to request this dance of me rather than the other way around. Why?"

The corners of her mouth curled a bit more. "Perhaps I dislike the idea of my lover risking himself yet again over another man's impetuous pursuit of that which cannot be attained."

"Is that what you think I'm up to?" he said lightly. "I know when to leave well enough alone, although your patron seems far less prone to fits of jealous rage than he has been made out to be. In truth, I find him quite agreeable."

"Don't let his pleasant demeanor fool you," she replied just as lightly. "He is neither pleased by your attentions to me nor willing to tolerate more than the utmost propriety on your part where I am concerned. He told me all about you, by the bye." She flicked a sidelong glance at him. "I know all about your banishment—and the reason for it."

"Then you have the advantage, for I know very little of you."

"Save what London's eager lips have whispered in your ear, you mean," she said with a low laugh. "You'll never be able to discern the truth from the fiction, I assure you."

"I will, if you tell me which is which."

"How can I, when I myself hardly know?" she quipped.

"Are we to dance, my lord? Or would you prefer to retire to a corner and debate the matter until your friend comes to claim me for the next dance?"

Actually, he'd love to do just that and tell his friend to sod off, but he took her point. "I suppose the same may be said of any person—meaning that very few people truly know themselves," he said, picking up the thread again. He held out his hand, and she allowed him to lead her to the ballroom floor. His hand tingled where she touched it, reaffirming his initial observation. "We all invent ourselves daily, do we not?"

Again, she shot him a sharp glance. "Indeed we do, my lord. Each day comes with just such a decision. Today is very nearly done. When I awake tomorrow, I shall have to decide whether to remain as I am now or choose to become something new."

"And if you had the choice of becoming something new, what would you choose?"

Her chin lifted, and she assumed an exaggerated expression of hauteur. "I should be a queen, of course. Not here, where women are looked upon as inferior, but of a place where women are revered, worshiped even. I think perhaps Cleopatra had it right."

It was his turn to laugh. "I think I begin to understand—you cannot abide being controlled by any but yourself, can you?"

An eloquent shrug lifted one shoulder. "What woman does not wish to determine her own destiny? But I've already seized control of mine. This is my world, and in it, I'm the ruler of all I survey. There is not a man in this room I cannot summon with a crook of my finger and then bend to my will."

A bark of laughter burst from him. "My, but we are confident! Pride goeth before the fall, you know," he tutted. The music began, and he made the first turn to pass her on the left, keeping his gaze fixed on her as they circled each other. He waited until she faced him again. "You name yourself the ruler of your world, yet in reality you're under the authority and auspices of your patron. If he should grow bored or displeased with you…"

With a soft chuckle, she broke pattern and came to stand before him. The crowd parted around them, creating an island of calm amid a swirling flow of brightly colored silk skirts and jackets. Her smoky sea-green gaze held him.

"My dear Lord Blackthorn," she said after a moment. "What in heaven's name makes you think I'm under his authority or that he is any less obligated to please me? As for boredom, I should think not." Her lips parted in a wicked smile that was as keen as any he'd seen on a man holding a winning hand of cards. "For those who have no fear of it, desire may be expressed in an infinite variety of ways."

Lucas suddenly found his mouth robbed of all moisture and his loins tightening with anticipation. Never had he encountered a woman as openly sensual as this! And yet… "Have you truly no fear?" he managed at last.

Her chin rose a fraction. "I was not forced to become what I am. I chose this path. After my reputation was destroyed, I could have gone to the church or become a servant, but I saw an opportunity for something better. I took it, and I have no regrets."

"This is better?" he asked, surprised at the scorn in his voice. "You'd rather this than to marry and have a home and children—a respectable life?"

Her playful, prideful demeanor vanished, and he caught a glint of cool steel in her gaze. "The one who betrayed me taught me a very important lesson, my lord. A so-called respectable life does not guarantee happiness. 'Happy' is a highly subjective term. I have a home. I have a lover who is both attentive and kind. My every need—and more wants than most women are granted—is met through our association. Perhaps one day I shall choose to marry, but only if doing so is sure to bring me greater happiness than that which I already possess."

The memory of her as a shy, nervous debutante flashed in his mind's eye. One "attentive and kind" lover was nowhere near enough to produce the jade before him now. Every instinct told him she was a lie. "You are a duke's daughter. You cannot tell me this is the life you desired."

Her gem-like eyes bored into his for a moment before her ripe lips twisted in a rueful smile. "Indeed not. Like any naive child, I wished for a prince to come and sweep me off to his castle far away, where he would lavish upon me his undying love and devotion. Unfortunately, not everyone is granted their childhood fancy."

"True, but—"

"I understand you feel I've sold myself. You are correct. I have." Her quiet voice was a razor's edge. "But so does every woman who marries and trades the use of her body for the sake of security and respectability."

He laughed a little to lighten the mood, which had grown entirely too tense. "The church would beg to differ, I'm sure."

"The currency may be different, and the church may sanction the exchange, but a calculated transaction it remains," she replied coldly. "Unless a woman marries for love, she is no less a whore than I, for she sells herself as surely as any dockside trull. I, at least, have chosen to sell myself to a man who pleases me in addition to providing me with comfort and safety."

"You have no shame at all, then?"

"Why should I?" she said with an indifferent shrug, and all at once her smooth smile and polite manner were back in place. "I can say with utmost confidence that I have more honor than most of the married women in this room, and I'm certainly more honest. I am a courtesan, my lord. I don't hide the bargain I made behind hypocrisy and call it by another name." Backing away, she rejoined the line to resume the dance.

· · ·

Diana felt like kicking something—like kicking *him*—right in his stockinged shins! Hard.

Why had she let him antagonize her into a response? She was supposed to have danced, smiled, and departed on the arm of another man before he could get under her skin. Instead, she'd practically invited him to ask a thousand more questions. She could see them swimming there, just behind his eyes, waiting.

He had lovely eyes. Gray as winter storm clouds they were, and framed by long, pitch-black lashes. In her opinion, they were far too beautiful for a man. Those eyes observed her now, too closely. It was as though he could see into her, as if he somehow knew the truth that lay buried deep inside her heart.

The music ended, she curtsied and walked away, head high, back stiff. If *that* did not tell him to leave her be, then he was a blind fool and deserved the slap she had waiting for him.

Just as she stepped off the ballroom floor, someone touched her elbow. She turned, ready to strike her pursuer and be damned the consequences, but it was Westing. In her haste to be away from Blackthorn, she'd forgotten about him.

"Lady Diana," he said, a bit out of breath but still grinning like an idiot. "What of our dance?"

She glanced beyond him to see Blackthorn still watching her. The look in his eyes told her he would surely come after her if she tried to leave alone. Fixing Westing with a regretful smile, she took the better part of valor. "The truth is I would much prefer to go somewhere quiet and sit for a moment. It's these new slippers, you see. I'm afraid my foot has become sore. Perhaps you might keep me company while I rest it?"

Westing's grin widened another increment, and he offered his arm. "It shall be my pleasure!"

Diana didn't dare to look behind her as they departed. Above all, Blackthorn must never think she cared one whit about what he'd said. Yes, she wanted a home—a *real* one—and a family. But both were impossible—for now.

They will certainly never be possible with him. Her stomach tightened with unease that such a thought had even occurred to her. Shaking herself to dispel her disquiet proved ineffective. Twice he'd referred to her former life, saying he'd known her. Perhaps that was what bothered her so. She frequently encountered those who'd known her before her downfall, but there were very few who didn't now look upon her with open contempt.

In fact, there were only a handful: Harrow, his wife, René, and now Blackthorn.

His curiosity was to be expected. Everyone wanted to know what she and Harrow got up to. Along with that, for the men at least, came lust. Blackthorn had certainly looked at her with an appreciative eye, but he'd also looked at her as though she was a person rather than an object—a rare occurrence. He'd seemed genuinely shocked that she might prefer the life she had now over what had been possible before her ruination. Morality was certainly the last thing she'd expected from a man of his reputation.

Reputation. It all came down to that one word. The word that had all but destroyed her. *How much truth is there in his reputation, I wonder?* Before she could give it more thought, her escort came to a halt before an empty chair. She looked around, surprised at how far away they were from the main gathering. She'd been so lost in thought she hadn't been paying attention.

"I can see my friend has managed to vex you," said Westing with a wry grin.

"Not at all." She sat. "I'm merely fatigued from the long day."

But his eyes twinkled knowingly. "Blackthorn has that effect on many people. He's not a bad sort, really. He simply knows not when to give up."

That much she'd already gathered. "Then he and I are not unalike, I'm afraid. I can be quite stubborn—or so I've been told. It's a quality that has often landed me in trouble." She threw him a saucy grin. "As you no doubt know."

Laughing, he nodded. His gaze then slid away. "I probably ought not to tell you this, but he's determined to puzzle you out. You, dear lady, are a mystery. And once Blackthorn gets it into his mind to solve a mystery, there is no stopping him until he has his answer."

Dread tightened her gut. "Oh? I was unaware I was so enigmatic. Pray tell me what it is he wishes to know?" She'd managed to ask it with just the right amount of insouciance.

"Everything," he answered with a snort. "He told me he met you once during your debut, claimed you were a shy little thing."

"I was practically still a child," she said, smiling. "Full of naive ideas. I dare anyone to accuse me of naïveté now." The seductive laugh she'd practiced for countless hours now came with hardly any effort at all. "After our dance—during which the man practically interrogated me, I might add—I should think he has all the answers he could possibly require."

"Hardly," said Westing, grimacing.

Wonderful. Still, she maintained a cheerfully indifferent facade. "Well, I'm afraid he'll have to settle for what information he's already gleaned." Fortune seemed to still be on her side, for she spied Harrow looking for her near the ballroom floor. "My lord, your company has been a true pleasure, but I fear my time with you has come to an end." She rose.

Turning around, he glanced in the direction of her gaze. "I see." He turned and bowed, disappointment evident in his eyes. "My lady, you are as lovely a person as any I've ever met, and I believe Lord Harrow the luckiest man alive. I do hope that one day you'll deign to dance with me."

"I shall be happy to do so at the next event where we are both in attendance," she promised, smiling.

Westing greeted Harrow and then politely took his leave.

"Why were you not dancing?" asked Harrow as soon as he'd gone.

Grimacing, she told him of her encounter with Blackthorn as well as what Westing had said.

"I should not be too concerned," said Harrow. "He'll lose interest soon enough."

Doubts plagued her, but she held her tongue. "How did your business go?"

"Precisely as anticipated. Where did you hear of Bolingbroke's plans?" he suddenly asked, changing the subject. "And why did you not mention them before?"

"A new associate of my uncle's—one possessing very little discretion—spoke out of turn in my presence," she replied. "I did not tell you about it because I did not wish you to become involved. I had planned to send an anonymous letter, but…"

"I see. Liverpool no doubt thought me far more informed than I am," he replied, an uncharacteristic frown marring his face. "The man has on numerous occasions tried to recruit me. Now, thanks to you, I'm sure he must think me ready to join the damned Tories."

"I'm sorry," she replied with genuine contrition. "I did not know."

"No matter." He sighed. "Now, I want to know exactly how you came into such information."

"Do you remember the Graftons' dinner party a fortnight past?"

"How can I forget? You nearly caused the man's wife to sue for divorce."

"Yes, well a few minutes after you stepped out for a pipe, Grafton told another guest of my uncle's plan to upset the election."

"Surely you jest. Grafton would not speak of such matters in front of—"

"I assure you he did," she cut in, annoyed. "Despite my presence and that of several other ladies playing cards, upon your departure it was as though Grafton felt the room had emptied of all but himself and his friend. They were quiet, and I had to listen carefully, but they were quite candid in their discussion. I can only assume that, like my uncle, they felt such a conversation was beyond a mere female's comprehension or interest. Birds of a feather, I suppose." She hadn't meant to say it with such bile, but it was damned hard not to resent having been treated like part of a room's decor, even if it had worked to her benefit.

"You really do hate him, don't you?"

She took a steadying breath. "My personal feelings aside, I don't agree with my uncle's views. The country is already divided enough. We need to put an end to the rift and soon, before it grows any worse. Our government must remain stable." She stopped and pressed a hand to her temple. "Despite my dislike for Bolingbroke, I've no desire to see him ruin himself through his bullheadedness, for it would only result in the suffering of my kin."

Harrow's reply was so soft she almost missed it. "I thought you'd cut your family out of your heart?"

"I thought I had, too," she replied sadly. "Over time, I've

come to realize my aunt was powerless to act any differently than she did. She could no more stand against him than I and had as little choice in the matter. She still has none. As for my cousins, they are completely blameless and at his mercy. Unfortunately, their father is thinking only of his own ambition and not of their safety and security. What I did was for them, to protect them from his folly."

"I understand," said Harrow. "I just hope Liverpool is discreet concerning the source of his information. While I fully support our new prime minister, I have no desire to become involved in his schemes and intrigues."

· · ·

"Is everything to your taste, my dear?" asked Harrow.

"It's truly lovely, and far grander than I imagined," Diana answered, a little nervous at just how grand it was. The move to Number Nine, Old Burlington Street had gone smoothly. This morning, a veritable army of men and maidservants had come and cleared her old house out, right down to the last lace doily. It was now evening, and here she was strolling through her new residence arm-in-arm with her benefactor and friend.

"A magnificent jewel deserves a proper setting," said he. "Kindly remember you are the daughter of a duke. Had your uncle been less of a cowardly fool, you would have married well enough to live in just such a house."

"That may be so, but there are many who will think me unworthy of such an address."

Stopping, he faced her with somber eyes. "Their worth is equal only to their purse. Yours is in here, and it is beyond any price," he said, pointing at her chest. "Never let anyone make you feel unworthy, Diana. Never. And for what you've given me, you deserve this and far more," he added, gesturing to their opulent surroundings.

"Your kindness is beyond measure," she said, smiling at him with genuine affection. Here, at least, there was no need for pretense. "I bless the day we met, and I'm honored to be your friend."

His answering smile was just as sincere. "Likewise. Now, what will you do with your old house?"

"I've decided to sell it," she answered after a moment. "When I leave, there must be nothing here to tie me down. I realize that day is still far off, but when the time comes, I want to be able to go quickly and quietly. With any luck, I'll be long gone before anyone even notices my absence."

"I feel no shame in admitting I don't look happily to that day," said Harrow. "I shall miss your company terribly."

"And I, yours," she replied, her eyes smarting. "You and René are my dearest friends. More than that, you're my family. I truly hope everything works as planned."

"We shall see."

His tone was confident, but she marked the crease between his brows. Monsieur René Laurent, his longtime lover and the guest at their recent little "*ménage a charade*"— though no one would know it thanks to his disguise—was to be installed as her music instructor a fortnight from now. Over the ensuing months, Harrow would publicly take a keen interest in the gentleman's compositions and become his sponsor. With his wife's help in the form of an apparent reconciliation, their connection would be solidified with no one being the wiser concerning its true nature. At that point, Diana would no longer be needed to maintain the complex web of deception that had kept her benefactor's neck from the noose. She'd be free to start her new life.

"This is your bedchamber," he said, stopping at a door. Opening it wide, he ushered her through with a flourish.

Diana's mouth hung agape as she entered. Everything

was decorated in cream and gold with a pattern of pale pink roses. It was elegant, lavish, and exquisitely feminine. A sweet fragrance filled the room from clusters of matching pink roses in vases set throughout. The coverlet on the bed was sprinkled with petals, and more trailed from it all the way to the door.

"It's a room for a fairy tale princess," she murmured, then shook herself out of her daze to bend and scoop up a handful of petals. "A bit overmuch, don't you think? I can only begin to imagine what people will say when they hear of this."

"They will say I'm besotted with you."

She turned to see the wry amusement in his voice reflected in his eyes. "Which is the point of all this, of course."

"Yes, but I selected the decor especially with you in mind."

"It could not be more perfect if I'd chosen it myself," she said, gazing around in delight.

"It was nothing," he said with a shrug. "Your liking for all things pink made it a simple matter, really."

She narrowed her eyes. "You asked Minerva."

A guilty flush rose in his cheeks at the mention of his wife, and his mouth crooked in a half smile. "You know me far too well."

Laughing, she let him off the hook. "I shall thank her when I see her next which, incidentally, is one week from today."

He nodded. "I'm glad the two of you became friends. I know not what she'll do when you leave."

The fact that she was his wife's confidante at times made her feel very odd indeed, despite the fact there was nothing more than friendship between her and the lady's husband. "She'll make new friends," she told him softly. "Minerva is sweet and caring. Once they come to know her, they will adore her, just as I do."

"If only she would take a lover of her own," he muttered,

his shoulders sagging. "Then I should not feel this terrible weight of guilt. She should never have agreed to marry a man who can never love her as a husband ought."

Diana rested a hand on his sleeve. "Minerva knew the truth long before the wedding and married you with full knowledge of how it would be between you. It was an informed choice on her part."

"Yes, but she still deserves better."

"Your wife has what she wants," she assured him, concerned over his sudden melancholy. "You've given her a beautiful home, a son to cherish, and while you may not love her as a husband, you *do* love her as a friend—her oldest friend who saved her from a terrible fate."

She'd heard the tale from Minerva's own lips. On learning her parents were arranging a match on her behalf with a brutish cousin who'd terrified her with uninvited touches and whispered threats, Harrow had offered himself as an alternative. Though she'd known of his preference for men, it had made perfect sense. He'd needed a wife and heir. She'd needed a way out. His lack of desire for her hadn't bothered Minerva, who was indifferent to all passion save that of a mother for her child. As long as her husband was discreet with his lover, the marchioness was quite happy with her marriage of convenience.

"Rest assured she is content," Diana continued. "Not *all* people desire carnal passion." Unbidden, thoughts of Blackthorn intruded. She pushed them into the darkest corner of her mind.

"Oh, to be one of that happy number," said Harrow, his gaze hollow. "At times, I almost wish I'd never met René. Had I not, I might have lived the rest of my life—"

"Without knowing love?" she supplied. "You once said a life without love is no life at all. And was it not also you who said we don't get to choose with whom we fall in love?" His answering sigh told her she'd tipped the balance. She moved to the mirror and tucked a loose curl back into place. "There now, you see? It was inevitable. Now cease your worrying."

"While we're on the subject of inevitability, let us discuss you and Blackthorn. He made you feel something, did he not?"

How had he known she was thinking of the man? "I…I suppose I found him somewhat attractive," she admitted grudgingly. "Which is why I intend to avoid him. We can ill afford distractions."

Coming up behind her, Harrow placed his hands on her shoulders and sighed. "My dear Diana, if I'm right, Blackthorn intends to be much more than a mere distraction."

She stilled, alarm stiffening her spine. "You anticipate a problem?"

"I know what it is to be attracted to someone, to be unable to put them out of your mind," he said. "I saw the way he looked at you when you danced with him. And I saw the way you looked at him. Ever since that night, you've been restless and preoccupied."

"Well of course I was. I was preparing to move across Town," she offered lamely. But she could see it didn't fool him.

"Diana, you cannot deny such an attraction—believe me, I know."

"And just what am I to do about it?" she snapped. "Offer him a night in my bed? He believes me to be your mistress, and I very much doubt you wish to disabuse him of that perception." She glared at him in the mirror. "No. We proceed according to the plan."

"And what if he won't take no for an answer?"

"He will. Of that, I can assure you." She turned away. "Come now, and show me the rest of this castle you've put me in."

Chapter Five

Closing his eyes, Lucas tried once more to blank out his thoughts and achieve blessed oblivion, but sleep was a fruitless pursuit. Rolling over, he grabbed his pillow and crammed his face in it.

It's been two bloody weeks! Why am I still thinking about that blasted woman?

It seemed he'd done little else since laying eyes on her. After struggling to find slumber for several more minutes, he finally gave up trying. Rolling over again, he stared up into the dark. Her words burned in his mind: *I am a courtesan, my lord. I don't hide the bargain I've made behind hypocrisy and call it by another name…*

Plenty of courtesans had crossed his path, and Lady Diana Haversham was definitely not one of them. He'd had abundant time to review and analyze their encounter, and he'd reached the same conclusion every time. The woman wore all of the trappings and played the part well enough to fool most, but her armor lacked the thickness and hard shine of the genuine article, and she'd made several cardinal mistakes.

Again, he thought of the way she spoke and carried herself. Hers was not the reckless manner of one who had no reputation left to lose, and—in spite of her allusion to the contrary—neither was her attitude that of a woman who thought herself a whore. No indeed, she wore her dignity like a royal mantle. Also, he'd never heard any courtesan call her patron "attentive and kind." Generous, perhaps, but not attentive and kind.

And he'd seen affection in her eyes when she'd looked at Harrow. Affection. Not love. And definitely not lust. What courtesan looked at her patron with affection? Fondness perhaps, but not affection. Most people couldn't tell the difference between the two, but he could. One could be fond of someone and not feel affection for them. Fondness was what one felt for one's valet or one's drinking comrades at pub. Affection was deeper than fondness, but nowhere near love.

Then there was the pain and regret she'd shown at the mention of her betrayal and the life she'd been denied as a result of it. A woman exchanging her favors for money and security *never* permitted her negative feelings to be perceived by a potential patron, for she knew that such men paid for pleasure that was blissfully free of any sort of emotional entanglement.

He doubted whether she even suspected her mask was so thin. She was definitely not in love with Harrow. And Harrow was definitely not in love with her. Westing was wrong. They would never marry. *Not even if the current Lady Harrow were to drop dead tomorrow.* For some reason this thought greatly pleased him.

Now that he'd determined once and for all his stance on the matter, curiosity ate at him. What was she to Harrow, really? And what was he to her? What was she like when she wasn't pretending to be a courtesan? Was she indeed content with her life?

As Lucas at last began to nod off, one coherent question stuck out from amongst all of the other disjointed thoughts meandering through his mind: if happiness was subjective, then what constituted happiness for Lady Diana? On the heels of that question followed another: *What constitutes happiness for me?*

In spite of the restless night, the cursed internal timepiece that awakened him at precisely eight o'clock every morning was without fail. Grudgingly, he rose and called for his valet, who responded bearing the coffee his employer required in order to properly function. Gulping it down, Lucas dressed and made ready.

There was no time to waste, for this was a red-letter day. It was moving day, and his prestigious new address awaited its lord and master's arrival. Number Five, Cork Street had quite literally fallen into his hands by means of a card game played only days after his arrival back in London. Happy chance had provided him with an overly confident opponent in the brash—and now much wiser—Honorable Mr. Rothschild, as well as plenty of witnesses to back his claim to the forfeit. Rothschild had not possessed the means to offer him a substitute of equal value and had had no choice but to honor the wager.

Lucas grinned, blessing his good fortune. He'd been kind enough to offer an exchange of residences rather than simply selling this place and sending Rothschild home to his father in disgrace. He'd been humbled so once himself and felt no young man ought to be subjected to such humiliation. At least the poor fellow would still be able to hold his head up in public—and he'd learned a valuable lesson: never wager something with which you cannot bear to part. Any prize offered up in a wager must be considered lost until one has won it back. So his father had always told him.

And so it is.

Everything had been drawn up right and proper by their solicitors, signed and sealed by both himself and Rothschild, and the exchange of deeds and keys would occur at the eleventh hour this very day. It was an excellent trade. A Leicester address was nothing to sniff at, but it was much more removed from the center of things and therefore far less desirable than Mayfair. Perhaps it would benefit young Rothschild to be a bit farther away from the friends that had urged him to make such a rash wager, but privately he doubted it. There were troublemakers aplenty in this part of London.

Myself being one—but not for much longer!

Looking in the glass held up by his man, he straightened his cravat. Mother would be pleased, at least. Now she'd be able to tell her friends her son lived in Mayfair. Of course, the move had its drawbacks. The pleasures of Covent Garden would be farther away—though that would likely please his mother even more.

Satisfied with his appearance at last, he turned to his valet. "Have the carriage brought around."

"What of breakfast, my lord?"

"I'm meeting Westing at Oxley's before seeing Rothschild. I'll breakfast there." He looked around at the sparsely furnished room with satisfaction. Most of his belongings had already been packed and awaited transport downstairs. It had been a very busy week. He'd had to hire additional staff, purchase new furnishings, and refurbish his wardrobe. Tonight, he would stay at the Rose & Crown. Tomorrow, he would take up residence in Mayfair and start anew.

The journey to Oxley's took an eternity thanks to an overturned cart they'd been forced to circumnavigate. By the time he arrived at his destination, Lucas was annoyed, hungry, and short of time.

"I was beginning to wonder if you'd forgotten," said Westing.

"The delay in my arrival was not of my making," Lucas told him, pausing to call a serving maid over and place his order. "It's uncouth to bolt one's food, but it seems I've little choice. Bloody thoroughfares are getting more congested every day. It took me nearly an hour to get here, and all because of a blasted overturned cart."

"It's only going to get worse," muttered Westing as he sipped his tea. "More people in Town this year than I can ever remember."

Thankfully, the service at the establishment was swift and the meal savory, mollifying most of Lucas's disgruntlement. Just as he was finishing, a conversation between two gentlemen seated nearby caught his attention.

"By the bye, I heard Harrow's ladybird sprouted wings," said one of the men. "Hart told me yesterday that he passed by her nest a week ago and marked it was being emptied. Said she'd gone and gotten herself a new lord and master." He sniffed. "I suppose we'll find out who the lucky bastard is soon enough."

The other man snorted. "Don't believe everything you hear, lad. I have it on good authority it were Harrow himself what moved her to Mayfair."

Lucas flicked a glance at Westing, whose face took on a distinctly discouraging look.

"Convenient, that," grunted the first man. "I should wonder what his wife thinks of it. It's one thing to keep a bit o' sweet on the side, but to move her into one's own neighborhood?" An incredulous bark of laughter burst from him. "M' wife would murder me in m' sleep."

"As would mine, but everyone knows Lady Harrow gets on well with her lord's lover."

"Think you it might be true, what they say? That the wench is servicing both master and mistress?"

"Damned if I knows," said the second man. "If 'tis, then I'll burn for envy. How bloody lucky can a man get?"

Lucas's ears grew hot. He'd heard of—and seen—such things before, but for some reason his gut rebelled at the thought of *her* doing it. He nodded at Westing, tossed coin on the table, and together they departed.

He couldn't help mulling over what he'd heard: she'd been removed to Mayfair. He'd find out her whereabouts quickly enough. If he didn't see her in passing himself, he was sure to learn the location from his no doubt scandalized staff or neighbors.

"Take us to Cork Street," he ordered his driver. To Westing, he said, "I appreciate your serving as a witness to the transfer. I'm sure everything will be in order."

"It's my pleasure."

They rode in silence for a few minutes, Lucas well aware he was under intense scrutiny.

At last, Westing spoke. "You know if you go looking for trouble, you're certain to find it. I should leave well enough alone, were I in your place."

"I *knew* you would be unable to bloody well keep off it," Lucas grumbled. "No, I don't intend to go looking for her. Do you expect me to walk the streets of Mayfair knocking on doors?"

"No, you're not quite that far gone yet," said his friend with a dry chuckle. "But I've known you a long time, Blackthorn. Once you set your mind to a purpose, you pursue it relentlessly to its end, and damn the consequences." He stopped and looked away. "Know that if you do so this time, I won't be able to second you."

A frown drew Lucas's brows together. Not that he anticipated needing one, but Westing had always served as his second. "Is there a specific reason why not, or have you simply tired of it?"

Westing's gaze rose to meet his. "I'm going to ask Lord Falmouth for permission to court his daughter."

"The red-haired hellion or her sweet blond sister?"

Westing's face colored. "The redhead, and her name is Charlotte."

A broad grin stretched Lucas's mouth. "Good man! With such a wife, you'll never suffer ennui. When is the funeral?"

"I have to win her heart and propose first," laughed his friend. "I was hoping you'd accompany me to see him this morning after finishing your business with Rothschild."

"I would not miss it for the world," Lucas replied. "But whatever am I to do once you've put on the leg iron? Besides find another friend to second me at duels, of course."

"You might consider marrying. After all, we are both of us thirty this year."

Lucas adopted a look of horror. "And ruin my reputation? Heaven forefend. And I'm well aware of my age. My mother reminds me of it at every opportunity."

"You need an heir. Don't you think it time to put the old wedding tackle to its proper use?"

"If I did, you would not be scolding me about my interest in Lady Diana—and how I choose to employ my 'tackle' is none of your concern. I shall thank you to kindly leave it out of the conversation."

"No, of course, you're right," said Westing at once. His sobriety lasted all of a few seconds. "Though you should probably get used to it surfacing in discussion, as I'm fairly certain your parents will be interested in its employment when they hear of you chasing after another man's bird."

A growl lodged itself in Lucas's throat, but he just couldn't stay wroth with Westing. Not when the man wore a look of such unrepentant impudence. "Toss-off," he muttered, giving in and laughing. "Were we not such good friends, I vow I would have shot you years ago for your cheek."

"I'm eternally grateful for your forbearance," said the other man with mock courtesy. "But truly, Blackthorn, you must know it's impossible to win the woman."

"Difficult, yes. Impossible? Never. Every woman has her price." *And so does every man.* Lucas had to admit she'd been right about that.

"Of all the women in London, you have to choose the one that presents the most danger to your continued longevity."

Lucas looked him squarely in the eye. "Something is not right about her, Westie."

"Something's not right about *you*. You're half mad."

He ignored the barb. "I don't doubt her loyalty to Harrow, but I *do* doubt the nature of their attachment."

Westing shook his head, clearly boggled. "I was wrong. You're *fully* mad. If you loved her, it would be different. God knows I'd stand for you in a blink if I thought you actually cared for the wench. I'm honestly beginning to question your sanity."

"I appreciate your concern, but I'm not looking to do anything rash. I'm merely curious about her."

"What in heaven's name do you need to know other than she belongs to someone capable of killing you?"

"Everything, starting with how a gently raised female like her came to be his mistress."

"Well, Fate has smiled upon you, my friend, because as it happens, I was present when they first met," said his friend, looking smug. "It was at the Whitfield ball. News of the scandal had just begun to travel, you see, when Lady Diana arrived. Having invited her, Lady Whitfield could hardly turn her away on the basis of a rumor. Once she was through the receiving line, however, no one would deign to speak to the poor thing."

"Except Harrow."

Westing nodded. "After Lady Whitfield retired in high dudgeon to the ladies' lounge along with Lady Harrow, he took pity on Lady Diana and danced with her. Everyone was scandalized, and I understand it caused a significant cooling between him and his wife. Two days later, it came out that Lady Diana had run off, that her family had disowned her, and she'd vanished. Then, a few months later, she pops up on Harrow's arm at an event his wife had declined to attend. A month after *that*, Lady Harrow invited her to tea. The three of them have been offending London's delicate sensibilities ever since. Satisfied?"

"Not by far," Lucas said drily. His innate skepticism wouldn't let the matter rest. "Lady Diana attended that ball fully aware of her situation, then," he mused aloud. "It was either a deliberate act of defiance to try and establish her innocence, or she was looking for a protector."

A shrug lifted his friend's shoulders. "Perhaps it was a bit of both. As for Harrow, I understand he was a right rogue before he married Lady Harrow, so it surprises me not that he snapped her up."

"I remember," Lucas said, a smile tugging at his mouth. "I wanted to be just like him and was rather disappointed when he put on the shackles. But I thought he was sensible about it, at least. He married a childhood friend, and I, along with everyone else, assumed it to be a love match."

"It certainly had every appearance of one in the beginning," said his friend. "They retired to his country estate after the wedding and disappeared from the London scene entirely for some time. When they came back following the birth of their son, Harrow seemed a changed man. Gone were his days of cheerful whoring, and there were no more high-stakes wagers. Everyone thought his fangs had been pulled until he took up with Lady Diana."

"You think she corrupted him?"

"I think that woman could corrupt a saint."

"I think you may be right about that," Lucas agreed, chuckling. "But I don't think she corrupted Harrow." He sucked a breath between his teeth. "I tell you, the air between them is not what it should be. There's a calculated quality to their interactions, almost as if they've been rehearsed. And they're far too cool for a couple having a torrid love affair."

"Not every man is ablaze with lust every minute of the day, you know."

Lucas looked at him steadily. "If she were *my* mistress, *I* certainly would be." He pressed on over Westing's groan. "I'm not sure what she is to him, but she's not his lover."

"Does it bloody well matter?" exclaimed Westing. "He's killed men over her—ran a man through only last year for putting his hands on her—and he's given a goodly number of nasty scars to several others for merely offering her insult. Whether or not she's wrapping his maypole is irrelevant."

But it does matter. For some unknown—and likely insane—reason, it mattered to him a great deal. Their arrival at the Cork Street address ended the conversation before Westing could further lament his apparent madness. A glum-faced Rothschild was ready and waiting for them, deed in hand, with his younger brother to stand as witness to the exchange.

Rothschild's manner was stiff, but not impolite as he shook Lucas's outstretched hand. "You'll find everything ready and in order."

Lucas could hardly blame him for being sullen. "Likewise."

The gentlemen exchanged no further pleasantries, for Rothschild chose not to linger while Lucas inspected the premises. From the kitchens below to the rafters above, the house's new owner filled his eyes with his winnings and was well pleased. The first-floor rooms were more lavishly decorated than those of his former residence, as were the private chambers upstairs. Even the servants' quarters in the attic were first rate as such things went.

They were walking through the ballroom's outer doors and onto a shallow terrace overlooking his new back garden when it really hit him. It wasn't a large garden, and it was in a terrible state of disarray, but it was private.

And it's mine. "Well, Westie? What think you? Have I risen in the world?"

"Indeed you have. Enough to warrant your mother's attention, I'm certain," said Westing. "Upon learning of your upward progress, she'll no doubt demand that you host a party at once. Your neighbors will certainly expect it."

Lucas grimaced. "I'll have my secretary discover their names and send out invitations once it's been arranged." Movement in his rear neighbor's much-larger garden caught his attention. His breath stilled. *Surely, it cannot be…*

"George's pudding prick," breathed Westing, coming up beside him. "Is that—by the dog's bollocks, it *is*. I don't believe it!"

Softly, Lucas laughed. "What was that you were saying earlier about Fate?"

"No wonder Rothschild was so sour," muttered Westing.

A slow smile formed on Lucas's lips. There, in the garden immediately abutting his own, dressed in a pale yellow morning frock, was none other than the woman who'd piqued his curiosity and robbed him of sleep: the one and only Lady Diana Haversham.

Chapter Six

"How *can* this have happened?" Diana railed, flapping the offending invitation in the air. "He had to have known. There can be no other explanation!"

"He could not possibly have known," said Harrow with irritating calm. "Everything was arranged and managed through my solicitor—a man I've trusted for the last twenty years. Neither Lady Buxton nor her solicitor knew me for the purchasing party until the sale was final, which was not until a fortnight prior. Rothschild lost his bet with Blackthorn nearly two months ago and only recently vacated the premises."

It sounded reasonable, but her panic wouldn't allow her to calm herself. "He'll find out. How can he not? He's probably watching us now." Her gaze flew to the window and across the space between their houses.

"Then we will make certain he sees only what we want him to see," insisted Harrow, taking her by the shoulders to gently turn her back around.

Diana burst into tears.

Her best friend's arms wrapped around her like a warm

blanket and pulled her close. "Hush now. You must stop this incessant worrying—all will be well."

"You *cannot* bring René here now," she choked out, taking the kerchief he offered and blowing her nose. The tender-hearted musician was to move in tomorrow under the guise of being her instructor. "It's too dangerous. In fact, you should sell this house at once, and I'll move elsewhere—back to my old one, since I've yet to sell it. The servants here are sure to strike up an association with the neighboring staff, and if any of them learn the truth—"

"As well as I'm paying this staff, even if they *do* see something, they will *say* nothing," he replied coolly. "Believe me, my dear, there are other men in London in situations similar to mine, and they've all managed to keep their secrets for many years."

"And what am I to do about this?" she asked, holding up the crumpled invitation.

"You will attend, of course." He dropped a kiss on her forehead. "And I'll be at your side. No doubt Blackthorn expects it and is well prepared to answer the scandal of having such a neighbor. We must likewise ready ourselves."

Anger surged through her, lending her strength. "How I wish I'd never laid eyes on that—that scoundrel!"

Her outburst elicited a gentle smile. "I fear there is little we can do about it now, save to play the hand we've been dealt."

Though his manner was calm and no doubt intended to be reassuring, her heart still raced. "And what will we do if he discovers us?"

A hard glint entered his eyes, and a chill crept into her bones, turning her upset to dread as he answered quietly, "One way or another, I'll ensure he keeps his silence." The dangerous look melted away, and he was once again her dear friend and not the deadly duelist. "In truth, I doubt it will come to violence. He seems a reasonable man, if a bit impulsive, but not the sort to be truly foolish. Regardless, I don't want you worrying yourself over it until there is reason. For now, there is naught but a cordial invitation to be answered."

She crushed the paper in her hand into a ball.

Laughing, Harrow took up her hand and removed the unlucky page. "Between my winning ways and your not-inconsiderable charms, we'll persuade him to be our friend."

She drew back in renewed alarm. "Our friend?"

Harrow's smile broadened an increment. "A wise man once said 'keep your friends close and your enemies closer'—and he was right. A strong public association will undermine the desire to reveal any discoveries he might make. He won't want others to paint him with the same brush."

Especially considering that particular brushstroke typically preceded a hangman's noose. It made sense, yet she still had misgivings. The idea of bringing Blackthorn into their circle both excited and terrified her—for reasons having nothing to do with her friends' continued longevity.

"Diana, I know you worry for me—"

"And René," she injected. "Have you forgotten yours is not the only life at risk?" Regret instantly set in as a wounded look entered his gentle eyes. "I'm sorry. I know you think of him before yourself. I'm just so afraid of what might happen if this goes ill."

"It won't," he whispered. "Trust me?"

There was no one on earth she trusted more. "Always."

"Then trust that I'll keep our safety—including yours—foremost in mind."

She nodded.

"And Diana?"

"Yes?"

"I know you don't want to hear this, but it must be said again that part of the reason you're so afraid of Blackthorn is that you're attracted to him."

Her throat closed, and her tongue cleaved to the roof of her mouth, refusing to deny it or form another excuse.

Harrow's eyes narrowed, and she could almost see the thoughts turning over in his mind as he observed her lack of response. "Ignoring it won't work," he eventually murmured with a soft smile. "I tried not to want René, you know. Impossible, of course, though I did everything in my power not to act on my desire. Even so, there was no hiding it from him. When he informed me the attraction was mutual, I was done. There was simply no denying what is between us. Just as there will be no denying it for you and Blackthorn."

An indignant huff broke from her lips. "I admit I find him pleasant enough to look at, and charming, to be sure—but not so much as to tempt me into endangering you and René." She'd never betray her friends over a handsome face. Never. "I'd sooner swim across the Thames in midwinter. *Naked*."

He chuckled and shot her an enigmatic little smile. "We shall see. The ball is not for another month, which gives us plenty of time to sort out matters. All will be as it should."

It was an answer which left her feeling no better at all.

The days stretched as Diana busied herself with settling in, adjusting to unfamiliar surroundings and becoming acquainted with newly hired staff.

Some feathers were ruffled when René joined her household and was given accommodation a mere two doors down from her own chamber. Teachers were normally considered above servants in the household hierarchy, but only just, and were typically quartered in the same fashion as the housekeeper, cook, and head footman. Diana made it clear at the outset, however, that she viewed him as more of a guest. She also bade Francine, her lady's maid who'd come with her from her old house, to warn any disgruntled staff against provoking her ire by showing any disrespect toward the man.

Diana was relieved to learn Harrow had elected to postpone further assignations with his lover until it was deemed safe. His prudence told her he'd paid more heed to her warning than he'd given her to believe.

She was determined not to let her unwanted neighbor's presence rattle her. Seeing nothing of its master, it was easy to pretend no one lived in the house behind hers. Within a week, Diana began to relax and enjoy herself. René availed himself of the drawing room's pianoforte daily, often for several hours at a time, gracing her home with the sweet strains of Pachelbel, Vivaldi, Rameau, and Handel.

The clouds had lifted yesterday, and today the sky was bright and the air unseasonably warm. Taking advantage, she'd had all the windows opened to allow fresh air into the house. The sound of René busy at the pianoforte drifted out to Diana's ears and mingled with the birdsong as she walked in her garden.

It was delightful to have a real garden again. Back when she'd lived with her aunt, she'd taken care of their tiny slice of earth. It had been her private retreat, a place of peace in a household full of simmering resentment and bitter disappointments. Her uncle's glower had never settled on her, and his voice had never barked at her from behind when she was outside in the sunshine. He disliked the outdoors, preferring to hole up in his library with his pipe and his ledgers. Her aunt had occasionally come out, but such visits had been rare. Usually, they'd only happened when she wanted to discuss something out of her husband's hearing.

This garden was much larger, and its previous owner had cared well for it. The roses were properly pruned, the flower beds free of weeds, and the hedges trimmed with precision. Harrow had hired a new gardener, but the fellow wouldn't arrive to take up his position for another week. Until then,

Diana surreptitiously pulled every weed she spied.

No sense in allowing them to gain a foothold.

As she meandered along the path to the rear, she marked the climbing vines on the brick wall that separated her space from that belonging to Lord Blackthorn. They'd gotten completely out of control and were hanging over its top. Examining them, she noticed fat buds protruding from the stems. Curiosity compelled her to pluck one and pry it open to see what color its petals would be. Pulling aside the thick curtain of leaves, she sought one that wouldn't be missed—and found the wall behind had changed from stone to wood. A frown pulled at her mouth as she widened the opening and discovered a latch and handle.

Had she not ventured a peek behind these vines, she might never have even known a gate was here. Tugging the foliage away, she examined the opening. It was small, just tall enough to let someone her height pass through without ducking.

The ladies who once graced these abutting gardens must have been good friends indeed to have installed such a passage. Rusted hinges that looked as if they hadn't moved in many years held the door in place. Bracing a hand against the wood, she pushed a little to see if it was still solid.

A commotion and a muffled curse sounded from behind the door, and Diana let out a surprised yelp.

"Hello?" said a voice on the other side. "I say, who's there?"

She cringed. Damned if it wasn't Blackthorn himself! "Hello? I'm so sorry to have startled you."

Silence held for a beat. "Lady *Diana*?"

Had she not exerted iron control, a laugh would've burst from her throat at how his voice had risen an octave.

"Whatever in heaven's name are you doing over there?" he asked. "Scaling the wall?"

Her face heated. "No," she retorted, indignant. "I was examining the vines and discovered a gate." Too late, she bit her tongue.

"A gate?"

"Yes," she replied resignedly. "There is a gate beneath the vines on this side." Clenching her teeth, she waited, and sure enough, a moment later there was a scraping sound as vines were swept aside on the other side of the door. Then, to her surprise, the door shook, followed by a loud *bang* and the screech of protesting hinges as it swung out, causing her to take a step back.

There in the opening, partially obscured by hanging greenery, was Lord Blackthorn. He stuck an arm out to clear the way between them and beamed at her. "I thought some animal was scurrying about over here, perhaps a cat trying to reach the top of the wall. How delighted I am to find *you* instead."

I'm sure you are. "I did not know anyone was over there, or I would have announced myself," she said, feeling more than a little awkward.

"No need to worry," he said, brushing it off with a negligent wave, which resulted in one of the vines escaping to slap him across the face.

This time, a laugh burst free before she could stifle it.

Sputtering, he shoved the offending foliage away and looked up at her, mischief dancing in his gray eyes. "It seems Mother Nature has it in for me. First the rain this morning spoiled my walk, and now the plants attack me."

"To be fair, we attacked them first."

"I shall have to retaliate," he muttered, eyeing them with feigned hostility. "At the least, they must be trimmed back so this gate can be repaired."

Alarm spiked through her. *Repaired?* "Why not leave them as they are? It's not as if this gate will ever be used again. I'm sure the blooms will be very beautiful once the buds open. It would be a shame to see them destroyed."

"Ah, but these vines grow all along this wall. A trimming here won't hurt them." He patted the wood fondly. "I'll have this put good as new straightaway."

Why? her mind shrieked. "For what purpose?" she asked innocently.

"Why, so we can be neighborly, of course. The people who built this between our houses must have been fast friends. I see no reason not to carry on their tradition."

Oh, no, you don't! "I doubt that would be considered proper, my lord."

A wide grin split his face. "Oh, come now, Lady Diana. People like us are little concerned with propriety."

Speak for yourself, rogue. "Lord Harrow might object."

"I doubt it," he replied, stunning her with the blunt answer. "He and I have become acquainted, and I now consider him a friend. Why, just yesterday he told me he was looking forward to bringing you to my ball so he could show you my garden. I've done a great deal to improve it."

Acquainted? When had *that* happened? And why hadn't Harrow informed her of it? She'd thought he'd forgotten about their discussion. Blackthorn was staring at her, awaiting her response. "I...I had no idea you were such an enthusiastic horticulturist," she replied brightly, her mind racing to find a way to extricate herself from this conversation so she could run back inside her house, lock the door behind her, and hide. *Coward.*

"I adore gardening such that I hardly need to employ any hands but my own," he said with a smug little smile. "Now you can come and see what I've done without having to wait."

What? No! "I really ought not to—"

"Ah, Harrow!" called Blackthorn, his gaze fixing on something behind her.

Whirling, she turned to see her protector strolling toward them, a quizzical look on his face.

As Harrow neared, his eyes took in the disheveled greenery, the open gate, and her neighbor's smiling visage. He returned it with a smile of his own. "The bill of sale neglected to include this charming detail," he said, gesturing to the gate.

"Indeed, I had no idea this existed," answered Blackthorn with a chuckle. "I was cutting the dead blooms off the rose bushes on my side and nearly dropped my clippers when it rattled. My surprise was complete upon discovering a door beneath the vines and this lovely vision beyond," he added, gesturing at Diana.

Harrow laughed. "A fortuitous find any day," said he, bending to drop a quick kiss on her mouth.

A courtesan would be accustomed to such open displays of affection, so she strove for cool indifference. She looked Harrow straight in the eye. "Lord Blackthorn is of a mind to have the vines trimmed away and the gate repaired," she said, careful to make it sound as if she thought it a fine idea in contrast to her unspoken protest.

Harrow's smile turned indulgent. "I don't see why not. After all, we are friends. Now we need not take the carriage around when we wish to visit."

Oh, bloody hell! She'd wring his neck later. For now, she had to play along. "Yes, indeed. I foresee many chats over evening pipes and brandy in this garden."

A thoroughly impish expression took over Blackthorn's features. "I had no idea ladies indulged in such things, but I shall be sure to make accommodation." She barely had time to register the joke and feel indignant before he went on. "You will of course be invited, as well, Harrow."

• • •

Damned if baiting her wasn't the most entertaining occupation in which Lucas had ever engaged! Her blushes and thinly veiled outrage were a delight.

He discussed the restoration of the gate with Harrow for a few more minutes before inviting them both to take a turn in his garden. He hadn't lied about improving the grounds. The garden had been in a shameful state when he'd taken ownership, and it had been one of the first things he'd set in order.

It had been necessary to take the entire area down to the dirt for a complete redesign. Now there were raised beds planted with tulips and other blooming plants, graveled walkways, ornamental trees and shrubbery, and rose bushes. He'd even had a small hothouse built in one corner for cultivating more exotic flora like orchids. In fact, ironically, the only thing he *hadn't* changed…were the vines covering the back wall.

He watched Lady Diana and Harrow as they admired his handiwork, his mind cataloguing their every word and action.

The mystery surrounding these two deepened with every encounter.

That chaste peck the fellow had given her in greeting had been all but brotherly, and he might as well have kissed a marble statue for all her response to it. Her sea-green eyes had lit upon seeing him, but there had been nothing more than pleased surprise in them. And now the man was advocating for an unguarded entry point into his mistress's garden. Certainly, no jealous lover would permit such a thing.

But if they are not lovers, then what are *they to each other?* Why would a man like Harrow keep such a beautiful woman in luxury if not to warm his sheets? From the vantage of his bedchamber window, he'd chanced to observe the lady several times over the previous fortnight. As far as he could tell, she lived quietly and maintained a proper household. As proper as any respectable lady.

At first he'd felt a stab of envy every time Harrow had come to visit her, but that had quickly faded once Lucas had become acquainted with the gentleman. It had come as a bit of a shock, really, Harrow extending the hand of friendship. He attributed the gesture as owing to the need to be on friendly terms with one's neighbor. Or one's mistress's neighbor, to be precise.

He'd developed a genuine liking for the fellow. Harrow carried himself with utmost confidence, yet he was unassuming. Humble, even, and far less intimidating than he'd been led to anticipate. Certainly not the taciturn, short-tempered figure people like Westie had painted him.

The musician who'd taken up residence in Lady Diana's household had given him pause, but he'd witnessed no late-night rendezvous, and they'd observed every propriety during their occasional walks in her garden. There were no furtive glances between them, no stolen kisses or impassioned embraces beneath the arbor.

It hit him suddenly that there'd been none of that during her garden strolls with Harrow, either. The instinctual doubt that had nagged him when they'd first met now spoke more strongly than ever—there was no way this woman was in an intimate relationship with Harrow. He'd be willing to wager good money on it.

Again, he wondered what they were to each other.

Their discussion with Liverpool rose to the fore of his memory. Her interest in her uncle's doings notwithstanding, the lady was awfully well informed with regard to both domestic and foreign politics.

Or is she? What if Harrow had merely fed her the information to give to Liverpool under the pretense of a personal vendetta? Was the marquess more ambitious than he appeared? More importantly: *Is she his cat's paw?*

But no. She'd been a shy little mouse when he'd first met her. The sophistication he saw now could only be a thin veneer, surely? He wondered what he'd find beneath if he scratched the surface...

"I'm uncertain as to whether it would be prudent," Lady Diana was saying.

His head snapped up. "I beg your pardon?"

Annoyance flashed in her eyes, but otherwise her demeanor remained unruffled. "I said it might not be prudent to create an open passage between our properties. The servants are sure to talk of it, and once it becomes public knowledge..."

The pointed look she leveled at him reminded him of nothing so much as a strict governess chastising a charge. "I would not have thought *you* to care so much for gossip," he quipped, raising a brow at her in challenge.

Again, the faint tinge of roses appeared in her cheeks. Again, not the reaction of a courtesan.

"I worry not for my good name, but yours," she replied, meeting his gaze with a raised brow of her own. "And yes, I know your reputation for wild living, but your escapades to date are the sort easily tolerated by Society." She slid a glance to their left, where Harrow meandered the path a short distance away, then her gaze returned to skewer Lucas. "Ours are less so. I'm sure you've heard tales."

Oh, he'd heard. "Indeed. But such rumors give no proof of veracity, especially when they originate from disgruntled former servants and the like."

A smug expression settled across her features. "Again, you'll never be able to decipher the reality from the fiction, unless...would you have me confirm which rumors are true and which are wild speculation?"

Now *there* was an interesting idea. He was almost certain to recognize it if she spoke falsely, but such would be a dangerous assumption this early in the game. *Perhaps not yet. Give it a bit more time.* "I would be no gentleman if I imposed upon you to reveal such intimacies."

A soft, derisive snort escaped her, surprising him. "No gentleman would suggest keeping an open passage between his property and that of another man's mistress."

She had a point. "I concede the argument," he said with a deliberate show of chagrin. "Very well. When the gate is repaired, I shall see that it is locked—and give you the key." He would persuade her to use it later.

The startled blink she gave him was yet another incongruity. "You would give up your advantage?"

Interesting choice of words. So she views this as a game, too. "And what advantage is that, pray tell?"

Once more, her cheeks pinked at his implication. "I'd be a blind fool not to acknowledge your interest in me, Lord Blackthorn, or do you deny that you seek my favor?"

He let a slow smile curl his mouth. "While I respect Harrow enough not to outright poach, I cannot deny my interest in you. You're a delectable contradiction: a courtesan who strikes me as more of a proper lady than any night blossom." He knew very well his turn of phrase narrowly skirted the edge of propriety. *He who risks naught gains naught.*

Right on cue, the rosy stain in her cheeks deepened. When she spoke, her tone was the morning frost. "I was once a 'proper lady,' as you put it. Old habits are slow to perish." At once, her manner shifted back to mischief. "Give me but a few more years of roasting at the brink of hellfire's flames, however, and I'm certain I'll be able to satisfy even your wicked expectations."

The tension seated in his gut twisted a little tighter. Was she flirting with him? Surely not, what with her protector so near? He decided to err on the side of caution and keep the banter light. "I have no expectations, madam," he said, giving her his easiest smile. "I learned long ago to assume nothing when it comes to women. For all I know, you may decide to seduce Prinny—or join a convent."

It earned him an honest laugh. The sight all but robbed his lungs of air. The curve of her mouth in laughter was perfection, the lift of her cheeks gentling her eyes with a tender light. She looked utterly angelic, a sharp contrast to the worldly-wise visage she usually wore. He could see the young woman she'd been before her tragic downfall.

Regret filled him. Had he been less focused on himself years ago when they'd first met, he might have *seen* her, and things might have turned out quite differently. He remembered she'd been painfully demure, declining to raise her eyes to meet his—and that had been *his* fault. He'd thought her a quiet little mouse unworthy of interest, and he'd passed her by without so much as a second glance. If only he'd taken a moment to politely address her and cause her to look up, he'd have been enchanted.

He was enchanted now. Years ago, she might have faded into the wainscoting, but now she was a scintillating presence impossible to ignore.

"Are you quite well, Lord Blackthorn?"

Her inquiry jarred him from his stunned reverie, and his mouth closed with a soft *pop*. "I...I was remembering when we were first introduced." His ears grew unbearably hot, and he knew he must be flushed to the roots of his hair. "It was at the Cheltenham ball. You wore white flowers in your hair."

The tightening of her face was almost imperceptible. Almost. "That was a long time ago. I am no longer that child."

"You were no child then," he quipped. "I, however, behaved like one. Please accept my humblest apology for my rudeness that day. I was no gentleman, or I would have made some effort at conversation and asked you to dance."

The depth of his chagrin was such that it sent another wave of heat across his face. Her gaze grew laden with some emotion. It could easily have been mistaken for regret, but he sensed more. He sensed anger. "I'm sorry to have made you recall what is doubtless an unsettling memory—"

"Not at all," she cut in, her face smoothing once more into an expression of nonchalance. "My prior life, while not always idyllic, was one blessed with few concerns. In fact, my only task was to marry a suitable gentleman." One shoulder lifted, and a small laugh escaped her lips. "Despite my obvious failure, I've managed to do quite well for myself. I want for nothing."

Save love. Perplexed that such a thought should even cross his mind, he let out an incredulous bark of laughter. Her askance look prompted him to make up a hasty explanation for his outburst. "Which is exactly why I've yet to wed, myself."

The instant it left his lips, he mentally kicked himself. "I-I mean, not that I *never* wish to marry, but why rush into it? I'm content with things as they are. I mean, I could. If I wanted. But I don't. Not yet." He was babbling. *Babbling.* Like an utter fool. *Stop talking. Just stop.*

One caramel brow had slowly risen as he'd spoken, and now a slight smile curved her lips. "One expects a gentleman to avoid the matrimonial noose for as long as possible. If one is content with one's situation, then I certainly see no reason to alter it. Like me, you've found happiness in remaining unfettered."

At this smooth handling of his blunder, Lucas's initial assessment regarding her level of sophistication underwent swift modification. She'd learned a great deal in her two years' exile. A great deal. "Then we are kindred spirits," he replied with an internal wince. *What is the* matter *with me?* First blathering on like a complete idiot, and now this? How did this woman turn him into a gibbering imbecile?

Yet despite every instinct screaming at him to hold his tongue, his mouth continued producing sounds. "I suppose you *would* marry, however, if the opportunity arose?"

Such was her look of astonishment at this inquiry that Lucas wondered whether any blood remained in his extremities, for it felt as though every last drop had risen to his face.

Her expression told him his question had clearly caught her off guard, and in that candid moment of surprise he again saw a young woman of surprising naïveté. "I suppose I might," she answered, the words seeming carefully weighed and measured. "But under the circumstances I doubt such an opportunity will ever manifest. I'm a courtesan, my lord."

"It's not unheard of for such women to wed their protectors," he replied, again astounded at his boldness. *In for a pence, in for a pound.* "I've heard it said that your Lord Harrow intends you to replace his wife in the event of her death."

Her reaction to *that* was as suspect as any he'd yet seen. Instead of the smug affirmation of a mercenary female assured of a coveted position, he saw sudden fury fill her eyes. It was only for an instant, but it spoke volumes.

When she answered, however, her voice carried none of that anger. "I consider Lady Harrow to be my friend. I know most people are unable to accept that a man's mistress can be friends with his wife, but it's quite true for us. I certainly hold no ill will for that lady and in fact wish her a long and healthy life."

He just couldn't help himself. "So you have no ambitions at all, then?"

"Certainly none that involve the untimely death of a good friend!" she hissed, the wrath returning to light her eyes and color her cheeks.

A thrill raced through Lucas as he realized he was now seeing the *real* Lady Diana. Anger often removed the masks people wore, showing the true self. What he saw was... astonishingly commendable. Loyalty, morality, altruism. Not qualities one would expect to find in a courtesan. His suspicion concerning her function in Harrow's life increased yet more.

As he considered the flushed, angry woman before him, he marked how the sun shone on her honey hair, turning it into burnished gold. His fingers itched to feel its texture, his palms to frame that lovely face and soothe it to calmness. He'd riled her, and he'd done it on purpose, just to get the true measure of her. Curiosity had compelled him, but now he almost regretted it, because knowing who she really was beneath the facade hadn't cured him of his attraction to her.

Indeed, no. It had only served to fling fuel upon the already burning fire.

Attraction and admiration, when combined, were the world's most potent aphrodisiac. Contending instincts warred within him, one driving him to do as he imagined, as he desired—to cup her flaming cheeks and kiss away her upset. The other, however, was thankfully far louder, telling him to keep his distance lest he end up facing his new friend Harrow on the field of honor at dawn.

Say something, you ass! Apologize. "I humbly crave your pardon, madam," he said, all nerves. It took all his willpower to keep from looking to see where Harrow was as he addressed her. "In giving voice to such distasteful gossip, I have again exhibited the most rude and un-gentlemanlike behavior. Tell me what I must do to regain your good regard."

Chapter Seven

Diana longed for nothing so much as to pull back her arm and slap Blackthorn with all her might, but Harrow, who was not far off, would hear, and then there would be trouble. Stuffing her ire back down, she regarded her neighbor with all the frigidity she could muster. "You may begin by never again speaking of my friends in so coarse a manner."

The bottom dropped from her stomach as, too late, she realized her mistake. *Did I just refer to Harrow and his wife as my friends?*

The subtle shift in Blackthorn's expression did not go unmarked. Contrition bled from his gaze, replaced by the distinct gleam of triumph, as if he'd just won a great prize. "Old habits are indeed slow to perish," he murmured, using her own words against her. "The lady may be removed from her raising, but the raising can never be removed from the lady. You're not at all as I've been led to expect."

Her heart tried to claw its way up out of her throat, but to her surprise, he elected not to further pursue that path.

"I have erred and offended you, madam. Deeply, I fear. I

must again beg your forgiveness. My curiosity got the better of me and led my tongue to incivility."

Curiosity be damned! It required great effort to maintain a placid demeanor when she was torn between the desire to run in terror and the need to repair the damage already done before it was too late. If it wasn't already. "I'm well aware of the speculation about me," she said, taking a steadying breath. "The mixture of truth and falsity is doubtless bewildering from your perspective."

"You have a gift for understatement," he said with a rueful half smile. "You'll pardon my shock, but I've never heard of a man's mistress referring to him and his wife as 'friends.' At best, the wife and the mistress tolerate each other, but friendship?" He left it there, hanging in the air between them.

So much for thinking he'd decided to leave it alone! It was time to put into action the contingency plan she and Harrow had formulated in the event of a break in their cover story. "Although Lord Harrow is my lover and indeed, my protector, I also consider him my friend. I'm privileged to have also found favor with his lady wife, who could have considered me a rival and a threat to her position, but instead welcomed me."

Of all the rumors about them, the idea that Lady Harrow was somehow part of a triangle involving her husband and his mistress was the most sordid. Minerva was well aware of it, yet held her peace. Better for people to think *that* than to learn the truth. Blackthorn's eyes betrayed him, telling her he'd most definitely heard the tale.

Dropping her voice even lower, Diana continued. "Few know it, but Lord and Lady Harrow have been friends almost from infancy. Their marriage was one of convenience rather than passion. Thus, when the physician who delivered Henry—their son—warned Harrow it would surely kill her to bear another child, he vowed never to touch her again. Theirs is an amicable arrangement, and I am part of it. I agreed never to sow discord between them or seek to usurp her, and she has rewarded my fidelity with her friendship and trust. My company may be paid for, Lord Blackthorn, but there are some things money cannot purchase. Lord and Lady Harrow have been good to me, and I would not betray either of them for the world."

So piercing was his clear gray gaze that she had to stop herself from squirming.

At last, just before her composure threatened to crumble, he spoke. "I begin to comprehend. Both you and your situation are far more complex than people assume."

"So it is with most things, I imagine," she quietly snapped. "Which is why one should be slow to pass judgment. Think what you will of my adulterous relationship with Lord Harrow, but leave Lady Harrow out of your crude conjecture."

He looked duly chastised as he conceded. "Rare is the occasion upon which I am humbled, but you, madam, have most assuredly put me in my place. I'm ashamed to say I've allowed myself to be guided by the opinions of others where you are concerned, when I ought to have ignored them in favor of forming my own. That error must now be corrected, as my findings are in direct opposition to almost everything I've heard."

"Almost?"

His eyes lit with amusement. "Well, you *are* quite the loveliest woman I've ever had the pleasure of knowing. I cannot contradict that general view."

She forced herself to look him calmly in the eye and breathe as if her heart weren't hammering against her ribs. "And what of your opinion concerning my character?"

His smile gentled. "Your cleverness is eclipsed only by your compassion and loyalty, Lady Diana. Lord Harrow is indeed quite the luckiest of men, for his wife is a saint and his lover unlike any woman I've ever known or even heard of. Had you not become his mistress, you would have made a wonderful wife."

Diana nearly laughed aloud over his visible discomfiture as he realized what he'd said. Pity moved her to be merciful. "I doubt many of the gentlemen that once considered a match with me would agree with you."

"That's only because none of them have taken the opportunity to get to know you."

The quiet statement sent a tendril of heat snaking down to coil at the base of her spine. "I'm far too outspoken for such domestic bliss," she said, hoping to steer the conversation into less treacherous waters. "Having been granted relative freedom to do as I please, I fear I would chafe under the yoke of a husband's authority. I prefer to remain untamed."

"To tame you would be an egregious sin," he replied, his eyes darkening dangerously. "Better to let a wild creature come of its own volition to an open hand offering an enticement than to trap it and risk forever destroying both its nature and inherent beauty."

And like some wild creature faced for the first time with a huntsman intent on taking it for a trophy, Diana froze, even as the coil of desire within her tightened. *This must stop. Immediately.* "I thought you were decided against poaching?"

A guilty look flickered in his eyes an instant before a wry smile tilted his lips and chased it away. "I am, indeed. And, unless I'm mistaken, no offer save that of friendship has been laid before you."

It was a blatant half-truth, but she could work with such. She squared her shoulders. "Then I accept your offer. As a *friend*, I hope you'll be discreet regarding our conversation today. I should be..." She chose her next words with utmost care, "disappointed, if Lady Harrow ever learned of it and became distressed."

At this, his smile broadened into something more genuine. "Then allow me to assure you of my unrelenting silence on the matter. The grave will be more forthcoming than I, should anyone inquire of me concerning our exchange. In fact, you may henceforth consider my lips sealed against all temptation to share our conversations with anyone."

Only time would tell whether he spoke true or if this was just another pretty speech from a right rogue. She raised her voice a bit. "Then I count myself fortunate to name you among my friends."

"Splendid. And perhaps we should celebrate our newfound friendship?" he suggested, matching her volume. Again, the smile widened an increment, giving rise to a dimple beside his mouth.

The sight of it sent an unexpected bolt of want lancing through her. Suspicion made her want to narrow her eyes at him, but she forced herself to maintain exterior calm. "What do you propose?"

"A picnic," he said at once. "Oh, I know I'm throwing a ball soon, but such events lack warmth. I've invited several of my closest friends to dine outdoors with me here in this very garden three days hence. I now invite both you and Lord Harrow to join us."

Harrow's voice preceded his appearance by only a moment as he returned to her side. "To what have we been invited, may I ask?"

Feeling a burst of affection for her protector for coming to her rescue, Diana took up one of Harrow's hands and held it between her own. "A picnic," she told him, nodding toward Blackthorn with enthusiasm.

Taking her cue, Blackthorn began to elaborate. As he did so, she again took his measure. If he kept his word and mentioned nothing of their conversation to his friends, which she would ascertain while at this picnic of his, then perhaps she might be willing to tolerate his neighborly presence.

Still, they would need to be extra careful. Harrow had visited her several times, but his first romantic rendezvous with René at this address was to occur tomorrow evening. As her protector graciously accepted Blackthorn's picnic invitation, she contemplated the situation.

Seeing how often Blackthorn's gaze flicked over to her as he was talking to Harrow, an idea began to form. The man could hardly keep his eyes off her. She imagined his curious gaze was frequently drawn toward her house.

A wicked chuckle lodged in her throat. Perhaps she might use Blackthorn's meddlesome nature against him. Instead of having all the curtains drawn before the couple's arrival, what if she left them open for a little while? Just long enough to let anyone who might be watching witness a bit of carefully orchestrated exhibition? Seeing her "entertain" Harrow and another gentleman—René would be unrecognizable—would sorely challenge any further assumptions on his part.

The idea almost made her laugh aloud. As soon as she and Harrow had a moment of privacy, she'd ask his opinion. Oh, it would be such fun!

And yet…it *had* been nice to have someone's genuine admiration, even if only for a little while. He *had* truly admired her.

Don't be a fool! He'd admired the facade. Not her. Not Diana. Though he'd come closer to uncovering her true self than anyone, Blackthorn hadn't managed to get under her armor completely. And she didn't intend to let him.

As soon as they'd extricated themselves from her neighbor and were once more safely behind walls, windows, and wainscoting, she told Harrow her idea.

A burst of delighted laughter was his initial response. But he quickly sobered. "You really are quite terrified of him.

And not, I think, entirely for my sake."

"I am," she admitted, hating herself for it. "He has this way of looking at me that makes me feel..." *Naked? Exposed? Vulnerable?* "As if he can see right through me. I fear even the smallest misstep, lest he know me for a liar and tell everyone."

Harrow's comforting grasp on her shoulders made her look up at him. "I've already begun drawing him in, my dear. Within a few weeks, our names will be irrevocably linked as bosom friends in the minds of the *Ton*. I guarantee it. All you must do is maintain appearances here. And I think your plan is a damned good one."

So it was that the following day René arrived incognito as "an acquaintance from the club" alongside Harrow, and Diana played hostess to the pair with extra gusto, joining in several games of cards and then charades in her cozy, garden view salon...with the curtains *open*. The abundant libations they consumed—diluted wine and tea-tinted water—rounded out the deception. When Harrow joined her and their new "friend" in an embrace in which Diana was caught between the two men, they made certain it was directly before the broad windows.

It was all an act, of course. For the most part, the hands that appeared to be all over her were in fact hovering a scant inch or so above her silk-clad form. René grasped her waist once to turn her around to face him so he could lean her back against Harrow and "kiss" her in a manner that hid her face from view. When he was done, Harrow swept her up into his arms and, followed by their "lusty" guest, proceeded upstairs to her bedchamber. There, before her unveiled windows, they slowly undressed her down to her chemise. As René worked at loosening her corset, Harrow divested himself of his jacket and sauntered to the window to draw the curtains shut, thus ending "the show."

As soon as he locked the door and they were safe from prying eyes, Diana waved the gentlemen off. Grinning, they slipped through another door connecting her bedchamber to the special one adjoining it, one built specifically *without* any windows. Harrow had decorated it all in black silk and had filled it with an array of items dedicated to love play. The servants all assumed the room had been designed for her, of course, but in truth the only time she'd been inside it had been the day she'd taken up residence here.

Undressing herself the rest of the way, Diana drew on her wrapper and set about unpinning her hair. The temptation to go and peek through her drapes to see if there were any silhouettes in the windows of the house behind hers was almost overwhelming. Throughout the entire farce, she'd felt as if eyes were watching her, but had no way of knowing. It was nerve-wracking. She and Harrow had been convincing enough that their own staff thought them passionate lovers, but never before had they attempted to fool outside eyes in so audacious a manner.

Diana hoped they'd had an audience in her meddlesome neighbor. For all she knew, more than one person might have been watching their faux *ménage à trois*, which was all to the good if it made grist for the gossip mill. If no one had seen the illusion, however, it had been a wasted effort.

Picking up the book she'd been reading earlier, she tried to ignore the occasional soft groan that bled through the wall separating her chamber from the one hosting the lovers. Harrow and René always tried to be discreet on her behalf, but passion was seldom quiet. Such things had shocked her in the beginning, but no longer.

Though she remained innocent in the strictest physical sense, Diana had acquired an astonishing amount of sexual knowledge during her two years with Harrow. It had been a necessity. She couldn't pretend carnal knowledge without at least knowing what the act might entail—in various configurations.

Suppressing a chuckle, she reflected that, despite being a virgin, she likely knew more about bed sport than most married women. If she ever *did* have a wedding night, she'd have to feign gross ignorance. *I wonder if even Blackthorn, with his black reputation, knows as much as I?*

And just like that, heat rushed into her face and made the tips of her ears prickle. That she should have such a thought after concocting this elaborate ruse for the sole purpose of throwing him off the scent told her just how dangerous he was. Still, if she had to guess, she imagined he knew quite a lot, and from experience rather than dry lecture. Harrow, bless him, had told her all the particulars, but it had been a purely clinical instruction.

Instruction with words is a far cry from the sort of instruction Blackthorn would likely give...

The faint noises that occasionally filtered through the wall suddenly had an entirely different effect on her. She found herself uncomfortably warm as she wondered if Blackthorn would muffle his groans or unabashedly howl his pleasure. And would her utterances be anything at all like what she'd voiced without any feeling for the benefit of eavesdropping servants?

Stop this. Stop it at once!

Too low to be heard outside her door, she began to softly hum to herself to drown out any other sounds. Harrow would doubtless laugh and call her a prude over such a reaction—if she ever chose to tell him about it, that is. Which she wouldn't. Ever.

The lady may be removed from her raising, but the raising can never be removed from the lady. That's what Blackthorn had said to her only yesterday. She would never reconcile her raising with...this. Or with these thoughts of Blackthorn that kept resurfacing despite all efforts to the contrary.

Diana tossed and turned in her huge bed long after all grew quiet and the lamps were put out. Over and over, she reviewed her interactions with Blackthorn, searching for something that would make him less appealing. It was a study in futility.

· · ·

On unsteady legs, Lucas walked away from his window in a state of both shock and undeniable arousal. Palming the stiffness between his legs to ease his discomfort, he put down the opera glasses he'd taken to carrying with him ever since what he'd dubbed "the Shakespearian farce" had been enacted, and sank into his favorite chair before the hearth. His gaze lingered on the glowing coals, the only light in the room, as he contemplated what he'd just seen.

He'd thought himself uninhibited. He'd even fancied himself a hedonist. But after just witnessing an exhibition fit for the Hellfire Club, he now revised those self-designated labels. He was in no way prepared to accept the reality that Diana, who'd seemed far too wholesome for such an occupation, was in truth utterly debauched. Indeed, the lady had clearly enjoyed being the object of lust for both Harrow and his guest.

As for Harrow, despite Lucas's earlier assessment, he had no choice but to admit he'd been wrong about the fellow. The man was a libertine and must have one hell of a penchant for voyeurism to allow anyone else to touch Diana, because heaven knew if she were *his*, he'd never let another man lay so much as a finger on her and live to tell the tale.

A ragged chuckle escaped him, its soft mockery competing against the fire's crackle. *Friends.* She'd told him Harrow was her friend as well as her lover. She'd also named his *wife* a friend. It now occurred to him that perhaps the other rumor Westie had spoken of was true, too, and Lady Diana was lover to both the gentleman *and* his wife.

Her relationship with Harrow might be lacking in passion—although what he'd just seen certainly challenged *that* assumption—but her outrage toward Lucas when he'd suggested she might one day replace Harrow's current wife had been too swift and genuine to be false. Her loyalty to that lady was strong enough to be called love.

But is it that *kind of love?* He supposed he'd have to see them together to form an opinion. *Westie did say the pair shopped and took tea together...*

A bark of laughter burst from his throat at the very idea of spying on his neighbor when she was out shopping with another man's wife to determine whether or not they were lovers—in order to decide if she could be persuaded into *his* bed! The knowledge he'd gained tonight had lessened his interest in Diana not one bit. If anything, it only made her more fascinating.

Unfortunately, Lucas wasn't into sharing. Which raised another question: *Is she?* Did Diana do it to indulge her own desires or only to satisfy those of her protector? *If she was being coerced, she hid her dislike well.*

Another thought hit him. They'd be coming to his picnic the day after tomorrow. He'd have to look them both in the face and act like he hadn't just seen...*that.* His eyes narrowed in the dark as he replayed it in his mind. Now that his arousal had abated, his thoughts were clearer.

What exactly *had* he seen? Touches. A few kisses. Diana nearly naked.

Nearly naked. The curtains had been drawn before she'd been deprived of all modesty.

Why?

His suspicious mind homed in on the question. Why had

Harrow drawn the curtains just before the lady was rendered completely nude? Why would a man who was wicked enough to have his mistress participate in threesomes with other men care at that point about them being seen? Especially when his reputation for such depravity was established. Especially in the midst of what ought to have been a moment of lustful abandon. Instead, he'd calmly tossed his jacket over a chair and walked across the room to close the drapes.

Just as in a play, when the curtain is lowered to allow for a set change.

Stinging heat swept across Lucas's skin in a great wave, gooseflesh rising immediately in its wake.

It was staged! The whole bloody tableau had been quite deliberately set up for someone's viewing pleasure, and he had a good idea who that someone was. Certainty thrummed in his veins, and with it, a sense of triumph. He'd wager that the scene behind those curtains was nowhere near as debauched as his lovely neighbor would have him believe.

Again, the question begged: *why?* Why the effort to make everyone believe they were so immoral? What were she and Harrow hiding behind their wicked reputations?

Of course, he could be wrong. About all of it. But again, certainty settled in the back of his mind. Rarely had his instincts led him astray, and he vowed to trust them now. A grim smile creased his lips. He was going to figure out Lady Diana Haversham—or die trying.

By the following evening, London's tattler columns had run amok with a witness account describing "Lord H's" latest erotic escapade with his mistress, confirming Lucas's belief that more eyes than his had borne witness to their little act. Unfortunately, from the visual perspective of the tale, it appeared said witness hailed from among his own staff.

Though offended one of his servants had to have been the culprit, Lucas could hardly blame them for it. There was good money to be had in trading information concerning members of the upper crust. As long as the servant kept their mouth shut concerning *his* activities, he could not grudge them the extra coin. After all, his neighbor *had* put on quite a show.

With the breaking news, preparations for his picnic had surpassed material concerns; mental agility would be required to safely navigate social waters in the wake of the storm. Thankfully, his was to be a small gathering. Westie would be there, of course, and Lucas knew he could count on his closest friend for support. The other attendees might not like being in the company of people who'd been the subject of such lurid gossip, but Westie, the only one he'd warned, was doubtless salivating over the prospect.

This was the thought that rose to the fore of Lucas's mind the following morning as he strolled out onto the broad terrace overlooking the gardens. Inhaling deeply, he grinned at the certainty that Westie would be the first of his guests to arrive that afternoon.

Gazing out over the wall separating his and Lady Diana's properties, Lucas saw his neighbor's windows were open to take advantage of the fresh air. The sound of a pianoforte and a sweet, high voice accompanying it drifted through those on the east-facing corner of the house—her drawing room.

Moving down the terrace as far as he could, he strained to see in, but his view was partially blocked by a potted tree. A curse on his lips, he wedged himself between it and the wall, crouching down so as not to be seen. First checking to be sure he was adequately concealed, he once more brought out the opera glasses.

Heat crept up from his collar to warm his face and make

his scalp prickle as he unfolded them. *If anyone sees me like this, I'll be the laughingstock of London.* Shame was a hot coal in the pit of his stomach, yet he didn't stop. He knew he was behaving like the worst sort of busybody, but damn it all, his curiosity would not be repressed.

Peering across the divide from his new vantage point, he could see about half the room's interior. There sat the infamous lady of the house at her instrument, fingers flying over the keys, voice lifted in song. Such was her skill at playing that he forgot for a moment to do anything but enjoy the piece.

Then movement caught his eye, and he watched her music teacher breeze into view. After a few minutes spent playing under his approving gaze, Diana stopped and scooted over to allow him to sit beside her—*close* beside her, Lucas noticed. His nimble fingers then joined hers as, together, they played the same song again. A moment later, the man's rich tenor rose alongside her clear soprano, adding a complementary counter melody.

Something dark twisted in Lucas's gut as he watched her throw her head back in open-mouthed laughter when they finished the rollicking piece. It eased only after she relinquished the instrument to the man and moved to a nearby chair beside the window to read while he continued playing.

Clearly, this wasn't a music lesson. Her fingers had lingered on the fellow's shoulder far too long as she'd risen, and her manner with him wasn't that of a student with a teacher, but rather that of someone much more familiar.

Why would someone as accomplished as she require an instructor to begin with? Lucas added the question to his ever-growing list.

A mistress with a passionless protector to whom she was unswervingly loyal. A sham show of carnality clearly meant to shock and distract any observer. A music instructor for a pupil who was, if his ears had told him no lies, equally as skilled as her supposed teacher.

What is *she, really?*

So deep was he amid his own thoughts that he almost missed it when the music came to an abrupt halt. Squinting through the glasses, he saw another visitor had arrived: Harrow, presumably to fetch her for the picnic, though it was still several hours off. Oddly, Diana didn't deign to stir from her chair to greet her protector. In fact, she only looked up from her book for the briefest moment in acknowledgment of his arrival.

The music teacher's reaction, however, was quite different.

Lucas's jaw went slack as the man practically leaped up from his seat at the pianoforte to greet Harrow with...a *kiss.* And it was no dispassionate kiss upon the cheeks, as between longstanding friends, but rather the hungry clashing of mouths reserved for desperate lovers.

"Blood-y hell," Lucas muttered to himself, drawing out each syllable as Harrow's long arms wrapped around the smaller man's shoulders and clasped him tight in an embrace that would make one think they'd been parted for years— *rather than mere hours.*

The epiphany brought with it an invigorating rush of elation. It *had* to be! He'd wager his inheritance that the gentleman "friend" who'd "shared" Diana's favors the other night was none other than her music teacher in disguise. *The height is about right, the build...*

Lucas's face stretched with a grin of pure delight. *Ha! Now I know your secret, madam charlatan!* Diana was no man's mistress after all. The clever actress had only fooled all of London into thinking it in order to hide her protector's romantic involvement with another man!

His smile grew smug as he watched the lady at last put down her book and rise. Going to the men, who were now talking animatedly, she embraced first one and then the other with almost familial affection. Then, as she was conversing with Harrow, Lucas saw the musician's hand absently drift down to the small of her back and remain there, gently massaging in small circles as he listened to the other two talk.

When she looked at him, Lucas saw her face in profile, and it was alight with a soft-eyed, adoring smile. Reaching around his waist, she then returned his affectionate gesture with a side hug and leaned her head on his shoulder.

The ebullience of a moment ago disintegrated in an instant, the fire of his delight turning into cold ashes. Part of him wanted to believe it was another ruse, but reason told him that since her drawing room wasn't within direct line of sight of his house, it couldn't be. Desperate, he searched for any clue the three might know they were being watched, but found none. The angles were all wrong, and there was nothing about their positions that smacked of playing to an audience.

Which could mean only one thing: Diana was part of a love triangle. Lucas sat back on his heels, numb. Harrow and Diana *both* loved the musician. The musician loved *both* of them. She and Harrow were friends, seemingly content to share in their lover's divided affections. That she should be involved in such a convoluted relationship baffled him entirely.

What sort of female mind could make peace with such an arrangement? Every woman he'd ever known was the jealous sort. The instant her man's attention wandered in the slightest, the green-eyed monster turned her into a vengeful lunatic. Some women even grew envious of their man's friendships with other men—the platonic sort. If he had to wed, and he *would* at some point, he wanted to marry someone like *her*, someone who wouldn't drive him to Bedlam over petty jealousies.

Determination filled him. Oh, he'd get to know his neighbor; he'd get to know her *very* well. He might be surprised at her apparent lack of inhibition and morality, but the attraction he felt remained undiminished. He'd sate it, if allowed, and while doing so seek his answers. There must be other women like her. He just needed to know what to look for.

Rising from his crouch, he stretched protesting muscles and pocketed the opera glasses. There would be no more spying. It wasn't necessary anymore, now that he knew the truth. With one final glance over his shoulder at his intriguing neighbor's house, he went back inside to attend to preparations.

Chapter Eight

Diana knew the instant their eyes met that something had changed. Blackthorn's speculative gaze all but impaled her as he offered her a friendly greeting at their shared garden gate. She barely contained a satisfied grin. Oh, yes. He'd seen! He'd seen exactly what they'd *wanted* him to see.

It was a small gathering, as promised, for which she was thankful. Aside from a few curious, sidelong glances cast her way, however, there were no untoward interactions. In fact, most of her fellow guests appeared to go out of their way to be friendly toward her.

Notoriety was a kind of celebrity in itself, it seemed.

She made a point of talking to Westing, whose pleasure in her company was a balm. They spoke of many things, few of which, if asked, she'd remember thanks to Blackthorn's rather obvious preoccupation with her. His eyes followed her everywhere.

It quickly became evident their little "show" hadn't put him off in the least. The man must be more of a libertine than they'd imagined!

An hour after Blackthorn's final guest had arrived, she and Westing were sitting beneath one of the oversized parasols pitched throughout the garden, chatting amiably and sharing a plate of elegant hors d'oeuvres, when their host came along with a bottle of chilled white wine to offer them a refill. The look he settled on Westing fairly sent the man scurrying, muttering something about fetching more strawberries.

Here it comes… She braced herself as Westing left them alone.

"You must be aware half of London is talking about your latest, *ahem*…exploit," he began, shooting her a wry smile as he sat beside her. But the question Blackthorn asked next wasn't at all the one she anticipated. "I wonder, have you and Harrow ever entertained a female third? I speak not of his wife, but of another," he hastily added.

For him to come right out and ask such a thing without preamble—and he'd used the appropriate term for it, too!—was startling. So startling, in fact, that she blurted out her answer without first thinking. "No." Taking a hasty gulp of wine, she forced herself to address him calmly. "Why do you ask?"

His steady gray eyes held her as he again managed to stun her. "I suppose you would become jealous if he required you to share him with another woman."

Oh good Lord. Think, Diana! "I had not even considered that possibility. After all, do I not already share him with his wife?"

"Yes, but not in a carnal sense."

What a conversation to be having at a picnic in broad daylight with a dozen other people wandering about! "Indeed, you are correct." *Think, think!* "I suppose I'm fortunate his affections are so restricted."

"Then, the addition of another bedpartner is for *your*

benefit rather than his?"

The trap's jaws closed with a snap, and Diana felt her face flush in an involuntary response so strong she hadn't any hope of concealing it. "My, but your curiosity is of the insatiable variety," she said, giving him an embarrassed little laugh to cover her panic. His eyes narrowed at her use of the word "insatiable," and she mentally kicked herself. Fine. If he wanted details, she'd give him ruddy details!

Bracing herself with another sip of wine, she forced a light tone. "The addition of another companion is for our mutual benefit. It enhances his enjoyment to watch as another brings me pleasure. Then, when he feels the moment is right, he joins us." She forced a cat-that-ate-the-cream smile onto her lips. "I can hardly complain, for we choose our companions well, and I reap the lion's share of the rewards in the arrangement."

The expression that crossed his face was one of grudging admiration, which confused her. She'd expected shock or disgust at the implications of her revelation. Danger warnings sparked in the back of her mind. *Time to turn the tide.* "Why do you ask such questions? Are you contemplating a similar arrangement with your own mistress?"

His scrutiny was unwavering. "Not exactly. I don't think I'm the sort to find enjoyment in sharing my bedpartner."

"Quite understandable," she said in a blasé tone, reaching for another berry. "Few men have the confidence to suffer the presence of another male while in so vulnerable a state. It's all too easy to begin making comparisons, which invariably spoils it for everyone." She popped the berry into her mouth and watched as the barb sank in. Maybe *now* he'd leave off the subject and find something else to discuss. Or, better yet, go away.

But again, he surprised her. "Comparison does tend to rob one of joy in all circumstances. I can certainly see why it would be intolerable in the bedchamber. My hesitancy to share has nothing to do with comparisons, however. I simply don't relish the idea of divided attention."

"You mean, of course, divided from yourself."

"I mean I prefer to devote my efforts wholly toward pleasing *one* person, with reciprocation in kind." With that he, too, reached for a berry. Holding it between his teeth, he smiled briefly before sucking it into his mouth with a pop.

Another flush rose in her cheeks, and she found herself laughing softly at how awry things had gone.

Surprisingly, this reaction seemed to offend him. "Has no man ever devoted himself solely to your pleasure without any thought to his own?"

It sobered her instantly. "As I said, I can hardly complain."

"That's not what I asked."

"That's the answer I choose to give," she said, showing him a hint of steel.

"You fear answering me truthfully—because you know the answer is no."

Her temper threatened to escape mastery. Closing her eyes, she took a deep breath before replying, "You clearly have little knowledge regarding such matters. I suggest you seek proper tutelage before we continue this discussion." She was just in the act of rising to escape his odious presence when his next words stopped her cold.

"Since you're so experienced in such matters, would *you* be willing to teach me?"

It took everything not to laugh at his transparent endeavor to get beneath her skirts. "That's hardly an appropriate request, given you and I have agreed to be *friends*, not to mention I'm currently engaged as another man's mistress."

"Ah, but your protector seems to have a different view of friendship than most," he said with a twinkle in his eye. "I thought perhaps you might share this view and extend it to *our* friendship."

She allowed herself a longsuffering sigh before answering him. "You must understand, Lord Blackthorn, Harrow is exceedingly discriminating when it comes to choosing our third."

"You said you made that choice together."

Damn. "Yes, well, usually it is he who brings a candidate to my attention. For approval," she rushed to add.

"Usually? You mean always," he said with a smirk, leaning a little closer and dropping to a whisper. "I think that a grave injustice, don't you?"

"I thought you did not enjoy sharing your bedpartner?" she shot back, irritated.

"Touché. But in your case, and in the interest of 'proper tutelage,' I'd be willing to compromise."

Oh, I imagine you would, you rogue! She pasted a saccharine smile on her face. "I would not hesitate to make a request, provided I liked the candidate well enough."

His lips curved in a rueful smile as he acknowledged her quick rebuttal with a nod. "Then I suppose I'll have to make you like me, won't I?"

Part of her wanted to laugh in his face. Another part wanted to melt at the look he was giving her. Fortunately, good sense prevented either reaction from surfacing. She settled for a cool smile. "I wish you luck in that endeavor."

"And if by some miracle I manage to pass muster?" he said, the hint of laughter in his voice.

You won't. But even as she thought it, she knew it was already too late. How long could she keep him at arm's length if he maintained a steady siege? Then, as if inspiration had been whispered by some invisible muse's lips at her ear, a new thought occurred to her: *Why am I trying to fend him off? If anything, I ought to grant him permission to do his worst—with one small caveat.*

Now, it was her turn to smirk. "If you manage to make

us *both* like you well enough, I won't *have* to ask." Wicked glee filled her as she watched his reaction to her inference. While he sat in gratifyingly dumbstruck silence, she took the opportunity to rise and brush the grass off her skirts. "I fear our friend Westing has become lost. Shall we go and find him?"

· · ·

As he scrambled up to join her, Lucas cursed his reckless mouth for leading him right into a dead end. She knew he'd never—

Bright as a sunrise, an idea formed. He'd call her bluff. She thought he viewed Harrow as a rival, but Harrow wasn't the obstacle here—the music instructor was. He'd happily cozy up to Harrow if it meant driving a wedge between her and her nimble-fingered Casanova. *All I have to do is make her fall* out *of love with him and fall* in *love with me.*

He glanced over to see Diana staring at him. "I've had a decent start, you know—with regards to befriending Harrow," he told her lightly. "We're not yet boon companions, but I don't doubt we'll soon become so. I like him a great deal."

A wry smile tilted her full lips. "Please don't take offense at my skepticism, but Harrow has a great many friends who 'like him a great deal,' but only a few have ever become close enough for him to trust in our bed."

Now *that* he didn't doubt. But however long Harrow had known his current lover was immaterial, as Lucas didn't intend to wait that long to achieve his purpose. He grinned. "I'm nothing if not convivial, and I'm hardly a man to judge another for his vices. I've quite a few of my own."

She stopped and faced him, a single caramel brow arched high. "So you would not mind being the subject of rumors placing you in his bed?"

Lucas bit back the correction that raced to the tip of his tongue: *your* bed. A knowing gleam in her eye told him her word choice had been deliberate, a subtle warning couched in literal terms. It was indeed Harrow's bed, as he owned her house and everything in it.

Being named a libertine was one thing; it was nothing he hadn't been called before. Harrow himself was often referred to in such terms. Because of the man's rank, most people left it at that and chose to believe—or pretend to believe—his sole interest was in the ladies.

Lucas knew better, however. And if the truth about Harrow ever became public knowledge, any man closely associated with him would be suspect. *No, he'd be tried and convicted in the minds of everyone he knows.* The idea of being called a molly behind his back—or to his face—wasn't one he relished. His parents would be fit for Bedlam. No matter what he'd told Westing about not giving a damn what his father thought, he wasn't certain he'd be able to withstand *that* sort of disapproval.

Still... as long as he made it clear once he achieved his goal that his only pursuit had been Lady Diana, the scandal ought to blow over fairly quickly and do no permanent damage. After all, his notoriety was securely entrenched in the overturned skirts of dozens of women, few of whom had been discreet about it.

Was it worth the risk?

Is she *worth the risk?* Looking at her, he felt it again. She pulled at something inside him. Whenever he was with her, it was as if he were being swept out to sea, caught in the inexorable grip of an outgoing tide and helpless to fight against it. It terrified him a little. Perhaps more than a little. But that fear was no match for her draw.

He decided to see how far she would go to put him off. "As long as you're in it, I should not mind in the least," he lied smoothly. "Don't forget—I'm already well accustomed to Society's censure."

Her gaze sharpened. "Gentlemen often boast of their own boldness but fail to follow through when their reputation is at risk."

Drawing close enough to breathe in her lavender scent, he gave her his best "I don't give a damn" smile. "My name is already blackened."

"It's not nearly as black as it could be," she countered, her mouth hardening.

How he longed to kiss those lips back to softness. "Is that an invitation to sully my name further?" He grinned. "Because if it is, I wholeheartedly accept."

"It's a warning," she murmured, her expression going utterly flat. "There are rules to this game, Lord Blackthorn. Rules of which you are clearly unaware. Such ignorance can be dangerous."

And the gloves are officially off... He sobered. "Then please, by all means, enlighten me."

A long pause followed in which he could almost see words being weighed behind her gem-like eyes. "For a man who prides himself on being known for his masculinity, accepting an invitation to join us would carry a most unpleasant consequence. No matter how you tell the tale—and we both know you would be unable to resist the temptation to boast—there would always be a question in the listener's mind concerning your role."

With unerring accuracy, she'd struck right at the heart of his misgiving. "You mean people might think I'm a—"

"Let us not give voice to ugly labels, but yes," she interrupted. "And there would be no way for you to unequivocally prove otherwise. It's a shadow you would live with for the rest of your life. So, I suggest you think long and hard about your next move."

The blatant innuendo wasn't lost on him, but he didn't dare smile. "I thought you'd know by now I'm not afraid of gossip. I'm—"

"Before you decide whether to continue on this path, there is something more you ought to know." She drifted a little closer and tipped her face up, impaling him with a seductive sea-green stare. "Since we have declared ourselves friends, may I depend upon your *complete* discretion?"

It was difficult to speak when all the breath had been stolen from him, but he managed to rasp out a rough "Yes."

Holding him captive with her gaze, she lowered her voice to just above a whisper. "Friendship is readily won, trust less so but not impossible. Both are required for what you seek. Yet even with these, you will never be issued the invitation you covet unless you convince Harrow your desire for him is equal to that which you feel for me. We never bed anyone we don't *both* want."

Pure shock skittered down his spine. *Well, I'll be damned.* The last thing he'd expected was for her to reveal Harrow's true inclination when it came to selecting his bedpartners.

This was a test, plain and simple. And the time had come to either withdraw or make bold. Was it a wise decision to pursue her? Definitely not. But it was something he absolutely *had* to do.

"Then…I must seduce you *both*…" Taking a deep breath, he leaped off the proverbial cliff. "Very well. I'll give it my best effort."

It was worth it, if only to see the look on her face.

"You cannot seriously be considering it?" she blurted, abandoning all pretense of cool sophistication.

The memory of Harrow kissing the music teacher replayed in his mind's eye. Unless he was sorely mistaken, Harrow's heart was already taken, so there was little danger of the man actually falling in love with him. He feigned confusion. "Why not?"

Her consternation gave way to a burst of incredulous laughter. "You cannot simply decide to like—" Glancing around, she lowered her voice back down to a barely audible hiss. "To like men in that way. From my understanding, such a thing is not a conscious decision. Harrow has *always* been attracted to both men and women."

Lucas shrugged, ignoring the lie she'd tacked onto the end of that statement. "Is there any reason it *cannot* be a conscious decision?" He enjoyed watching her sputter as she searched for a rebuttal capable of holding water. When it was clear none was forthcoming, he went on. "I'm not immune to curiosity, you know, and I'm not inhibited by any particularly strong sense of morality."

Her mouth fell open, and he saw sheer panic enter her eyes.

The same sort of panic roiled in his gut, but his gambler's mask remained firmly in place. *It's all or nothing, now.* "I daresay Harrow *is* quite a good-looking fellow, now I think on it," he mused, watching her carefully. "One might even go so far as to call him handsome. And he certainly seems to like me well enough. I'm—"

"But—"

"—certainly up to the challenge. In fact, I find the whole idea rather invigorating." Her increasingly flustered reaction further bolstered his courage. "But then, I've never been one to shun new experiences. And as for my reputation—"

"But—"

"—that's already well in the gutter. Let people assume what they will. I care not. Should anyone inquire, I'll simply deny there is anything more than friendship between us. After all—"

"But—"

"—as long as we are discreet, no one will be able to

prove anything one way or another. Yes," he said in a tone of finality. "I'll do it." He waited for Diana to object, but the lady appeared to have finally been rendered speechless. Her expression was beyond price, and he took his time memorizing it.

At last, she found her tongue. "Do you have even the slightest idea how to court a man of his tastes?"

He rubbed the back of his neck, at last allowing some of his nervousness to show. "Not in the least. I don't suppose I can depend on your advice?"

That brought her up short. "You're asking *me?*"

His anxiety was mitigated by amusement at her discomfiture. "I am." But if he'd expected her to answer back with all manner of ridiculous suggestions guaranteed to earn him Harrow's undying enmity, he was wrong.

"I'm afraid I have little to offer. His expectations of me are not those of our other companions. But, as you said, he already seems to like you, which means you're doing well enough on your own. You don't need my guidance."

This time, the smile he gave her was genuine, borne of pure glee at her discomposure. "I'm glad to know it. But I suppose the question I really ought to have asked is how best to gain *your* favor."

The calculating look returned to her eyes. "Treat those whom I love with love, and you'll have no trouble winning my heart."

And just like that he knew. He *knew* she wasn't in love with the music teacher. Had she been, she never would have said her heart was even capable of being won. Did she harbor an honest affection for the fellow? Yes; he'd seen as much with his own eyes.

But she's not in love.

Happiness flooded him at the thought. "You are as intelligent as you are beautiful," he murmured. "I shall endeavor to be the best possible beau—for you *both*. But come, let us find Westie, and then I think we ought to find Harrow so I can begin winning his heart as well as yours." He frowned suddenly. "You won't tell him anything, will you?" he asked, knowing her answer would be a bald-faced lie.

Chapter Nine

"And spoil the romance? Of course not," Diana lied, unable to refrain from sarcasm. "If you truly want my advice, *you'll* tell him of your interest—and sooner rather than later. He prefers people to be direct when it comes to such matters. I'm sure you can understand why."

Facing forward, she pretended utter indifference, as if this entire conversation hadn't bothered her in the least. Inside, she was an absolute disaster. But she mustn't let him, or anyone else, see it.

The annoyance at her side flashed her a wry grin. "I do indeed. Not everyone is easily discerned regarding their most intimate preferences. I, for instance, would not have suspected a man like Harrow of having a foot on either side of the fence."

What have I done? Fear spiked in her belly as she mentally castigated herself for being a fool. Exposing Harrow had been an incredibly dangerous move on her part, even though she knew it would be impossible to find any evidence to support a criminal conviction. Still, the scandal of such an accusation would at best be damaging. People might whisper about them now, but as long as she and Harrow maintained that *she* was the focus of their third's attentions, the law called it "immorality" rather than a "criminal perversion" deserving of the noose.

As they rejoined the other picnickers, she forced her features into a pleasant smile that gave away nothing of her inner turmoil. Spying Westing, she practically dragged Blackthorn over to him, hoping to rid herself of the millstone 'round her neck. "You abandoned me," she accused, giving the man her prettiest pout.

She didn't miss the wary glance he shot at her escort before answering. "My apologies, madam. It's said two is company, and I had no wish to overburden the conversation with a third voice. I hope he did not bore you too much."

Beside her, Blackthorn chuckled. "I believe our exchange was lively enough to stave off ennui," he said, lading the words with intimate overtones. "Would you not agree?"

Diana wanted to fling her parasol at his head. Instead, she pasted on a sweet smile. "Oh, indeed, yes. I found your advice on cultivating roses fascinating, though I hardly do more than reap the benefits of my gardener's hard work. He manages the thorns and the manure, you see—and the pruning. He's absolutely merciless when it comes to pruning. I merely enjoy the results of his tender care."

His eyes lit with merriment rather than ire. "Manure and pruning are indeed necessary evils if one wants the best blooms. But one must wield the watering can as well as the shears, for beautiful roses require constant, devoted attention. As for the thorns, I've found that most beautiful things often have them."

Damn him. The speculative look on Westing's face told her their not-so-subtle verbal swordplay hadn't gone unnoticed.

Thankfully, Harrow chose that moment to come and save her. But before she could greet him, Blackthorn moved between them, leaving her standing rather awkwardly behind him while he began to talk to Harrow.

Westing stepped in at once. "It seems our friends have things to discuss. Why don't we find those strawberries?"

Grateful for having been rescued from any further embarrassment, she took his arm and let him lead her away. Harrow would find her when he was ready. She'd love to have given him some warning concerning what was about to happen, but he was a grown man and could handle himself. In fact, it would likely give them a great deal to laugh about later tonight.

A chuckle escaped her as she imagined his reaction when Blackthorn began flirting with him.

"You have a lovely smile, but I suppose you hear that on an all-too-frequent basis."

Indeed, she did, and always from men who wanted something. She looked at Westing, not bothering to suppress her mirth. "It never hurts a lady's vanity to hear it said."

"May I inquire as to what amuses you so? Was it what Blackthorn said about gardening?"

"It was indeed," she said with another laugh. Peering at him sidelong, she made a snap decision. "Roses were, in fact, not at all a topic of our discussion."

The man's eyes lit with quiet humor. "I thought that sounded a bit far-fetched. The analogies you exchanged were rather obvious. You know, of course, he means to seduce you?"

"I know he means to *try*. He made that abundantly clear," she told him with a long-suffering sigh.

"And does our friend have any chance at all of succeeding?"

"I won't *entirely* rule out the possibility," she answered

lightly, earning a look of patent disbelief. "But it's doubtful. I'm no green girl to be swayed by a handsome rogue or a lot of empty promises." Pausing their progress, she pinned him with a hard stare and watched his eyes widen. "If you truly are his friend, you'll tell him I'm no easy conquest. Since becoming Harrow's mistress, I've had all manner of men try to tempt me away, from penniless painters to peers. The man who persuades me to leave my lover will have to offer me something he cannot."

"And what is that?" breathed Westing, looking as if he were about to be told where the Holy Grail lay hidden.

She let a wry smile tilt her lips and tried to ignore the empty ache in her heart. "When I discover it, I'll be happy to tell you."

He released the breath he'd apparently been holding. So dejected was his demeanor that she could hardly stand it. Threading their arms, she patted the top of his sleeve, hoping to buoy his spirits. It worked, for his smile returned, but it was a bit less bright than before. "But what of you?" she asked him. "You'll pardon my saying it, but you don't seem the sort to befriend someone like Blackthorn. You're far too wholesome for his company."

Now Westing laughed outright. "Don't let my splendid, angelic appearance deceive you. I'm quite equally as bad in my own way, and I flout Society's rules on an almost daily basis."

"Oh? Do tell, for I delight in rule-breaking."

What followed was quite likely the most unexpectedly pleasant conversation thus far that day. Westing wasn't the rotter he claimed to be by a long shot. He was, in fact, truly far too nice a gentleman for Blackthorn's circle. Yet she could tell by the way he talked of him that the two were like brothers. She vowed not to ruin his good name if she could help it.

Blackthorn, on the other hand, had stubbornly put himself on the board and was fair game. She watched him from the corner of her eye as he hovered near Harrow, and it took all her self-control not to let her smile turn smug. Given the way her protector currently looked as if he might asphyxiate, Blackthorn must be making an utter cake of himself. In a way, she supposed it was a good thing she hadn't had time to warn him what was coming; his startled reaction to Blackthorn's doubtless unsubtle approach was a genuine one.

Oh, yes. The after-dinner conversation tonight was going to be simply grand! René must be warned that his beloved was now the object of a determined pursuit by a man who thought himself entirely too clever for his own good. She could hardly wait. Blackthorn had no idea the trouble he'd put himself in with this rash move.

Although Harrow's face appeared dangerously flushed, Diana was confident in his ability to handle whatever was thrown his way and had no qualms about setting Blackthorn on him. Her dear friend would know *just* how to manage the fellow. By the time Harrow was finished with him, the cocky roué would likely be questioning his own leanings.

She almost regretted doing this to him. Almost.

If only things had been different…

No. She couldn't afford to think about could-have-beens that would never be. Her plan was the right one. She'd let him think her amenable to his advances and allow him to chase his tail on that front while his attentions were divided trying to seduce Harrow.

Her surprise at his reckless desire to throw what little reputation he had straight to the dogs just to sleep with her had been real enough, but she knew he wasn't serious about Harrow. True, he'd called her bluff, but he wouldn't actually follow through. He'd put on a show of trying to win Harrow's affections for her sake, all the while truly intent only on cozening her into his bed.

Harrow was right. By the time Blackthorn accepts that he's playing an unwinnable game, even if he discovers the truth, his name will be so deeply entangled with ours that he won't be able to reveal it without implicating himself.

She felt no guilt. He'd been warned.

When Harrow at last extricated himself to fetch her, she found herself reluctant to leave Westing's easy company and distance herself. But such was necessary if she didn't want to see his name smeared. She understood why Blackthorn liked him; he was congenial, kindhearted, and without pretension. The perfect friend. How Blackthorn had come to earn his confidence was a mystery.

The back of her neck tingled as they were saying their goodbyes, and she knew *he* was staring at her again. Giving in to the impulse, she glanced over her shoulder and confirmed it. Blackthorn's eyes conveyed the expected desire as he gazed at her, but they also held unconcealed irritation.

He's jealous! The blood in her veins surged with victory, but she quashed her excitement. She had no business being pleased to see him that way. When she turned back, she marked Westing's gaze had followed hers. The benign gentleman's smile had faltered, and she suddenly knew it wasn't Harrow reclaiming her that had set Blackthorn on edge, but her easy acceptance of his friend.

Perhaps distancing herself from Westing could wait a little while. It might be wise to hold that card in reserve in case things didn't unfold as anticipated. If it all went pear-shaped, they might need his help later to make Blackthorn see reason. She gave Harrow's side a surreptitious double nudge, silently telling him to invite the person in front of them to further socialize.

He did so without question, again proving his trust in her.

The look on Westing's face was one of transparent pleasure as he accepted an invitation to join them next Tuesday for an evening of cards. He would round out their group by partnering her while Blackthorn, who'd already been invited, would partner with Harrow.

She felt bad leaving Westing to bear the brunt of his friend's imminent displeasure at having been made part of a larger group rather than the more intimate trio he'd wanted, but it couldn't be helped.

The look Blackthorn directed at her when Harrow revealed this news as they were taking their leave was accusatory. She met it without flinching. If he thought she was going to make this easy for him, he had another thing coming. Arching a brow at him, she gave him one last chance to withdraw. "We'll see you Tuesday evening, then?"

• • •

The only thing required was a plausible excuse, and he'd be out of this fool's game with nothing lost but a bit of dignity. He could say he'd forgotten about another obligation, but that would be letting her win. The gambler in him wouldn't stand for that.

Lucas acknowledged her challenge with a raised brow of his own. "I would not miss it for tea with Prinny."

Inwardly, he seethed as he bid them farewell and closed the gate between their gardens. After his impetuous decision to call her bluff, he'd gone straight to Harrow to prove he meant business. It had been…uncomfortable, to say the least. But he'd done it, and not without finesse. The man's reaction to his attentions had been…well, in truth he didn't know whether or not he'd succeeded in his ploy now that Westing had been invited along to join their Tuesday party.

Westing. Of all the people Harrow could have invited,

Westing was the last he'd have chosen. And he knew she'd had something to do with it.

I should never have left her alone with him.

Not only had he experienced an unpleasant twinge of envy at seeing how easily his closest friend had ingratiated himself with Diana, but he was worried for another reason. Westing had never been known for being particularly tight-lipped, and his temptress of a neighbor had doubtless spent the better part of an hour wheedling from him all sorts of information Lucas would rather she not know.

A sinking sensation gathered in his gut. He could have initiated his plan to "pursue" Harrow another day, but he'd been impatient. And look where it had gotten him—now Westing would be there on Tuesday, making it all but impossible to achieve any progress.

Unless…

He could tell Westie, bring him in on the plan, and perhaps even obtain his assistance.

Lucas trusted his best friend with his life, but he wasn't certain he could trust him with this insanity.

The jokes would be unending. Westie would give him absolute hell. For years to come.

And what about keeping the secret? His best friend's greatest fault was that he was a friendly, talkative drunk who loved to tell wild stories of friends' exploits whenever there was plenty of alcohol and an enthusiastic audience. Whether or not Lucas succeeded in achieving his goal, this little escapade would provide infinite fodder for such storytelling.

He'd make Westie swear on his beloved grandmother's grave *and* threaten to reveal his humiliation at the hands of Miss Evangeline Worley if he spoke of it to anyone before all was said and done. Lucas hated using that intimate knowledge against his friend, but if he was going to enlist Westie's help, it was necessary.

Now that he'd made a decision, the tension within him eased. It would be good to have a friend on his side. But first, he needed at least a few days' respite to finalize his hastily made plan of attack and then figure out how best to tell him and exactly how much to reveal.

• • •

"You're going to *what?*"

Lucas, having anticipated Westie's outburst, maintained an expression of utter calm. "None of it will be real, you understand. I'll only be pretending interest in him in order to appease *her*. They have this agreement never to bed anyone they don't both desire."

Lucas had elected not to tell him about the music teacher. Westing need never know, as his sole purpose in this would be to help him keep her from sabotaging his efforts.

"You're completely out of your head," murmured Westie, his eyes like saucers. "You *know* what they do to people who—"

"I can assure you I won't be doing anything to earn myself a hemp cravat," he drawled. "My end goal is her, not—"

"And I warned you of Harrow's views on poaching," his friend cut in, his look changing from one of outrage to trepidation. "Going after her in itself is dangerous enough, but God forbid he should realize you're cozening him only to get to her. You'll get no quick bullet to the brain when he calls you out, but a slow, painful death. *No* woman is worth that."

But Lucas knew better. Harrow may have earned a deadly reputation, but he wouldn't be foolish enough to actually risk his life challenging someone equally as skilled as himself. Because Harrow wasn't actually in love with Diana. She was his societal shield—who happened to also be sharing his lover. And therein lay Lucas's advantage. Harrow might consider her a friend, but surely he wouldn't mind it if her affections were willingly transferred to someone else, leaving the music teacher solely to him?

But Westing didn't know any of this. "You're *asking* for a bad end," the man ranted. "If you truly wish to die, I can suggest a hundred less painful ways."

Lucas knew he wasn't going to be convinced unless he told him the truth. *Or part of it, anyway.* "Harrow has another lover." He didn't have to reveal he knew who it was.

Westing's eyes bulged even more. "Of course he does, you blithering idiot! All of London knows they had an overnight 'guest' only a couple of nights ago."

"No, I mean there is an *established* third, and it's not Lady Harrow. It's another man."

Boggle-eyed silence greeted this statement for several heartbeats.

"You're even madder than I thought," said Westing at last. "You propose to intrude where you well and truly ought not. If the pair of them are sharing a mutual longstanding lover, that's a whole different game, my friend. A much more complex one."

"I know it, and there's more. Harrow and Lady Diana both desire the same man, but not each other."

His friend's gaze narrowed. "How can you know this?"

"I just know," Lucas replied, his face warming.

"You've been *spying* on her."

The breath exploded from Lucas's throat. "I could not help seeing what I saw," he lied. "My bedchamber windows face hers, Westie! It's a clear view across our bloody gardens!"

"You could have chosen to draw the curtains or look away."

"As I suppose *you'd* have done if put in my position?" Lucas drawled. As expected, it elicited a look of chagrin. "I've never seen her show carnal interest in Harrow or vice versa. Not once. Her affection is restricted to the other man, as is Harrow's. They appear to...*share* him," he said with a nervous swallow.

"And you propose to replace this fellow, is that it?"

"With regards to Diana, yes. If I'm right, Harrow will be happily rid of her when he has his lover all to himself. He can always find another faux mistress—one who won't be a distraction to his amour."

"What if you're wrong about their arrangement? What if your spying has only partially revealed the relationship between the three of them?"

Lucas shook his head. "She's Harrow's protection from persecution, his employee. They've become friends, but they are nothing more to each other. I've been observing them, Westie. Her relationship with Harrow is purely platonic."

"As platonic as can be when they both love the same man, you mean?" scoffed Westing. He all but squirmed before continuing on to ask, "Do they...interact...with him separately, or together?"

"I don't know," Lucas answered truthfully, his insides twisting. "Every instinct tells me separately."

"*Instinct?* George's bollocks, man, but you put a lot of faith in your gut! You need to know for certain, not guess at answers."

"How can I find out anything more without actually joining their circle?" But his spirits were already lifting. His friend had moved from "abso-bloody-lutely not!" to telling him he needed to know more, which meant there was hope.

Westing's face showed all the signs of a fierce internal debate being waged behind it before he answered, "I'll help you—but only insofar as to learn the truth of it. I've my own life to consider, and Charlotte's family won't tolerate her suitor being associated with a scandal. Certainly not one of this nature. If you mean to cozen the man into thinking you're falling in love with him, you'll have to do it when I'm not around. And *that* is certainly something I never imagined saying to *you*."

Relief washed over him. "You have my undying gratitude, Westie. You won't regret it." Rising, he went to his brandy decanter and poured them each a drink.

"I had better not," his friend warned, eyeing him dubiously. "Good Lord, man. Why could you not have chosen an easier mark at which to aim the arrow of your ambition? Of all the women in London—in the whole of England, for that matter—*you* decide only the most difficult one to obtain will do. Aside from the queen, that is. Although, at this point, I'm not even certain of that. She might be easier to persuade. And safer."

Lucas thought about it for a minute. He didn't know why *her*, exactly. But he couldn't tell Westing that. "I like a challenge," he finally said with a shrug.

"A challenge?" Westing's voice had risen an octave, and his eyebrows looked as if they were trying their best to meet his hairline. "If a challenge is what you seek, climb a mountain or sail the seven bloody seas—your chances of survival would be better!"

Laughter came easily now that he had an accomplice. "Something about her draws me, Westie."

"You and every other male that sees her," groused the other man over the rim of his glass. "I'll not deny she's damned attractive. However, *some* of us have better sense than to be lured onto the rocks by feminine wiles."

If that's what happened, then so be it. "It's too late to turn this ship. I've set my course, and I mean to stay it."

But Westing had more questions in store. "And what if you find out she *is* in fact...*with*...both of them? Will you still want her?"

"Why would I not?" he answered drily. "It's not as if I'm

looking to make her my wife."

"God forbid!" said Westing with a shudder. "Your father would never allow it."

"Forget my father—it's my mother I'm concerned about. She'd part my head from my shoulders with the sharp side of her tongue."

"Indeed. So your only motivation in this is to verify the color of the lady's bedsheets?"

"You've met her, what do you think?" Lucas waited, but his friend's answer was slow in coming.

"I think if I were not already nearly engaged to someone else, I might consider pursuing her, myself," said Westing at last. "She is not at all what I expected."

The way he said it made Lucas's jaw tighten. "Yes, well. The most interesting people tend to thwart all expectations."

"Indeed they do," said his friend with a pointed look that quickly turned droll. "In truth, were she not a courtesan, I think any man would count himself damned lucky to have her for his own."

Now Lucas knew he was being deliberately goaded. "Do I have to count you among my rivals, as well?"

"Rival? Me? As if she'd even consider me."

"She seemed to like you well enough. You certainly spent a long while talking at the picnic."

"I did indeed, thanks to your desire to chase after Harrow. I must assume your charm had the desired effect, as you're to be there Tuesday?"

He ignored the mild gibe, knowing it was warranted. "What did you tell her about me?"

"Oho! So *that's* your aim, is it? Nothing."

"Oh, come now, Westing. She knows we're close friends. Surely my name had to come up in conversation."

Westing's expression grew smug. "The only thing she said concerning you was to ask me to warn you that she's not an easy conquest. What was it? Ah, yes. She's had both paupers and peers try to convince her to abandon Harrow, but the man who succeeds will offer her something he cannot."

"But Harrow is not the one I have to persuade her to abandon," Lucas grumbled. Frowning, he took another sip of brandy. "I know nothing of her true lover," he lied. "How am I to compete with an unknown quantity?"

"I suppose you'll have to trick her into revealing what's lacking between them and then try to provide it."

It sounded so simple; however, he knew it was anything but. "She truly did not ask anything at all about me?"

Westing cast him a knowing smirk. "Contrary to your perception of your own importance, there are many other subjects on which to expound besides you. But if it's any comfort, you can rest assured I'm not her sort. She thinks me too wholesome."

A chuckle burst from Lucas's throat. "Did she actually say so?" The withering glance he in turn received told him she had indeed. "I'd happily correct her terrible error in judgment, but I suspect it works in my favor. Well, at least I don't have to worry she'll fall for the wrong man. Best have an eye on Harrow, though," he teased. "He appeared to take quite a liking to you."

A flush rose up from beneath Westing's collar, and he muttered, "I'll thank you *not* to encourage him in that direction."

"Perhaps you ought not to have accepted his invitation, then?"

"Perhaps not, but *I* accepted it under no false pretenses," said Westing, coloring further. "All speculation aside, he's a wealthy marquess, and I currently cannot afford to appear rude to my betters. I merely looked to befriend the man. It *is* my right."

"Of course, as long as you remember who was your

friend first." He hadn't meant it to come out so sharp, but there it was. Shame filled him at the crestfallen look on his oldest friend's face. "Forgive me, Westie. I've not been myself of late," he confessed.

Westing's speculative gaze settled on him. "I've noticed," he said drily. "Bloody hell, you really are the jealous sort. And I'm flattered, by the bye."

Good humor restored, Lucas smiled into his brandy, taking a sip. "You should be," he quipped. "It's not every day I'm caught being so sentimental."

"Save it for Harrow," laughed Westing, holding up a hand. "*He's* the one you must impress."

When it arrived, Tuesday's game night was accompanied by inclement weather. Lucas half expected Westing to show up at his house early so they might go together, but he didn't. Part of him almost hoped he'd chosen to bow out. Thus it was a surprise when he was shown into the salon to find his best friend already seated before the hearth, sipping mulled wine, and chatting amiably with Lady Diana.

Again, jealousy boiled up within him at how at ease they appeared with one another. But that had been the plan; Westing was to keep her occupied while he mainly concentrated on Harrow. They could trade company later, *after* he'd convinced Diana he'd taken her advice to heart.

Harrow was as affable as ever, though Lucas could have sworn the man was watching him more closely now. He dismissed it as nerves. He'd never tried to flirt with a man and didn't quite know what to do, so he fell back on what was comfortable. Talk centered on the usual topics discussed between gentlemen, and he slowly began to relax.

He liked Harrow well enough that the idea of being friends with him was agreeable. But every time he thought about deliberately attempting to make the man think he was interested in more, his palms began to sweat, and his cravat seemed to constrict around his throat.

The longer he sat there, the more he worried he'd be unable to do it. Worse, he grew concerned Harrow would sense his unease. The mulled wine helped, but too much would be a bad thing, so he practiced the art of balancing on the knife's edge between alcohol's comforting embrace and sobriety's unloving grip.

Chapter Ten

Diana watched as Blackthorn took the seat opposite Harrow at the card table. His distracted, fidgety demeanor had her caught somewhere between laughter and pity. How Harrow was maintaining such a calm exterior was beyond her. When she'd told him what had transpired between them at the picnic, he'd laughed so hard he'd cried.

On several occasions, she marked Westing's nervous glances in their direction. Within twenty minutes of Blackthorn's arrival, she knew the two were in each other's confidences. It was only fair. After all, she and Harrow were a team, too.

Playing cards seemed to have a strangely calming effect on Blackthorn. She attributed it to distraction at first, but then realized it was more than that. He was a skilled player. They all were, but his focus seemed a bit too intent for a friendly match. Several games in, she realized his was the manner of a professional gambler, and another piece of the puzzle fell into place.

His willingness to take what most would consider a

dangerous risk suddenly made sense. He wasn't the sort to back down from a challenge. His very nature demanded that he rise to meet it. In that area, they were very alike.

The games ended in a dead tie, which Blackthorn likely attributed to Westing's skill rather than hers. It didn't matter to her in the least. In fact, it worked to her advantage to let him think her less clever than she was.

Throughout dinner, the four of them covered a range of subjects, the conversation flowing easily between them. Blackthorn's gaze rested on her a bit more frequently than before, but she noticed he made a marked effort to look at Harrow often, too.

Harrow, bless him, returned each glance with just the right amount of intensity to make the fellow squirm and look away, pink-faced.

She had to give it to Blackthorn—he was indeed giving it his best effort.

As for Westing, he was excellent company and admirably fulfilled his role as a distraction. In her case, a welcome one. Anything that kept her from paying too much attention to the sensations elicited by Blackthorn's nearness was a good thing. She revised her earlier decision to exempt him from her company for his own benefit. Could she help it if he'd thrown his lot in with Blackthorn? He'd made his choice. She'd try her best to see he didn't regret it, but would make no promises.

Following dinner, the four retired to the salon for more games. This time, they swapped partners, and she ended up with Blackthorn. They made a surprisingly good team. He was an intuitive player, at times seeming to know what cards she held before they were revealed. She suspected he did.

After playing with him for an hour, she realized she'd erred in thinking he didn't respect her skill. Rather than making her a passive partner, he worked with her to maximize their cards. Winning against the other pair was all but effortless, a fact greatly lamented by their opponents, who'd been roundly drubbed.

Blackthorn's open admiration of her ability warmed her inside. As much as she'd intended to see him make a fool of himself trying to flirt with Harrow, she was rather glad he hadn't.

As the men were preparing to depart, however, he appeared to remember his promise.

When Harrow reached out to shake hands in farewell, Blackthorn held on a bit longer than necessary and shot him such an intense look that it elicited a twinge below *her* navel. To her shock, it appeared to have an effect on Harrow, too. His eyes widened a fraction, and a tinge of color entered his cheeks before he managed to compose himself and bid their guest goodbye.

The look Blackthorn gave her when he bowed over her hand a moment later was one of smug triumph. A shiver of heat ran through her as it changed to one even more intense than that to which he'd subjected Harrow. Blackthorn's hot, dry fingers slid beneath hers, setting off little sparks deep inside. Those sparks ignited into a bonfire when his warm lips brushed against her skin.

A melting sensation swept through her, eliciting tingles in unmentionable places, simultaneously scrambling her brain and setting off warning bells. Keeping her distance was going to be much harder than anticipated.

As soon as their guests were on the other side of the door, she went straight to the decanter and poured two stiff drinks, one for herself and another for Harrow.

Harrow didn't even blink. "George's gout, what have we gotten ourselves into?" he muttered as he accepted his.

She swallowed a mouthful of fire, barely refraining from making a face at the burning trail it left in its wake before answering, "Trouble. Let us hope not more than we can manage." Eyeing her friend, she smirked. "I thought you immune to his charms?"

He huffed a laugh. "So did I, but I was unprepared for *that*. I swear if you had not warned me he was going to pretend an interest, I might have thought it genuine. A body would have to be cold in the grave at least three days not to have been affected. You're certain he's only playacting?"

The hint of wistfulness in his tone broke the tension, and she released the laugh she'd been holding in all evening. "Should I warn René he has competition?"

"Bite your tongue," he replied with mock severity, knocking back his drink. This more than anything told her it had affected him more than he was happy to admit. "He may be a handsome devil, but so is René, and *he* has my heart." His look turned sly. "I was not the only one flustered by the man. I saw the way you blushed every time he looked at you tonight, especially just now."

"I'm sure I don't know what you mean," she said, putting her nose in the air. The effect was ruined by the giggle that erupted from her lips, however. Her head felt light, and she grasped the back of a chair to steady herself.

Harrow's eyes narrowed. Before she could protest, he gently took the glass from her hand. "I think you've had enough. It won't help anyway, not really. And you don't wish a headache in the morning."

It was probably too late for that, but she conceded without argument. As for helping, the alcohol seemed to have the opposite effect. If anything, it made her feel more vulnerable and at the mercy of her emotions. "How am I to endure this, this...*wanting?*" she asked, beyond caring how embarrassed she ought to have been.

"You're not," answered her friend. "I told you it would become more than you'll be able to bear. If you think it's bad now, just wait." He downed the rest of her drink and set aside their glasses. "Giving in too soon would be a mistake, however, so we must plan ahead."

"Easy for you to say 'wait' when you have René," she grumbled.

A guilty grin flashed across Harrow's face. "I do, indeed."

Heat flared in her cheeks, and she pulled a face. "I don't want to know," she half sang before giving in to laughter.

Coming over, he wrapped an arm about her shoulders and pulled her into a hug.

Diana leaned in and let herself be comforted for a moment. "I'm glad you have each other," she said, determined not to feel jealous.

"As am I." He placed a kiss atop her head and whispered, "You won't be alone forever."

She let out a sigh. "Sometimes it feels as if I will. All my old friends are married now."

"Trust me when I tell you it's likely better you waited," he said, leading her toward the stairs. "So many women marry young and come to regret it. When *you* wed, it will be for nothing less than love."

"You're thinking of Minerva again and making yourself sad," she murmured, shaking a finger at him.

"She'll never know love the way she deserves."

"We've talked about this," she admonished.

Now he was the one to sigh. "I know, but it was still selfish of me. And it was selfish of me to make you part of my facade."

"Nonsense. What would I have done if not for you?" She didn't wait for an answer before changing the subject. "What shall we do next with regards to Blackthorn?"

"Continue to let him think he's succeeding."

"That should be easy, given both our reactions tonight. I imagine he must be quite proud of himself at the moment, having made us blush. Any idea how long we should let it go before entering the next stage of the game?"

"You'll know when the time is right, and you'll tell me," he said, steering her down the hallway and into her bedchamber.

Diana let him lead her over to the bed and sit her on its edge. The room was spinning ever so slightly. She really ought to have had better sense than to try and drink brandy on top of all the wine she'd had with dinner and the sherry she'd enjoyed during cards. She'd been worse off but knew this was still going to bite her in the arse tomorrow morning.

The sound of Harrow closing the curtains behind her filled her with intense relief. Knowing there would be no eyes watching from across the way as he helped her strip down to her chemise was a blessing. Ever since moving here, she'd felt like she was on display.

On impulse, she leaned over and planted a kiss on Harrow's cheek. "Thank you for being such a wonderful friend."

The corners of his kind eyes crinkled as he smiled. "Don't thank me yet. We've yet to see the end of this tribulation."

"Nonetheless, I thank you," she insisted, peeling off her stockings. "And I promise I'll do whatever I must to keep you, René, Minerva, and Henry safe. He *won't* find out."

"I know," he said, his tone placating as he helped her into bed and tucked the covers beneath her chin.

She felt a bit ridiculous, a grown woman being put to bed like a small child, but it was also more comforting than she'd ever admit. As Harrow trimmed the lamp's wick, she grimaced. *What would Blackthorn say if he could see me now?*

"Try not to think about it anymore," murmured Harrow as he opened the door to his and René's room. "It will all become clear in time, and you'll know what to do."

"I hope so," she said, stifling a yawn.

. . .

Lucas refrained from getting the opera glasses back out again, but only just. The sight of Harrow leading Diana into her bedchamber had him pressing his nose against the glass, glad that he'd declined to light a lamp. It was just as well that he hadn't gone to the trouble, because the man shut the drapes only a moment after depositing her on the bed.

Seeing them together didn't bother him at all. He was more confident than ever there was nothing between them, especially after his little experiment with Harrow had resulted in a rather spectacular blush from the man.

The sight of the music teacher leaving his room a moment later, however, tied his stomach in knots and made his hands clench into white-knuckled fists.

Lucas knew exactly where he was going.

All the desire he'd seen bloom in Diana's eyes when he'd kissed her hand would be spent on someone else tonight. Envy coiled like a venomous serpent in his gut, filling him with its poison until he felt it was oozing from every pore. He didn't even know the fellow, and the man had done him no ill save that of being the lover of the woman he wanted for himself, yet Lucas despised him.

The musician was probably a very amiable person. He *must* be, if two people felt so passionately about him they'd be willing to share his affection. But Lucas knew he'd never be able to meet him face-to-face. So strong was his dislike that he wasn't sure he'd be able to hide it.

More than ever, he regretted turning down Westing's invitation to finish out the evening at their favorite tavern. Now he wished he'd taken him up on the offer, because the last thing he wanted to dwell on was what was happening in Diana's bedchamber, and that's all he could think about.

He nearly ripped the curtains off the rod as he yanked

them shut, blanketing his room in total darkness. Determined to forget about his neighbor, he went downstairs to find a bottle of brandy.

It was time to get drunk. Exceedingly drunk.

The brightness bleeding through his closed eyelids was an unwelcome intrusion, chasing away the blessed oblivion that had enveloped him after downing far more liquid comfort than any man ought. He dared not open his eyes.

Unfortunately, his valet wasn't the merciful sort to allow him to rest in peace on the day his mother was to visit. The smell of coffee mitigated Lucas's disgruntlement only a little, but it was enough to entice him to take a peek. He cracked one aching eye open. The morning sun streaming through his windows carved directly into his pounding head with the precision of a surgeon's blade.

Lucas let out a stream of curses so foul they'd likely make a dockside whore cross herself and pray for his immortal soul.

His valet cheerfully went about his duties, behaving as if he hadn't heard. "Coffee, my lord?" he murmured, wisely keeping his voice down.

"God, yes." Dragging his legs from beneath the covers, he planted his feet on the rug and just sat there for a moment, willing the room to stop moving around him.

A steaming cup of what looked like tar appeared before him. He took it and proceeded to drink what had to be the strongest coffee he'd ever tasted.

His valet continued bustling around the room, laying out clothes. "A bath has been drawn if you'd—"

"Yes, yes," Lucas cut in. He reeked of alcohol and sweat. His mother certainly couldn't see him in such a state. "What time is it?"

"Half past ten, my lord."

George's hairy arse. He had only an hour and a half to make himself presentable and cognizant enough to handle conversing with his mother. Not that she wouldn't necessarily expect him to have a hangover; his profligate lifestyle was her favorite subject of complaint.

Resigning himself to the discomfort, he levered himself up slowly off the bed, groaning with each subsequent step as fresh pain assaulted his cranium. As always after a night of excess, he vowed never again to imbibe so much alcohol. But he knew damned well it was a vow he'd never be able to keep as long as Diana lived within sight.

He had to get her out of his blood, and there was only one way to do it.

Although his desire for her was much stronger than any he'd previously experienced, this wasn't the first time he'd wanted a particular woman to the point of distraction. It hadn't happened in several years, but he remembered well enough what it was like. Until he knew everything there was to know about the woman and tasted pleasure with her, the thought of her would drive him mad with curiosity and want.

But within a few weeks of finally scratching that itch and sating his curiosity, he knew his attention would drift. No woman had ever held his interest for very long. It was the reason he'd never kept a mistress. Mistresses required a certain level of commitment not required by the occasional willing wench he availed himself of whenever his desire grew beyond his own ability to sate.

As he stepped into the tub and sank with a soft groan of pleasure into the warm water, he reflected on his current predicament.

For all his reputation, Lucas hadn't really been with that many women. There were a few notables he'd given a good tumble in his first years on his own in London. He'd not disappointed them, and they'd done him the favor of bruiting about their pleasure in his company enough that he hadn't had to do much to maintain his roguish reputation since. Which suited him just fine.

Because the truth was, women were trouble. His mother, for all he adored her and was actually looking forward to her visit today—not that he'd ever admit it to anyone but himself—had taught him that much. She'd fooled his father into thinking she was in love with him, when in fact she'd been in love with another, and he'd been nothing more than a means to an end. Learning the truth had made his father wretched for many years, and Lucas had vowed never to let that happen to him.

Marrying for love was an impetuous act that could only end in misery. He couldn't blame women, really. Their hearts were by nature fickle, and their dependence on men for means and security made them mercenary. When he married, it would be a practical union made for the sake of duty, and it would be to someone who had no reason to deceive him into thinking otherwise.

That wasn't to say his eventual bride wouldn't be likable and attractive, of course. Just not enough to cause trouble. *Not like Lady Diana Haversham.* Just the thought of her made him wince with discomfort as the pressure in his head increased with the quickening of his pulse.

Again, he condemned the idiotic idea of drinking away his problems. It hadn't helped. If anything, it had made it worse. All he'd been able to think about last night as he'd nursed a newly opened bottle of very expensive brandy was her and that damned music teacher.

How had such a man managed to make her *love* him? The soft-eyed look he'd seen her give the musician on the morning of the picnic had convinced him she did. Lucas denied wanting her to look at *him* in such a way, of course.

Yes, he'd come to the conclusion that the transference of her affection was the only way to get her into his bed, but that didn't mean he had to love her back.

It struck him that he ought to feel at least some guilt for planning to destroy what was clearly a happy arrangement, but he just couldn't. He wanted her with a selfish desire that brooked no pity for his rival.

And what of her? If she gave him her heart, he'd only break it when he lost interest.

He couldn't bring himself to feel guilty about that, either. If she foolishly decided to take her fickle heart back from her nimble pianist's fingers and give it to someone else, well, that was her prerogative. She was a grown woman capable of making her own choices.

Even if they are bad ones. Again, the image of her adoring expression as she'd looked up at her lover assaulted him. Taking up a face cloth, he scrubbed at his scrunched eyelids in a vain attempt to scour the picture from his mind's eye. He almost wished he had that bottle of brandy here with him to help stifle the memory and silence his nagging conscience.

Ultimately, the choice *would* be hers to make, not his. He was merely offering her an alternative, nothing more.

By the time his mother arrived, Lucas was feeling much more himself. Her pleasure in his new address was, as expected, expressed in no uncertain terms. He welcomed the rare praise. The immediacy of her subsequent inquiry as to when he expected to install a wife there, although also anticipated, was somewhat less welcome.

"I'm only just preparing to host my first ball," he reasoned, offering her another scone, which was declined. "Give me some time to settle myself in the neighborhood."

"A wife would help you do so with far greater efficiency," she shot back, glaring.

Lucas allowed himself a small laugh. "Yes, Mother. I

know, but I'm not yet ready for a wife."

An elegant brow arched in an all-too-familiar look of disapproval. "Indeed, as all of London knows after you invited Lord Harrow and his mistress to your picnic."

Ah. Here it comes. "They are my neighbors, Mother."

"No, my son. *They* are not. *She* is."

"The invitation was addressed to him, and where he goes, she also attends. I can hardly dictate who he chooses to accompany him."

"It's shameful," she declared, putting her nose in the air. "He flaunts his lover to the whole of London while neglecting his wife."

"From what I understand, it's a mutually satisfactory arrangement."

Her gray eyes, which he'd inherited, grew icy. "According to whom? The woman sleeping with her husband?"

Surely his mother had heard every rumor he himself had, possibly more, but he decided to play the game. "From her lover, actually." *Or, at least the man pretending to be her lover.* It was better to be blunt than to allow the conversation to travel any further down this path. "Like your own, his marriage is without passionate sentiment. It was a marriage of convenience."

A harrumph of discontent erupted from her. "Marquess or not, I don't like you associating with him. He has a terrible reputation."

"So do I, or have you forgotten?"

"Not like his." Worry sparked in her pale eyes. "He is a deviant. They both are. I know you've heard talk of their depravity." Color flooded her cheeks. "Not only does he keep a mistress, but he brings...others...into their, their—must I say it?"

"Their bed?" he offered bluntly, enjoying the discomfort that flashed across her face. "Yes, I've heard all of the as-yet-unsubstantiated rumors." The fib rolled easily off his tongue. He could hardly tell her it was even worse than she imagined. The next lie was just as smoothly delivered. "I've observed no such unseemly behavior. In fact, the lady lives far more quietly than even I expected."

"Then the most recent tale that came out last week was nothing?"

He bared his teeth in a cool smile. "Considering every window I could see was dark that night when the event supposedly took place, I must assume so." Then, he realized how it might sound. "It was warm, and I was restless. I came out onto the terrace to smoke that night. When I saw the story in the papers, it made me laugh because I knew it to be untrue."

Her expression grew skeptical. "Perhaps, but the rumors cannot *all* be fictitious. Regardless, you should distance yourself from such people lest their taint ruin you. Be polite, of course—he *is* a marquess—but no more than the necessary due deference."

Anger over being ordered around like a recalcitrant child made his face stiffen. "*I* choose my friends, mother. And I form my own opinions. I neither require nor want parental advice pertaining to my social life."

The faint lines bracketing her mouth turned white. "As much as I dislike meddling in your personal affairs, I feel it necessary to warn you about these people. Harrow is bad enough on his own, keeping dubious company and allowing filthy tales to spread without offering so much as the slightest denial or protest. You've befriended questionable men before, but none like him. He is a shameless libertine. As for the Haversham woman, I find her particularly worrying. Several of my friends' daughters have complained of her turning their suitor's heads, distracting them. Duels have been fought over her, as well. She is nothing but trouble."

He narrowed his eyes. "You've never before complained about any of the people with whom I've associated. Why now?"

"You were young and brash then. You're older now, and I thought you were moving toward wisdom when you settled in this house and expressed interest in your father's seat at Parliament. That you were ready to take the next step as a responsible gentleman and the future Earl of Markham. Now I know the truth, that you took this address because of *her*."

It took him a moment to tamp down his fury so he could speak with relative calm. "I was unaware she lived there when I won this place—and yes, Mother, I *won* the deed to this property in a wager." He knew how much she despised his gambling, and to tell her he'd won the address about which she'd doubtless bragged to all of her friends was guaranteed to provoke her ire. He didn't care.

Indeed, her face paled on hearing it. But she wasn't ready to give up the fight yet. "If you persist in this foolish association, I cannot vouch for your father's reaction."

A laugh slipped out of him. "What will he do? Send me out of the country again? I think not. Father stopped having control over me the day I amassed my own fortune, and he bloody well knows it."

"He may have allowed you to run wild in your youth, but I anticipate that will soon change. Wealthy or not, you *are* his heir, and you will be expected to behave like it."

"Or what?" He let out a soft snort. "I will continue to conduct my personal life as I please, and thank you to keep your nose out of it. Whom I choose to befriend is *my* business."

Her lips thinned. "Well, I sincerely hope your *friends* don't make it impossible for you to marry appropriately."

Again, he laughed a little. "If by marrying appropriately you mean taking the bride of your choice, I'll pass. I'd rather marry someone I've come to know on my own."

Now it was her turn to snort. "If your recent judgment of character places you among such infamous personages as Lord Harrow and that shameless harlot, then—"

"Careful, Mother." His earlier amusement vanished. Lady Diana was no angel, but she was someone he liked, and he didn't care to hear her so disparaged, even if the label was technically true. "These are my friends you speak of."

She blanched at his chilly manner, but her gaze remained steady. "You know how she came to be his mistress, yes?"

"I've heard."

"Well, here is something you may not know. The gentleman the Haversham woman was to have married, Grenville, told someone that a few days before he'd intended to propose to her, he learned she'd gotten herself with child by another man. She was going to tell everyone Grenville had compromised her and pass off her lover's offspring as his. He eloped with the current Lady Grenville to avoid becoming a cuckold."

Indeed, he'd *not* heard this version of the tale. "Who told you this?"

"It's not important," she replied, a triumphant gleam in her eye. "What *is* important is that you know the type of people with whom you associate and select your circle with more care."

A frown pulled at his brow as he folded his arms and contemplated his mother. "And where *is* this child?"

"Lost," she said with a negligent wave. Her face darkened. "Presumably, your *friend*, Harrow, paid to be rid of the inconvenience when he made her his whore."

He didn't believe it. Not for one instant. Of either of them. Sighing, he passed a weary hand over his face. "I happen to know them both well enough to know neither of them would do such a thing." He pinned her with a hard stare. "You know, I would not have expected *you* to be spreading such fabrication."

Her eyes widened. "You doubt your own mother? I'm only trying to help you—"

"No, you're trying to help yourself by ensuring I don't embarrass you," he drawled. At once, her look went from wounded to sullen. "Again, from whence did you obtain such enlightenment?"

"Lady Atherton said she overheard it when her husband was talking to Grenville one evening at a dinner party. May I now assume my information is acceptable, since it reportedly came from the gentleman himself?"

"Reportedly," he retorted drily. "I find it…interesting… that this new information comes from Lady Atherton, who happens to be one of London's worst gossipmongers, *known* for embellishing hearsay and propagating whole-cloth lies. That woman is a menace, and I cannot believe you tried to sway me with such twaddle."

The offended look she wore now was quite genuine. "I have only your best interests at heart—"

"Save your protestations, Mother." Tired of playing games, he held up a hand to forestall any further objection. He loved her, but she could be such a trial at times. "I'll do as I please. Your disapproval of me is already well known to your friends and liberates you of responsibility for my actions. I don't see how my befriending Harrow—*or* his mistress—can make one jot of difference."

The Countess of Markham drew herself up, her face reddening. "Then you are blind and deaf to reason. Your past disregard for Society's sensibilities may be owed to youth and forgiven, but no more. People are saying things about this friendship of yours. Unpleasant things. Things no girl of decent lineage will forbear to overlook in a potential husband."

Now his temper *did* get the better of him. "Any woman that refuses my suit based on the opinions of others does not deserve the honor of bearing my name. When I finally marry, my bride will know exactly what she's getting and accept me as I am. I, in turn, will grant her the same courtesy. You have my love, Mother, but I won't change who I am or desert my friends in order to impress anyone."

The careful mask his mother had built over the years crumbled, and he saw she was, in truth, quite distraught. "Then you may expect your father to make a show of his displeasure, as well. He asked me to speak with you first in the hope you would alter your course for my sake. That failing, he will do what he feels he must."

He stiffened, surprise sending his eyebrows skyward. They'd not communicated in years save through their solicitor. "You're speaking to each other again?"

"Briefly, yes," she said in a clipped tone.

Somewhere in Hell, the devil is building a snowman... A smirk tilted his lips before he could prevent it surfacing. "I must have committed a grave offense to warrant such a miracle."

Her glare should have turned him into a pile of smoking ashes. "It was a *most* unpleasant meeting. And now I shall have to write and tell him of your disappointing answer. I've little doubt but that you may expect to see him not long after he receives it."

"I'm not leaving London to answer the summons," he said with a cool smile.

"You won't have to."

When it dawned, comprehension sent a feather-brushing of alarm skittering down his spine. "He's here? In Town?"

"He is, and I don't expect his mood will be congenial when you see him. You know how he dislikes leaving his lair," she added, her lip curling with contempt.

His father loathed London, preferring the "smaller, but infinitely more wholesome" society of the English countryside. He was a man content to live like a country squire rather than a wealthy earl, and Society would likely have forgotten him entirely but for his notorious prodigal son.

Lucas couldn't let her know the thought of his father coming to chasten him in person gave him any concern. Adopting an expression of supreme indifference, he sniffed. "Then I hope for his sake the visit won't be a lengthy one."

"As disagreeable as I find your father, I hope you won't say or do anything foolish enough to truly anger him," she replied. "Tread carefully with him, my son. He fears for your future. As do I. We only want what is best for you."

He'd expected sarcasm and bile, but her manner was instead both sober and sincere. Instead of snapping back with a biting retort, he looked her in the eye and nodded. "I cannot promise to alter my course, but I'll hear what he has to say and make every effort not to speak rashly."

Maternal affection softened her features. "If I could, I would tell you to do whatever makes you happy." The faint smile faded from her lips, and she laid a gentle hand on his cheek. "But the world does not often reward such people. Often, we must do what we dislike in order to survive, which means putting needs above wants and practicality before sentiment."

Though Lucas had grown up knowing she'd broken his father's heart, he'd never been able to hate her for it. For all that she was a terrible wife, she'd been a wonderful, loving mother. "Then it will comfort you to know I'm not a man governed by sentiment." He'd found most desires could be fulfilled without emotions getting in the way.

"No, you're not," she replied with sad eyes. "But neither are you ruled entirely by reason. You may not require your father's support or approval to be happy, but consider how much easier life would be if you have them. Weigh your choices carefully."

When his father called later that evening, the discussion between them was brief and disagreeable. Battle lines had been drawn. He would either end his friendship with Harrow or lose all support for his ambitions with regards to Parliament.

Lucas bid his father farewell with the expectation of the latter and the understanding this wasn't over, that there would be more unpleasantness to come.

As the door closed behind his normally mild-mannered father, he reflected that it wouldn't be the first time he'd done exactly as he pleased and managed to make it work. Even his trip abroad had worked to his benefit in the end. Not only had he avoided escalating the conflict that had set him on such a course, but the journey had provided him the means to both ingratiate himself with the Crown and enrich himself through profitable investment.

Same as then, his gambler's mind weighed the risks against the potential gains—only this time, the margin was far slimmer than any he'd previously justified. His mother was right. Regardless of whether he succeeded in this game, Society would always remember his association with Harrow. Whether that was for good or ill depended on the man maintaining plausible deniability concerning his true nature.

But could he count on Harrow's discretion? After all, *he'd* managed to catch a glimpse of the truth. What if someone else did, too? It might just as easily have been a servant who'd seen them as himself.

Fingers of apprehension marched across his scalp.

But it's not as if people don't already wonder... As long as he wasn't caught in the act by at least two witnesses willing to testify before a magistrate, however, it was nothing more than gossip. Harrow had many powerful friends who'd clearly decided to turn a deaf ear to the rumors. He had his detractors, too, but they were lesser men.

Lesser men are often envious, ambitious, and cunning. To discount them entirely would be very unwise.

If he was going to continue on this path, he'd have to befriend Harrow in truth and then somehow tactfully warn him to be more careful. In this game, the only one Lucas wanted to see gain the upper hand was himself.

Chapter Eleven

Diana encountered Blackthorn far too many times in the weeks following the picnic.

When the garden gate was repaired, he called to present her with the key, as promised. But it wouldn't do to simply leave it with a footman. No, he had to be the one to place it in her hands directly, necessitating a conversation.

Two days later, he presented her with tulip bulbs to brighten a corner of her garden she'd complained of being dull. And not just any tulips, but a rare new hybrid, quite coveted. Of course they had at once found her gardener to instruct him as to their immediate placement. They'd chatted for nearly two hours before he left again via the shared gate.

Every few days he'd found an excuse to visit her early in the afternoon, usually bearing some sort of token—a book on growing orchids, some seeds—that, while they couldn't necessarily be construed as "gifts," were certainly meant to please.

They met four times at mutually attended balls and danced at least twice at each. Harrow was not neglected at these events, for Blackthorn made it a point to include him in discussions while she danced with other gentlemen.

And then there were the evening card games on Tuesdays and Thursdays to which Harrow had invited him. Westing was there for some, but not all. Some nights there were others from their circle. Blackthorn managed to win them all over with his charm.

Her Tuesday appointment with Minerva was followed by a trip to Fisk's, since both required new gowns for upcoming events. On the way back, they stopped for refreshment—and who should be at the café but Blackthorn and Westing.

By the time Diana spied them it was too late to alert Minerva and make a tactful retreat—they'd already been spotted. Her stomach dropped, but all she could do was paste a smile on her lips and pray the situation didn't become too awkward.

Blackthorn's brows rose high—an unpromising sign—as they were led to a table right beside his. His speculative gaze darted between them as he and Westing rose. "Lady Diana, what a pleasure."

Careful not to clench her teeth, she did what was expected and turned to her companion. "Minerva, allow me the pleasure of introducing Lords Blackthorn and Westing. My lords, this is my friend, Lady Harrow."

Blackthorn bowed respectfully. "It is an honor to make your acquaintance, my lady."

"Indeed, my lady," echoed a suddenly florid Westing, also bowing.

He looked so guilty and abashed it nearly made Diana laugh aloud. In that moment, she knew he'd given ear to the sordid tales concerning herself and Lord and Lady Harrow. She took a modicum of satisfaction in watching him squirm now that the lady stood before him in the flesh.

Minerva, though she also very likely knew the reason

for his blush, was the epitome of sweetness and poise. Diana watched as she favored the two men with a disarming smile. "My husband speaks highly of you both. I'm so pleased to finally meet you."

Now Blackthorn had the good grace to flush, too, though only a little. He gestured toward the table behind him. "Would you and Lady Diana care to join us? We only just arrived, ourselves, and there is plenty of room."

Diana knew Minerva would say yes. Their tables were so close they might as well. As her friend agreed, she resigned herself to what was sure to be at least an hour of awkward conversation.

Making small talk while her protector's wife looked on with curious eyes was enough to cure Diana of any desire for food, but she nonetheless made herself nibble at a scone and sip her tea. They spoke of upcoming balls, and Blackthorn told them of the improvements he'd made to his new residence.

Westing's failure to contribute more than the briefest answers to the conversation didn't go unnoticed by Diana. While Blackthorn was engrossed with Minerva's account of Harrow's plans for the renovation of their country estate, she took the opportunity to address his apparent discomfort.

"You seem preoccupied, Lord Westing. Is all well with you?"

His face pinked as he raised startled eyes. "Please accept my humblest apology—"

She forestalled him with a gentle gesture. "I meant no reproach."

His shoulders relaxed, and a rueful smile tugged at his mouth. "My thoughts of late are generally not where they should be, I fear."

She returned his smile with one of her own and followed her instincts. "Who is she?"

The widening of his eyes told her she'd been dead on the

nose with her guess.

Blackthorn chuckled and answered for his friend, "Lord Falmouth's daughter, the Lady Charlotte."

She didn't know the woman—a fact for which she was immensely grateful. "I thought it must be a lady," she said, lacing her words with just the right amount of mischief before sobering. "Is all going well with your pursuit?"

"Indeed. I could not be more pleased." But the worry that sprang into his eyes belied his too-quick affirmation, and the telltale glance he sent to the tables nearest them told her everything.

He's concerned about being seen in my company! It ought not to have come as a shock, and it ought not to have hurt, but it was, and it did. Her ire faded as quickly as it had arisen, however. She couldn't blame him. Everyone in this room would be talking of this meeting today, and all of London would know of it by tonight. If—no, *when*—his Charlotte heard of it, she'd likely question his devotion regardless of any legitimate explanation he might offer.

Blackthorn appeared to reach this conclusion at the same time as her. "Indeed, Westie has been intolerably smug about his success on that front," he said jovially, turning to his friend. "The lady would be a fool not to accept your suit, old fellow."

Minerva seemed to pick up on the undercurrent also. "Lady Falmouth and my mother are acquaintances," she said softly, eliciting a comic look of surprise from Westing. "They attended finishing school together and wrote each other faithfully for many years. I was only a little girl when Lady Falmouth last visited us, but I remember well her sweetness. I shall be delighted to tell my mother of our mutual acquaintance and give her an excuse to renew their friendship. I'll be sure to have her recommend you, should an opportunity arise."

Oh, well done, Minerva! She watched as Westing's manner relaxed a bit. Minerva's mother was a duchess, and no matter what Charlotte's parents thought of Harrow, they couldn't deny such an influential connection. Perhaps they might even overlook Westing's less palatable acquaintances. The sting of knowing she'd be numbered among that lot was lessened only by the certainty that it wasn't really her that people disapproved of, but rather the facade she'd taken on.

If they knew the truth, would they think better of me? Would Blackthorn? The stray thought jolted her out of her melancholic slide. Caring for his—or anyone else's—opinion of her was both dangerous and stupid. *Harrow, Minerva, and René know the truth and love me. No one else matters.*

Looking up, she saw Blackthorn's gaze had settled on her. How long had he been staring? Her pulse quickened. The man looked as if he knew what she'd been thinking.

Ridiculous! Her thoughts were her own, of course. *Unless you wear them on your face like an inexperienced little fool.* She glanced away and schooled her features into a look of supreme indifference.

But it was too late, and she knew it. She didn't know what exactly he'd seen, but the knowing glint in his eye told her it'd been entirely too much. A tiny smile quirked his lips, and her traitorous face heated. Silently, she cursed his uncanny ability to unsettle her.

When she looked elsewhere to compose herself, she made the mistake of choosing Minerva as her refuge. Her friend's arched brow made it clear nothing of her blushes and fidgeting had been missed.

The next half hour was quite possibly one of the most uncomfortable Diana had experienced within the last year. Being caught between two people who knew too much—one of whom should know nothing at *all*—tied her stomach in knots.

Minerva waited until they were safely ensconced within her carriage before beginning her interrogation. "Charles told me of your admirer. Until today, I merely thought Blackthorn another of the same sort as has pursued you prior."

Nettled, she answered with a bit more sharpness than was probably warranted. "He's no different. Others have attached themselves to my skirt in hopes to overturn it. Rest assured, I'll shake him off my train just as easily as I did them."

"Oh, I think not," countered Minerva with a chuckle. "The way he looked at you tells a different story, my dear. He's quite serious."

Her temper got the better of her. "About what?" she exploded. "About bedding me? Of *course* he is! They *all* are. But it's nothing more than that—nothing more than lust. How could it be anything else?" she spat bitterly. "The day he bends knee and begs me to marry him with the whole world watching, *then* I'll believe it's more than just a desire to get between my legs."

Minerva, unfazed, stared at her in contemplative silence for several heartbeats before answering softly, "You may well inspire such an act." She ignored Diana's unladylike snort of contempt. "You really don't see it, do you? The way he looks at you? He knows you're not what you pretend to be."

Fear spiked in her belly, and she knew it was written all over her face. She didn't even bother trying to put up a brave front. "If that is so, then we are all in trouble. Such curiosity will be our undoing."

Her friend laid a hand atop hers and gently squeezed. "Charles will handle him if he comes too close to the truth or calls the ruse into question, but I doubt it will happen. Blackthorn may be interested in you, but he's no fool."

The laugh she let out had a desperate, near hysterical edge to it. "Men are all fools when it comes to lust."

"I won't argue with you on that," said Minerva with a

wry smile. "But I think there is more at play here. I think he's falling in love with you—if it has not already happened."

Diana's heart all but seized in her breast, but she was determined not to show fear. "You're wrong. He's like all the others, and I'll manage him just as I did them."

Thankfully, she was spared any further questions. But Minerva's words stuck in her mind, and she couldn't help it if every interaction thereafter was colored by them.

The very next night, she and Harrow bumped into Blackthorn at the Theatre Royale. Naturally, Harrow invited him to join them in his box for the performance and then to share a late meal afterward at Rules. A good time was had by all, with many a story told over superb wine and delicious pheasant, heavily spiced with laughter from all three. The whole time, she kept careful watch, trying to see what Minerva claimed to have seen.

Did he look at her with more than curiosity and lust? *Was* there more to his interest in her? She told herself no, tried to quell the spark of hope that flared inside each time their eyes met and his held a warmth that, despite all her cool reasoning, appeared to be genuine affection.

Every time Diana was with Blackthorn, speech seemed easier and grew more familiar. The tension inside her, however, wound ever tighter. She knew they held each other's gazes for too long. She was well aware her face warmed at even the smallest implied compliment. She cursed the liquid heat that pooled at the base of her spine every time he was near.

Over the course of these visits, they shared with each other childhood memories and spoke of their likes and dislikes. She was always careful not to tell him too much, but even so it felt like she was sliding further and further down a slippery slope, at the bottom of which lay she knew not what.

With great amusement, Harrow continued in his

plan to befriend her neighbor, a task aided by the man's own determined attempts to garner favor. Her protector responded with all fervor to the slightest flirtation as though unable to help himself.

Despite her misgivings, the pointed looks he occasionally shot her when Blackthorn couldn't see made it doubly hard for her to refrain from laughing every time triumph wrote itself across their mark's face in the wake of an apparent victory.

She had nearly let out a snort on hearing Blackthorn compliment Harrow on the superior cut of his jacket.

A giggle had almost worked its way out of her throat when he was so bold as to actually reach out and straighten Harrow's lapel while requesting the name of his tailor.

Asphyxiation had become a real threat when Harrow had subsequently pinned him with a steady gaze and invited him to come along with him for a fitting appointment later that week so that he might personally recommend him to the fellow, who was very exclusive and only took on new clients by such means.

Blackthorn had turned several beautiful shades of scarlet while accepting the invitation in a distinctly cracked voice.

That night, together with René, she and Harrow had celebrated their fine performances, not to mention ironbound restraint, with a bottle of champagne.

But no matter the hilarity throughout, nothing could alleviate Diana's growing disquiet at the thought of where all of this was leading. Especially when both Blackthorn and Harrow separately confirmed the book at Whites was beginning to see a great number of wagers on whether or not "Lord B." would become their next overnight guest. There were also quite a few in favor of an impending duel between Lord H. and Lord B. over Lady D. Bets on the outcome had yet to be posted.

On the morning of Blackthorn's ball, Diana awakened to a surprise package from Harrow. The gown within, a Fisk's, stole her breath.

Deep teal silk with a fine silver mesh overlay embroidered with tiny sparkling jewels fell in graceful swaths, bound just beneath a shallow bodice by a darker sash of velvet edged with silver. Its train was a glorious pale aquamarine silk so fine it was nearly transparent, also dotted here and there with gems. The miniscule puffed sleeves were of the same material.

Though still daringly low cut, it was more modest than those she typically wore when Harrow wanted to show her off. She couldn't wait to put it on. Another, smaller package was tucked inside the larger box. This one held matching slippers, a silver reticule, and aquamarine jewelry.

As the day wore on, she grew more and more nervous. She'd been to countless balls, but this one was different. It was *his*. He was their host, and they were now considered by all of London to be friends. Which meant she would have to act…*friendly*.

Exactly how friendly was the question. A sudden bout of nerves made her feel faintly nauseous.

Harrow, upon seeing her pale cheeks when he arrived, tried to set her mind at ease. "We've nearly achieved our goal. The flirtations must become a bit bolder tonight—from all parties—so expect some ruffled feathers from the less tolerant of his guests." A predatory look entered his eyes, and she recalled how much he loved pitting his wits against an opponent, a trait they shared. "This is our first real opportunity to plant the seeds of suspicion in the minds of the public, and it must be done right. Hopefully, he plays his part."

"And if he fails? If he tries to distance himself?"

A faint smile played about his mouth. "I've a contingency

plan at the ready."

"What is it?"

But he merely shook his head. "It's best you not know. If I must enact it, it's vital that your reaction be genuine."

Dread made her heart pound inside her chest. "I'm frightened."

His gentle hands cupped her shoulders, warm and reassuring. "You've no cause for worry. I'll be with you the entire evening. By the time we're done, he'll be unable to say anything damning without also condemning himself."

Despite her faith in him, Diana was a mass of nerves as she sat through the finishing touches of her toilette. When she was ready, however, Harrow told her to remain seated and dismissed Francine from the room, closing the door behind her.

"Why are we not leaving? He'll expect us to be among the first to arrive."

"I intend us to be fashionably late," he answered. "I want everyone present when we enter."

Trusting his judgment, she contented herself with reviewing the finer points of the plan in her mind while he read the *Gazette* and she pretended interest in her copy of *Magazin des Modes Nouvelles*. Half an hour later, he rose and held out his arm, ending her torment. On arriving downstairs, she was surprised when he led her not to the front of the house to board his carriage, but to the back. At her askance look, he held up an oversize brass key she recognized as belonging to her garden gate.

A devil's grin curved his mouth. "Tonight, I want everyone to know just how very neighborly we are."

Her breath caught, and she knew her eyes must be like saucers. The consequences of what they were about to do would be irreversible. If Blackthorn had any hope of escape, it was about to be crushed.

. . .

Where the bloody hell are they? Surely she cannot have fallen ill since taking her morning constitutional? Perhaps something has happened. Perhaps Harrow is late... Lucas's teeth were practically itching with irritation. They ought to have put in an appearance by now.

It was all he could do to stop himself sneaking out and going up to the terrace to try to see what the devil might be causing their delay. Prying himself away from his guests, he edged toward the rear of the ballroom and its bank of garden-facing French doors. He wouldn't be able to see over the wall from down here, but he could at least catch a glimpse of her second floor windows. Several were lit from within, but not the ones belonging to Diana's bedchamber. Nor were the music teacher's windows aglow.

Perhaps she decided not to attend? His heart sank. Then he felt a flash of anger—immediately followed by trepidation. If she'd told Harrow what he was on about...

Light and movement amid the darkness caught his eye. Moving toward him, a lamp bobbed along the garden path. Moments later, the servant bearing it was revealed, immediately followed by Diana and Harrow.

Why are they coming through the back rather than around front? Had something happened to Harrow's carriage on the way to pick her up? But even so, Diana had her own. Perplexed, he opened the doors to let them in.

As soon as Lucas saw Diana's dazzling smile, he forgot his annoyance and puzzlement. She looked a vision. Bowing over her outstretched fingers, he bid her welcome before shaking Harrow's hand in greeting.

Harrow's earnest face was full of regret as he covered their joined hands with his other and apologized profusely for their lateness. "The fault is entirely mine—an unexpected visitor prevented my departure at the appointed time, and as we were already so late, I thought to avoid any further delay by taking our little garden shortcut," he said with a conspiratorial wink, releasing his hand with a final pat. "Don't worry about formally announcing us. We'll just pretend we've been here all along, and no one will be the wiser."

Except they would. Because several of his other guests had witnessed their entrance. Granted, none were near enough to have heard the exchange, but they had eyes.

Lucas's stomach did a somersault as the implications sank in. Whether intentional or not, the result of their unconventional arrival was *fait accompli*. Everyone would soon know he and his neighbor were on *very* friendly terms, such that they had private access to each other's grounds and felt familiar enough to enter unannounced through the back door. The warmth of Harrow's greeting would not have been missed, either.

Indeed, heads were already turning toward them as whispers doubtless raced from mouth to ear, spreading like ripples across a still pond.

There is no going back now. Squaring his shoulders, he mentally prepared to brazen it out. Forcing muscles twitchy with nerves, he smiled broadly. "Now you've finally arrived, we can truly begin the festivities. Come, let me introduce you to some of my other friends. You already know Westing, of course…"

He'd worry about the consequences of this later. For now, he could only manage the cards dealt him and play as best able. Making the rounds and seeing familiar, friendly faces helped dismiss the panic threatening to set in. As did remembering all the bets placed at White's.

People already thought the worst and were merely awaiting confirmation. He hadn't planned on giving it to them tonight, but that's the way the dice sometimes rolled.

His mind raced, searching for a way to turn this around to his benefit.

It had already occurred to him that he couldn't discontinue his flirtation with Harrow tonight without revealing his deceit. The only way around it was to flirt *only* when both Diana *and* Harrow were present, making sure to always end on her, thereby allowing others to assume his attentions were directed toward her alone.

By the time the dancing began, confused and doubtful expressions had given way to knowing looks and even grudging nods of approval from some of the men. Through it all, he maintained a calm exterior, as if he'd expected nothing less.

The deal was sealed when Harrow, who took Diana's first and second dances, walked her over to Lucas and presented her to him for the third. The significance of that number was not lost on Lucas. Nor was it lost on the keenest of their spectators. Brows rose, and whispers followed the gesture.

He couldn't keep the smile off his face as they took their places for the waltz. "You look like an angel in that gown," he said on impulse, internally kicking himself for sounding so trite.

When she laughed, her face transitioned from beauty to divinity. "Flatterer," she teased, arching a caramel brow. "Most here would sooner name me the devil."

"Was not the devil once heaven's most beautiful angel before the fall?"

"Have you no shame?"

"None. I lost it in a foolish bet with a clever angel."

Mischief twinkled in her sea-green eyes. "Beware, lest the esteemed matrons overhear you and caution you against corruption at my hands."

"I should consider myself the luckiest of men if you deigned to corrupt me." The music began, and he swept her away across the ballroom floor, happy to admire her graceful movements from up close. "In fact, I hereby issue a standing invitation to attempt it."

A combination of desire and wariness flickered across her face for an instant before she smoothed it over with a low, sultry chuckle. "Were I to accept, you would be forever ruined."

"Have I not said before that I care nothing for other people's opinions?"

"Indeed." Her lashes lowered, and her gaze became molten. "But I was speaking of a different sort of ruination."

Her words sent a dizzying bolt of pure desire lancing down through his vitals and straight into his suddenly aching crotch. The swiftness with which he grew hard was almost painful. It forced him to reevaluate his plan. He'd thought to have Diana once and get her out of his blood, but the strength of his want for her was such that he wondered if a solid month between her legs could quench it.

Every look that passed between them stoked the fire. Every touch made it burn hotter. Everything in him clamored to claim Diana, to make her *his*. The impulse to kiss her and damn the consequences was almost overwhelming. He bit back a nervous laugh on realizing his muscles were trembling with the effort of holding himself back.

Her lush mouth curved up at the corners. "I see I've managed to silence you at last."

All his senses were heightened by unrelenting want as he focused on the woman before him. The color had risen in her cheeks, making her eyes appear even brighter as she teased him. The pulse at the base of her throat was a rapid flutter. Her small hand was hot and dry in his grasp as they slowly circled the ballroom. As he watched, the pink tip of her tongue darted out to moisten her ripe lips, leaving behind a pearly sheen that begged his attention.

He knew she wanted him as badly as he wanted her. The thought sent another lightning-flicker of need spearing through him. Something had to be done about this before he was driven to act recklessly. "Speaking of invitations, has there been any hint of my receiving the one we spoke of before?"

Perfect lips parted in a gentle smile. "He certainly seems quite fond of you."

A sinking sensation settled the pit of his stomach. "I had hoped by now that you—*both* of you—would be more than just 'fond' of my company."

Something like regret flashed in her eyes, but she didn't have a chance to answer as the waltz drew to a close. Before he knew it, she was gone, led away on the arm of another gentleman who appeared far too enamored of her for his liking.

Black jealousy pricked him sore as she turned her brilliant smile on the poor, dumbstruck bastard. Bad enough he had to compete with the bloody music teacher. The last thing he needed was yet *another* rival. The supreme irony of it elicited a quiet laugh. He was competing with a man he didn't even know for the affection of another man in whom he wasn't the least bit interested. And all for her.

There had to be a way to hasten this along before it grew any more complicated. He knew he was making headway with Diana. They'd spent a lot of time together and talked enough now that he could see the signs. She wasn't quite there yet, but soon. As for Harrow, he was but a hair's breadth from infatuation.

This thought made him squirm a little, and not merely from discomfort at the idea of being lusted after by another man, but from guilt. He was playing a cutthroat game, and its victim was a capital fellow, a genuinely good man in a city full of bad ones. In the beginning, he hadn't been concerned for anyone's feelings but his own. Now...

But damn it all, he couldn't walk away. Not when he was so close to winning her over. He stuffed the guilt away in a dark corner and shut the door on it. Sentimentality had a nasty habit of getting in the way of obtaining what one wanted. It wasn't as if he'd be leaving the man broken and alone. Harrow had his lover to console him.

When Diana complained of sore feet later in the evening, Lucas invited her, Harrow, and Westing to join him in a game of whist in the drawing room, where he'd had several tables set up for his guests' pleasure. The first few rounds were full of jests and friendly banter. When Harrow rose with the intention of having a smoke, he could have followed him and Westing, but decided Harrow had been the focus of enough of his attention tonight and remained with Diana.

He gave her a disarming smile. "Have your poor, abused feet recovered?"

She winced and with a little huff of rueful laughter shook her head. "I'm afraid I won't be dancing anymore tonight. Lord Burlington trod upon my toes without mercy, and he is no small man. I shall count myself lucky should I manage the return home without having to be carried. Shall we continue playing, or did you have something else in mind?"

Lucas marked that although the words were suggestive, her tone wasn't. "Cards it is, then. A round of Speculation, since it's just us two?" As she nodded agreement, inspiration struck. "What say we learn which of us is the better player?"

One brow arched. "Is that really fair, considering gambling is your profession?"

"Don't tell me you're afraid of losing?" he teased, continuing to shuffle the cards.

A slow smile stole over her lips as she held him with her eyes. "Do I look afraid? Deal."

Within half an hour, he realized any losses the lady

suffered were the result of pure bad luck rather than any lack of skill. Several games later, the tally showed them tied for the number of wins, with her slightly ahead in currency, which up to this point had been only markers, as it would've been ill-mannered for a gentleman to play against a lady for actual money.

Several of the room's other occupants had abandoned their games to watch them. Eventually, Harrow and Westing returned and joined the gathering, but neither expressed an interest in rejoining the game.

Another half hour passed, and he was down by two wins and a few markers. Losing was never a pleasant experience, but in this particular instance he was exactly where he wanted to be. "You're a masterful player," he conceded. "Shall we raise the stakes and make it a little more interesting?" he suggested as she was dealing another round.

She kept her gaze trained on the table, where she was laying out cards. "What do you propose?"

"Five rounds. Both players begin with fifty markers, and the one with the most markers at the end wins. Loser grants a forfeit to the winner."

Sea-green eyes flicked up to meet his. "Care to be a bit more specific?"

Giving her a lazy grin, he answered lightly, "No." He watched as her gaze became wary while she contemplated her response.

Before she could answer, Harrow chuckled softly and came up behind her chair to place his hands on her shoulders. Bending, he murmured at her ear, loud enough for those closest to hear, "Go on, Diana. You're the best player I've ever known."

Tipping her head back to meet her protector's eyes, she gave him a look full of uncertainty.

Then Harrow shocked him and everyone present by

leaning down and pressing a brief kiss to her upturned lips, and whispering, "Show him how it's done, my dear."

Lucas's gut clenched as a flush tinted her cheeks, turning them rosy. Doubt resurged at her telltale response. Harrow's hands still rested on Diana's shoulders, absently stroking them as he stared at Lucas with a faintly amused expression.

Are they, in fact, lovers? Unease rippled through Lucas, and feather-brushings of panic caused his stomach to knot. It took all his self-control not to show how unnerved he was as Diana returned her attention to him.

No smile graced her lips now, and her gaze was clear and sharp. "Very well. I agree to your terms."

Their audience's collective exhale was a soft susurration that raised the hair on the back of his neck.

Hoisted by my own petard. There was nothing for it but to play. He briefly considered letting her win in order to save the situation, but with so many onlookers there was no way to do so without being caught. If he went easy on her, everyone in London would know he'd thrown it and wonder why. *Play to win, then.*

She won the first round. He won the second and third. The area around their table was ringed with faces as the room became crowded. More were trickling in, having been alerted to the titillating nature of their wager. She won the fourth.

The fifth game would determine the winner of the forfeit. Tension rose as the cards were shuffled. The atmosphere in the room fairly crackled with it. Harrow's face was inscrutable as he looked on.

Lucas had a moment of sincere regret for having brought it to a head in so public a manner. "We can stop now and call it a draw, if you prefer," he offered her quietly, ignoring the small noises of protest echoing around them. "I won't hold it against you if you do so."

Irritation sparked in her eyes, telling him it'd been the wrong thing to say. "Now who is afraid of losing? Deal the cards. Unless, of course, you wish to concede and grant me the forfeit now?"

Oho! So that's how you want to play this, then? Very well. You asked for it. In a flash, his reticence vanished, and all at once he became the cool hand that had won this house and most of his fortune. Picking up the deck of cards, he offered them to her. "You deal this time."

Without breaking eye contact, she picked them up and shuffled them a few more times before dealing. The crowd ringing them seemed to collectively hold its breath as they played the game out to its end.

When the last of the cards was laid out, a bolt of pure elation ran through Lucas. He met her eyes, seeing his own shock reflected in their sea-green depths.

He'd won.

Her voice quavered a little as she bowed her head in acknowledgment of her loss. "Name your prize."

A choice lay before him. Ever since proposing their wager, he'd been going back and forth, desire wrestling with conscience, trying to decide what he'd do if he won. He had the option of requesting something safe, something that would offer no offense, yet put him one step closer to his goal. Something like: *all of your first and last dances at every ball we both attend for the remainder of the Season.* Or perhaps even a little more daring: *a kiss.*

It was there, on the tip of his tongue. All he had to do was say it, and this would be over.

Chapter Twelve

A strange calm blanketed Diana as she awaited his answer. It was almost as if she were floating somewhere outside herself, watching the scene play out as on a stage.

When he spoke, she heard it as if from far away. "One night of passion with you."

Gasps broke all around them.

Blackthorn's face had gone quite pale, but he held her with an unwavering gray gaze, awaiting her response.

Damn. She'd hoped he might ask for something innocuous, hoped that he'd know better than to claim a prize that might earn him a ten-pace walk on the field of honor. But in her heart of hearts, she'd known exactly what he would request. "I'm afraid that is not within my power alone to grant."

In the silence that followed, Harrow's warm hands again enveloped her shoulders, and she peered up at him expecting to see a look of grim resolve. But to her surprise, he appeared almost amused as he gave her a miniscule nod of agreement. Prickles broke out across her skin in a sweeping wave. *He* wants *this to happen!*

Numb, she turned back to again address Blackthorn in a serene voice that utterly belied the turmoil inside. "It appears my lover has no objection. Very well then. As you wish." She raised her voice just enough to be heard above the crowd's subsequent murmuring. "I would prefer that we discuss the exact terms of fulfilment in privacy." She glanced up again at Harrow for confirmation, receiving it in the form of another small nod, before continuing. "As such, I invite you to call on us at my residence tomorrow at two o'clock to settle the details."

Blackthorn's glance darted between her and Harrow as he answered, "I look forward to it." His Adam's apple bobbed as he swallowed, betraying his nervousness.

Ramifications sinking in, are they? Afraid you've gone too far? Good. She had no sympathy to spare him. Too many other emotions were already crowded inside her, all in disarray as each fought for supremacy. Part of her dreaded the encounter, but the larger part of her was far more excited than afraid.

She was used to men lusting after her. What she wasn't accustomed to was reciprocating their desire. Even now, though her insides shook with apprehension, she wanted Blackthorn. Briefly, she wondered if she would've been bold enough to request the same forfeit of him had *she* been the winner.

Those bearing witness to tonight's battle certainly would've expected it of someone like her. *Mistress. Harlot. Whore.*

She was, in truth, none of those things, but these people couldn't know it. *Blackthorn will find out soon enough.* Another wave of panic threatened, and she quashed it. Until that moment arrived, she had a job to do. Donning a mask of cool sophistication, she rose, forcing her erstwhile opponent to follow protocol and rise also. Harrow immediately offered his arm, which she took before again addressing Blackthorn. "Until tomorrow, my lord."

When she turned around, it was all she could do not to falter on seeing a veritable sea of bodies between her and the door. The room had filled to capacity while they'd played, and now all eyes were on her as the crowd slowly opened a path before her and Harrow.

The silence was so thick it was practically palpable. She wondered how anyone in the room could even breathe for it. Harrow's arm kept her steady, granting her a measure of security as they ran the gauntlet. It was less crowded out in the hallway, at least. As they entered the ballroom, faces swiveled around to regard their passage.

Gossip travels faster than dawn's light. It had been one of her mother's favorite sayings. Everyone here tonight would know of this before the ball ended. By mid-morning, all of London would know.

As they walked, her toes ached where Lord Burlington had bruised them. But she felt the pain as if from a great distance. It was a queer sense of detachment, this. As if someone else were experiencing these events, as if someone else were causing her legs to move her forward a step at a time. Even the music seemed weirdly muffled to her ears.

It was only belatedly that she realized Harrow was leading her once more to the back of the ballroom. *Of course.* They'd come in through the gardens, after all. Though she knew it would only add fuel to the fire for them to leave by the same path, she couldn't find it in herself to be anything but grateful. She'd be home within just a few minutes.

Before they made it to the exit, however, Harrow stopped and turned.

As he swung about, Diana saw they'd been followed by their host. Blackthorn joined them at the door, his expression full of uncertainty as he extended a tentative hand.

At once, Harrow reached out and clasped it, granting him a broad smile as he pulled the other man close enough to murmur something at his ear. She didn't catch his words, but whatever he'd said caused Blackthorn to shoot him a relieved smile as they parted. The message to all observing the exchange was clear: what had transpired tonight had caused no enmity between them.

Diana took her cue from this, so that when Blackthorn bowed over her hand, she forced her lips into a sultry smile. The look he cast up at her as he straightened was filled with a mixture of apprehension and naked longing. He'd won the prize he sought, and he'd managed to circumvent the obstacles she'd thrown in his path, but it was clear he had misgivings.

He's not the only one. She stood and waited while their host summoned a servant with a lamp to light their path back across the gardens. The ache in the toes of her left foot had become a painful throbbing now, and all she wanted was to be home, soaking them in hot water. *Just a little while longer...*

As soon as they crossed the threshold, Harrow surprised her by swooping down and picking her up. Grateful to be off her feet, she laid her head on his shoulder and let him carry her without protest. The walk back through the gardens felt a mile long and seemed to take forever. So many words perched on the tip of her tongue, but she dared not speak until they were inside.

The moment the door to her house swung open, Harrow gave the gate key to the servant posted there to await their return, along with instructions to secure the gate and then give the key to the housekeeper.

A soft laugh broke from Diana's throat, easing the tightness there as he climbed the stairs still carrying her. "I can only imagine what they must all be thinking." Blackthorn would know it was her sore feet which had prompted her protector's gallant act, but no one else would. They'd all think Harrow gone mad with jealousy, hauling her across the gardens and upstairs to doubtless ravish her the instant they arrived in her bedchamber.

Relief flooded her as Harrow deposited her on her bed and told Francine to have the kitchens ready water for a bath and bring it up in half an hour. She didn't move until he came back, shut the door, and drew the curtains. Then, knowing it was safe, she finally addressed him. "You knew he'd win."

His face was a study in serenity when he answered, "I thought he might, yes."

"I'm still a virgin," she reminded him, not bothering to mince words. "Or have you forgotten?"

"What difference does that make?"

Her temper flared, making it an effort to keep her voice down. "It will make a world of difference the moment he discovers it!"

"Then you *do* intend to go through with it," he said, a faint smile curving his mouth.

"As if I have any other choice." But her words lacked any real bite.

"Of *course* you have a choice, Diana," he scolded, kneeling on the floor beside the bed to take one of her feet into his lap and gently remove one of her dancing slippers. "If you don't truly want him, I'm happy to negotiate different compensation." He looked up at her with sorrowful eyes. "I would have thought by now you'd know me better than to think I'd allow him to touch you without your enthusiastic consent. Had I thought you did not want his attentions, I would have called him out for his cheek. I still can."

That he would risk his life to protect her—not for the sake of his own reputation, but to preserve her virtue, should she want to keep it... The backs of her eyelids stung, and she blinked back tears. No, she didn't want Harrow to call Blackthorn out, and she told him so. "But the problem of my virginity remains. As soon as he discovers it, our ruse is ended."

Harrow peeled off her stocking and examined her foot, cursing under his breath at the purple bruises already visible. "Burlington is a menace. There ought to be a law prohibiting the man from dancing," he growled, making her laugh in spite of herself. "I won't tell you to pretend otherwise because, as a man who once took a virgin bride, I know all too well it is not something that can be hidden. But our actions tonight guarantee his silence on the matter. He may discover the truth, but I can promise you he will never speak of it."

"You're as bad as he is, taking such risks," she grumped, wincing as he liberated her other foot. It was even worse off. "This needlessly jeopardizes everything we've worked to build."

"Love is never needless."

She felt the blood leave her face at his words. "Love has nothing to do with it."

"Does it not?"

Something in her chest tightened. But it wasn't. It couldn't be. "We hardly know each other."

He pulled a wry face. "I've seen the way you look at each other. If you're not in love, you soon will be. As for him? He's already long gone over the edge of that cliff."

Astonishment stole all her words for a moment. She ignored his assertions about her feelings, instead addressing those concerning Blackthorn's. "Do you mean to say that you think...you think he's in love with me?"

Her best friend chuckled as he grasped her legs by the ankles and swung them up onto the bed. "A blind man could tell, although he likely has no idea yet, himself. Men like him are often that way."

Diana didn't question it. Harrow was very good at reading others, and she trusted his opinion. But believing Blackthorn was in love with her changed nothing. "It makes no difference. As soon as he realizes he's been lied to, he'll figure out the rest of the truth, putting you and René in danger. No. I won't do it."

Harrow sat on the edge of the bed beside her. "If he had not already suggested raising the stakes tonight, I *would* have," he confessed, again surprising her. "But I'm glad he did it without prompting. Allowing this to unfold the way it has means I won't be forced to call him out—because the prize is being willingly granted rather than taken by force. Lean forward."

She did as he bade, allowing him to unfasten the back of her gown as he continued talking.

"When he comes tomorrow, I'll set the terms of your debt's fulfilment. The first is that it will be carried out *here*. That will be non-negotiable. The second is that he will speak to no one concerning the details of what happens between you."

The way his hands hesitated as he untied her sash told her there was more. "And the third?"

Harrow's cheeks flushed as he leaned back to look her in the eyes. "Not to detract from the sentimentality of it all, but there are certain practicalities to be considered. He *will* discover you're a virgin. He'll guess why, and you'll have to tell him the truth about René and I and your part in our lives. If a child should be born as the result of this wager, Blackthorn must claim responsibility for it. I will brook no dispute over Henry's inheritance."

The thought of bearing a child out of wedlock elicited all sorts of panicky sensations. "The herbs you spoke of to prevent conception, we must obtain some so I may begin taking them at once. But even they are no guarantee. Should it happen, there is no way to force him to acknowledge the babe as his own. You know this."

"I beg to differ." A grim smile thinned his lips. "If he should think to refuse, I'll threaten to let slip that he was interested in more than just *you* when he made that wager."

Alarm tightened her stomach. "But that would expose—"

"That was my foolish temper talking just now," he said ruefully. "Pay it no heed, I beg you. I promise it won't come to that. Blackthorn may have been willing to dance at the fire's edge with regards to his reputation, but he won't wish to leap into the flames direct. He would not survive the scandal of it. I would. I *have*. My reputed penchant for sharing your charms is widely accepted as debauched *but* within the law."

"Because there are no witness accounts to say otherwise and because we've fed the assumption that your interest is in me and not our overnight guests," she supplied as he eased the gown down off her shoulders.

He let out a dark chuckle. "They certainly won't assume the same of Blackthorn after the way you had him chasing my coattails this month. Why do you think I was so friendly with him when we left tonight? Trust me—he'll cooperate."

Diana had to admit he'd tied it up rather neatly. "Your ability to manipulate others into doing your bidding is a little frightening at times, you know."

"The man did this to himself," replied Harrow, spreading his hands wide. "He was so eager for you that he was willing to take wild risks."

Shifting the skirts of her gown out from beneath her, she settled back against the pillows in her chemise to await the arrival of her bath. "I should be flattered," she said on a sigh. "Instead, I'm afraid. Afraid he'll be wroth when he finds out I'm not really what he wants. I'm no courtesan—I have knowledge of love play, but no experience."

Reaching out Harrow tucked a stray wisp of hair behind

her ear. "My dear, I think he would want *you* no matter what your occupation or experience."

"He did not want me when I was a debutante," she retorted softly, fingering the fine linen of her chemise. "I was too boring for him then. I can only imagine his disappointment when he finds out I'm the same person I was when he first met me."

"But you're not," he said, his voice gentling. "Not even close. You've learned more about yourself and the world in the last two years than most of your peers could even begin to imagine. If he is disappointed with you, then he's a damned fool."

A knock sounded at her door. Standing, he leaned over, planted a kiss atop her curled head, and whispered. "As soon as they've gone, I'm going to signal René to come through so we can fill him in on what's happened."

It meant bathing in her chemise behind a screen for decency's sake, but she didn't mind. The last thing she wanted right now was to be left alone with her thoughts and fears.

• • •

Watching Harrow carry Diana across the gardens made Lucas's stomach do an odd little flip. *He knows her feet are sore. That's all it is.* Still, it made all the appearance of a man determined to wipe out all thoughts of other men from his lover's mind.

"I say," said Westing, eyes bright with curiosity as he joined him. "You, my friend, have bollocks of solid granite. Congratulations. I cannot believe you managed it without getting called out."

"Neither can I," Lucas grated, snagging a glass of wine from a passing tray and downing it. "But don't congratulate me quite yet. Nothing is final."

"You think the lady may try to renege?"

"I don't," he replied, certain. "But the details must be worked out. With Harrow."

"But you're *friends* now, are you not?" murmured the other man with enthusiasm. "I saw the way you parted company—that was not an angry or jealous man. If anything, he looked pleased," he added with a good-natured elbow nudge. "You've done it, my friend! O happy man, to have been welcomed into *that* elite circle." Stopping, he faced Lucas and puffed out his chest. "I know you'll make England proud."

Laughing, Lucas brushed past him. Yes, he'd done it. But at what cost? Westing had known of his plan from the beginning, but he was the only one. Everyone else here must make assumptions based solely on observation—and what they'd seen painted him in a very questionable light.

His reputation as a gambler and lifter-of-skirts was one he'd built with great care and deliberation. Had he just taken the first step in destroying the latter? He *had* won a night with Diana, but he'd also played the part of Harrow's shadow now for weeks. He'd even gone to the man's tailor with him, for heaven's sake.

Then again, Harrow's known vice was specific. Diana had told him her protector liked to watch. *Well, he won't be watching me.* Of that much, Lucas was certain. He wanted her all to himself. No voyeurism would be permitted.

But what if it was one of Harrow's requirements? Could he do it? He'd tupped a willing wench with other men in the same room before. It shouldn't feel any different. But Lucas knew it would. Those had been his university mates, and as far as he knew none of them fancied other men. Harrow did. Even though they were on friendly terms, and even if the fellow never laid a finger on him, it would feel…awkward.

The very idea made his palms sweat. *I'm beginning to regret making that wager.*

But even as he thought it, her image rose in his mind's eye. The memory of her smile, her laugh, the way the sun glinted in her hair, turning it into spun gold. Her soft voice, the way she looked at him as if seeing into his very soul. She was utterly captivating.

And he liked her. Her forthright manner held such appeal. He didn't like people who dissembled. Especially women. She was different.

He liked her a great deal. Enough to admit to himself he wanted more than one night. *The original plan, then. Persuade her to leave Harrow and their lover.*

It still rankled that he didn't really know who the fellow was. He'd seemingly come from nowhere. As skilled a pianist as he was, he ought to have had some patronage before becoming Harrow's lover.

Lucas's step faltered as another thought struck.

What if he did? He'd assumed Harrow had known the man first, but what if it was the other way around? What if the pianist was in fact the unknown lover who'd caused Grenville to abandon the idea of marrying Diana? It all made sense. Upon being discovered and subsequently cast out, she'd become Harrow's mistress and then had introduced him to *her* lover.

How ironic it must have been for her to learn that Harrow and her musical amour had developed a taste for one another. He'd give a lot to know how it had ended with the three of them coexisting in seeming harmony. But he couldn't ask her about it until she revealed his identity herself, or she'd know he'd been spying on her.

One slip, and… Such an error didn't bear consideration. He locked his curiosity away, determined not to let it get the better of him. Again. It had already landed him in far too much trouble.

The atmosphere in the ballroom had begun to noticeably

shift. He could feel questions hanging in the air like gathering storm clouds. Everyone would want to know the details. He would provide none. He couldn't. At least not until he knew what he'd gotten himself into.

· · ·

At precisely two o'clock the next day, Lucas found himself settling into a chair opposite Harrow and Diana in her drawing room. The gentleman had greeted him with surprising warmth, as if they truly were good friends, and Lucas had relaxed, secure in the knowledge that his host wasn't jealous.

And for good reason. His lover was doubtless waiting for him upstairs. *Her lover, too.* The thought made him clench his teeth. No matter how hard he tried not to look at it, Lucas's traitorous gaze kept wandering over to where the pianoforte stood by the window.

Harrow's voice jarred him from his increasingly black thoughts. "Though you've never asked me about it, I'm certain you must know by now that Diana and I are accustomed to this sort of thing."

"I've heard a few rumors," he replied carefully, striving to appear calm.

One corner of the other man's mouth quirked upward. "Then you must have heard something of *my* role in such assignations."

Indeed, he had. When he tried to speak, Lucas found his mouth devoid of moisture. He'd been a bold liar when he'd told Diana he wouldn't mind taking them both on. Now his bluff was being called. Though his innards trembled, he forced himself to meet the other man's gaze. "I try not to pay heed to idle gossip, but yes." He was pleased at how nonchalant he sounded, as if it didn't matter to him in the least whether or not it was true.

Harrow's smile deepened, and something like approval flickered in his eyes. "Allow me to set you at ease by assuring you that, although I'm quite fond of you and consider you a friend, I have no interest in making you my bedpartner." He leaned forward a little and winked. "Handsome as you are, you're simply not my sort."

It was only with the utmost self-discipline that Lucas refrained from sagging in relief. Despite his effort to conceal his reaction, however, he suspected Harrow knew. Giving up the charade, he allowed himself a small huff of laughter. "Fond as I am of you, as well, I cannot say I'm offended by your rejection."

Soft laughter followed the admission before Harrow carried on. "I'm glad that's cleared. As to your interest in Diana, you should know it was her decision, and hers *alone*, to accept and follow through on this wager. I asked her if she would prefer I offer you alternative compensation. She refused."

She does want me! Again, Lucas was filled with exultation as he looked to his hostess. Part of him was peeved over her attempt to cozen him into embarrassing himself through a public pursuit of Harrow, but he was too happy and relieved to sustain his ire. Of course she'd tried to dissuade him! She had a great deal to hide, and he understood she viewed him as a risk of exposure. "I'm glad you chose to honor our wager, and I promise you won't regret it."

"She better not," said Harrow before she could reply. "Nor should I." Now Lucas saw the deadly duelist in the face of the man he'd, surprisingly, begun to genuinely think of as a friend. "Which leads me to the requirements for this rendezvous. It must be held here, and you will vow never to reveal to anyone the specific details of what occurs beneath this roof. I don't expect you to deny the assignation—all of

London knows of the wager—but if and when you speak of it, you *will* be discreet. I'll not tolerate Diana being denigrated by *anyone*."

A frown pulled at Lucas's brow. "You may count on my utmost discretion, of course. And know that I'll be the first to set my fist to any man's face should he speak ill of her in my presence." The vehemence with which he said it shocked him a little. He mellowed his tone and addressed the lady directly. "My desire for you has nothing to do with being able to boast of any conquest."

At last she spoke, her soft voice cutting the thick silence that had fallen. "I'm aware, or I would never have agreed to this."

Again, as Lucas looked at her, he realized one night with her wasn't going to be enough. But it was a start. He'd make it the best night of her life, a night to make her want many more just like it. A night to make her forget the pianist and every other man she'd ever known. "I'm glad. You have my word as a gentleman that I won't share the details of our assignation with anyone."

"Thank you," she murmured, demurely looking down at her hands, which were folded on her lap. He briefly marveled at the sudden rosiness of her cheeks but had no more time to reflect on it as she continued. "Then I invite you to dine with us here tomorrow evening at seven o'clock and remain with me thereafter as my guest until the following morning."

"It will be my honor." A frisson of excitement ran through him such as he'd not experienced since he'd been a green youth. Mingled with it, however, was a bit of affront at the thought of Harrow chaperoning them. But he couldn't begrudge it.

After all, she is playing the part of his mistress, and she is his friend. It stands to reason he'd want to remain close to see to her safety. Briefly, he wondered what her nimble-fingered lover must think of this arrangement. Before he could ponder it, however, Diana rose suddenly, startling him.

"No, please don't get up," she said, stopping him from doing likewise. "If you'll pardon me, gentlemen, I have another matter to which I must attend."

Lucas watched in consternation as she exited and shut the door behind her. Looking to Harrow, he saw the other man was watching him with contemplative eyes. "Is anything the matter?"

Harrow's demeanor remained calm and relaxed. "She is nervous, and rightly so. It's not often we invite people into our most intimate circle. I imagine it would shock you to learn that though it may appear otherwise, that circle is quite small."

Knowing it wouldn't do to let on just how small he knew it really was, Lucas remained silent.

Rising, Harrow went to a tray laden with decanters and proceeded to pour them both a drink. "I'm not surprised she decided to honor the wager, however," he said with a small sigh. "I've marked the way she looks at you. And the way you look at her," he added as he brought over two glasses of whiskey. "I knew you were going to be trouble the moment I saw you."

It was said in a good-natured manner free of rancor, but still Lucas felt the sharp sting of guilt. She'd clearly been quite happy with her life as it was, and he'd deliberately set out to disrupt it. Taking the glass proffered, he sampled the amber fire within, giving an appreciative nod to his host as its warmth slid down his throat. "I won't deny my desire for her. Given that you're known to share her favors, I'd thought to satisfy it without causing anyone pain. Was I in error to assume it possible?"

Harrow let out a small huff of laughter as he took a sip of his own drink. "Indeed, but not the sort of pain you think. Diana *is* precious to me, but her heart is not mine save in friendship. I feel the same kind of love for her. Though I *am* protective, mine is not a jealous love as so many have assumed," he added with a wry twist of the lips. "As such, I can 'share' her with others without taking injury. But I cannot do without her friendship and affection. I'm not willing to give those up."

It was the last thing Lucas expected the man to say, and he couldn't hide his surprise. So stunned was he that he could form no response whatsoever.

Which was fine, because Harrow wasn't finished. "Whatever happens between you, I won't stand in the way. She deserves happiness. But please don't take her from me entirely. I could not bear it. I consider her part of my family."

Lucas remained dumbstruck. He knew he ought to reply, but nothing would come out of his mouth. Desperate to avoid the embarrassment of having been rendered speechless, he knocked back the rest of what was in his glass, hoping it would loosen his tongue. "I mean to make her mine," he blurted in the wake of the whiskey's fire. *Why the seven hells did I tell him that?*

Harrow smiled faintly. "Of course you do. I cannot see you doing anything else."

"It would be her choice, you understand," Lucas rushed on. "But if she agrees to become my mistress, she will be mine—I won't share her with *anyone*, including former lovers." He thought of the other man upstairs and knew his host was likely thinking the same.

"If you can persuade her to your course, I would like to hope we will remain friends," said Harrow, his gaze narrowing speculatively. "And I don't just mean Diana and me. I was being quite honest when I said I'm fond of you."

Amazingly, Lucas was warmed by the compliment, which was a bit unsettling. Now that the danger of being considered fair game for a bedchamber adventure had passed, he supposed he could afford to feel flattered. "I'm honored to call you my friend, as well," he said at last. "Truly. You're one of the most remarkable people I've ever known. In the interest of furthering our friendship, let us be entirely frank with one another. You're not in love with Diana, and you seem resigned to her leaving you."

The other man rotated his glass, seemingly intent on watching the light play in the prismatic crystal. "Indeed. I've always known it to be inevitable."

Well, there was *that*, at least. "Is there anything else I ought to know about the situation in which I seem to have become entangled?"

The silence grew so thick between them he could hear the soft ticking of the clock on the mantel across the room.

Harrow took the opportunity to finish off his whiskey before continuing. "I fear I cannot speak further without betraying her confidence, and that is something I won't do." Rising, he went back to the tray and retrieved the decanter. "You'll learn the rest of it when she's ready for you to know."

It was a most unsatisfying answer, and Lucas was tempted to reveal his knowledge of their secret to force the issue. But he held his peace. If he spoke now, it might ruin any chance he had with Diana. And he wanted that chance. Badly. Yes, this was an almighty tangled web into which he'd fallen, to be sure, but he couldn't see any way out of it that didn't involve either cutting himself off from her or going forward blind. *Well, almost blind.*

"What do you want out of this?" asked Harrow suddenly as he bent to refill Lucas's glass. "I know Diana means more to you than a simple conquest. What do you intend to make of her once you have her?"

Lucas stared at him as if he'd spoken in an alien tongue. "Make of her?"

Harrow's brow furrowed. "When I first took her on as my mistress, it was to be for five years, after which she'd have wealth enough to do as she pleased. She was planning on taking a new name and building another life for herself somewhere far away where no one would know about her past."

Leaning forward, Lucas peered at him in consternation. "You only intended to keep her for five years?"

"In the beginning, yes. But then our relationship became...complicated. I grew to love her. You're correct in that I'm not *in* love with her; however, my feelings regarding Diana are quite powerful. I adore her in the same way I adore my wife. I've shot and skewered men over an insult to her. I've lied industriously to more people than I can count, including you, in an attempt to preserve her happiness. I've even ruined the lives of some of those who've injured her. I would do almost anything for her sake."

Now Lucas was thoroughly confused, and feeling more than a little threatened.

It must have shown on his face, because Harrow let out a bark of laughter. "Do you think the human heart so small it cannot love more than one person to such an extent? Lady Harrow was and remains my oldest friend *and* the mother of my heir. I may not love her in the carnal sense—she cannot again conceive without grave risk to her life, which I will not give—but I *do* love her. Deeply. She feels the same affection for me—*and* for Diana. The two look on each other quite as sisters. If you decide to make Diana your own, you should know *we* have become her family. The only way you can truly have her is if you're willing to share her in that capacity."

Lucas tried to wrap his mind around this strange new development. Harrow loved his wife *and* his mistress *and* the pianist whom he'd as yet failed to mention. Libertinism was one thing. *That*, he could comprehend. But this? This was…he didn't know *what* this was. He'd never heard of such a thing. *Tangled web, indeed.* "How am I to maintain such ties if she agrees to become my mistress?"

"In befriending me, you've already taken the first step. She would never have agreed to honor the wager did she not feel your fondness for me was genuine, and vice versa." He paused to take another sip. "Clearly, you weighed the possible consequences of a close association with me and found them acceptable, or you would not be here now."

"She did warn me certain assumptions would be made," Lucas muttered, taking another swallow of whiskey, too.

"They are already being made. And it will likely only get worse. You must be prepared to answer such assumptions as are voiced in inquiry, whether direct or otherwise, with resolute misdirection or silence. They might speculate, but no one can know what I really am—and what they already suspect *you* of being."

The urge to squirm was almost overpowering, such was his discomfort at confronting the issue. "You must pardon my ignorance, but I hardly know how to define that, myself."

Another laugh, this one gentle, full of patience. "You know what I am. If you must put a name to it, the least unsavory term I've heard is 'amphibious'."

Lucas had heard it said before of those attracted to both men and women. He nodded. The question nagged at him until he couldn't stand it anymore. "And you truly don't find me at all…?"

One of Harrow's brows arched high. "Are you disappointed?"

"Not in the least," he laughed, draining his glass. "Though I'll admit I was a tiny bit flattered to think you might be when Diana first tried to use the idea to frighten me off." Their easy laughter mingled, and the tension between Lucas's shoulder blades eased.

"Ah, vanity," said Harrow wryly. "As I said, you're handsome but not my sort. After all, just because you're attracted to women does not signify that you're attracted to *all* women. The same applies to people like me. We all have our individual preferences." He settled a long, weighty stare on Lucas. "Do you really want Diana enough to do whatever is necessary to make this work?"

At this point, the decision had already been made. *I must be insane.* "I suppose I can withstand a bit more of Society's disapproval."

Chapter Thirteen

Diana's nerves were stretched to the breaking point. Harrow was *still* downstairs talking with Blackthorn. "What in heaven's name is taking so long?" A warm palm pressed down on the back of her hand, and long, elegant fingers interleaved between hers, giving them a gentle squeeze. She looked at René, seeking reassurance.

"All will be as it should, *mon amie*," said René, leaning close so she could rest her head against his shoulder. "Trust in Charles. He won't fail."

"I *hate* this," she confessed, ashamed of the rising panic in her voice but unable to control it. "I wish we did not have to deceive him in this manner."

"There is no other way—or, rather, there is no *safer* way—to do this. Not if you are to have what you desire."

Now it came to it, she regretted letting said desire sway her. "I knew better. I knew I would be unable to resist him. I should never have allowed him to get near me again. I should have run away."

"Do you think he would have allowed it?" the Frenchman

asked, again squeezing her hand. "If he feels as strongly about you as you do him, then I'm afraid there is nothing on this earth that would keep him away. *Non. C'est mieux.* Be patient."

"And if he betrays us?"

"He won't. Charles will make certain of this. I've known him long enough to know there is nothing he won't do to protect those he loves, and he loves you, *chérie.* Trust in that love."

She wanted to believe him but had no idea what Harrow might be telling Blackthorn. When she'd asked him, he'd told her he'd know how much to say only when it needed saying, which would all depend on Blackthorn's reactions. That had given her no comfort. Today's reactions aside, could he be trusted to keep his word once he knew the truth?

Every fiber of her being wanted to get up and pace the room, but she knew it wouldn't help and that it would only make René anxious. She glanced at her friend, wondering how he could remain so calm in the face of this catastrophe.

Her heart leapt painfully in her chest as the door opened, admitting Harrow. A bemused smile hovered on his lips, but she refused to allow herself to hope until he spoke the words that would release her from this torment of uncertainty. "Well?" she demanded, unwilling to wait even a moment longer.

"I think he'll do admirably."

A relieved sigh burst from her throat. "Tell me everything, and don't leave out a single detail, no matter how small." She listened as he spoke, taking it all in. His observations, his predictions, all of it. He was holding something back; she was sure of it. But what he did say calmed her considerably.

Beside her, René chuckled. "Did I not tell you, *chérie?*"

Harrow reached out and took the other man's hand between his own and kissed its palm. "Such faith you have in me," he whispered to his lover. "I hope you're not disappointed I felt it best not to reveal your part in this?" When René indicated no displeasure, Harrow again looked to Diana. "I disliked misleading Blackthorn about my true nature, but it was the only way to preserve his view of you until he learns differently for himself. Once he realizes neither of us is a threat, that certainty should dispel any remaining jealousy. It might even turn him into an ally. If he can help us maintain appearances…"

A lump rose in her throat as she looked at her two dear friends sitting with their hands entwined. Love, tender and ferocious, rose up inside her. She wouldn't allow anyone to harm them—or Minerva and Henry. *Certainly not because of my selfishness.* "I assume he knows this won't end well for him if he makes the wrong choices?"

"Indeed, he does," affirmed Harrow softly.

"Good. We cannot afford any mistakes." *Any more mistakes, you mean…*

"Diana…" Harrow's tone was hesitant. "There can be no coming back from this. The man is besotted, and once he knows the truth it's especially unlikely he'll be willing to let you go after just one night. There is still time for you to change your mind."

"No," she answered at once. "This—*he* is what I want. At least once." It frightened her to bits, but she'd regret it her whole life if she didn't do this.

"Even if it means giving up the future you had planned? The likelihood he'll marry you is all but nonexistent. Any children born to you would be illegitimate. And you must face the possibility that he might one day marry someone else."

His worried expression went straight to her heart. "I know. But this is something I must do for myself. And if, in the end, I'm unhappy, well…I'll still have my savings, won't

I? The world will still turn, and I can still sail with the tide."

At last, he nodded. "True enough."

The three talked until the evening meal, making plans for every contingency they could come up with. Part of this included her extracting a promise from Harrow to make advance arrangements for his and René's escape should the worst happen and they were somehow exposed. He didn't seem to feel there was any danger of this happening, but he finally agreed, if only to allay her fears.

That night as she put out the bedside lamp and settled beneath the covers, Diana feared she'd be unable to sleep. It was silly, but she felt like a bride on the eve of her wedding.

In a manner of speaking, I am. She was about to take an irreversible step off the edge of a proverbial cliff. By this time tomorrow, her virginity would be a thing of the past. There would be some pain, but she knew enough about her own body to ensure there would also be pleasure. Still, her stomach fluttered with nerves. She was wise enough to comprehend that all the foreknowledge in the world couldn't prepare her for the reality of the act itself.

Her feelings for Blackthorn were a tangled morass. She wanted him. She liked him, too. A lot. Harrow thought him in love with her, and she wanted to trust his judgment, but how could he possibly know for certain? He'd also suggested *she* was on the verge of falling in love.

Which couldn't be true.

Could it? If anyone ought to be able to tell, it should be me. It unnerved her that she couldn't verify it one way or another with any confidence. *If I am, then shame on me for having reneged on my promise to never be so foolish.* And on the other side of that same coin: if she wasn't, and she intended to let Blackthorn make her his mistress, then she had to convince him she was.

She grimaced in the dark. *That should be all too easy.*

She'd thought the part of herself that wanted to be loved and cherished was dead and buried with her past, but living with Harrow and René had convinced her otherwise. The pains they suffered and the hurdles they leaped simply to be together had taught her love was real, precious, and infinitely desirable.

The evidently incurable sentimentalist in her wasn't content with things as they were anymore. Although she was loved and had a family again—a *chosen* family—she wanted more. She wanted a husband, a home, and children. She wasn't naive enough to think Blackthorn capable of giving her those; reality was implacable. Even if he *did* love her, even if she *was* coming to him a virgin, he would never marry a woman with her sullied reputation. Love didn't wash one's name free of taint in the eyes of Society.

But tomorrow night wasn't about love. It was about passion. She just hoped Blackthorn wouldn't be so disappointed that he'd lose all further desire for her. Despite her virginity, she was determined not to fall short of expectations and resolved to employ all her knowledge to make the experience a pleasurable one.

When morning came, Diana was shocked to find she'd slept soundly. The house was already bustling with activity by the time she made her way down. In fact, it was quite busier than she expected. "What is all of this?" she asked a passing footman, gesturing toward two others bearing a chaise up the stair.

"Lord Harrow's orders, madam," he answered. "The claret guest room is being reappointed."

Reappointed? "Thank you, carry on." She would have gone upstairs to see for herself, but Harrow's voice stopped her.

"Ah! You're awake. Excellent. Come and have breakfast with me."

Over tea and toast, she learned he'd selected the room in question for tonight's tryst and was having it redecorated to suit the occasion.

"As your apartments are rather specially designed for another purpose, I thought it best to designate another room," he quietly confided. "I did not think you'd mind."

"Not at all," she assured him. "Now I consider it, I would not have been comfortable in my own chamber for fear of him making an accidental discovery. But why redecorate?"

Harrow smiled slyly. "I'll show you when it's ready."

As if she weren't already suffering enough anticipation. The day sped by. At a quarter past five, the head footman came to inform them the room was prepared. Her stomach tightened as she followed Harrow upstairs to inspect it.

The sight that greeted her eyes made them sting with unshed tears. Roses of a deep red hue had been brought in to grace every corner of the room, echoing the color on the walls. Clusters of candles had been placed on pedestals throughout the chamber, unlit as of yet, but Harrow informed her he'd give orders for them to be lit while they took their evening sherry.

One item that had mystified her as she'd seen it being hauled up the stair earlier in the day now jumped out at her: an enormous, gilt-framed mirror from her ballroom. It now stood propped against a wall to one side of the bed. She regarded it with a frown. "That seems a bit too large for this room, don't you think? And should it not be hung on the wall?"

Harrow's chuckle made her turn to see merriment dancing in his eyes. "It's not really for decoration, per se. It's more for...well, you'll find out tonight."

She continued her perusal. The heavy, wine-colored velvet bed curtains had been tied back with gold sashes and the bed scattered with pillows and rose petals. A tray bearing libations in sparkling crystal decanters stood over by the window. On approaching the bedside table, she saw it bore an array of items she recognized from Harrow's earliest tutorials on love play: several feathers of differing lengths and shapes, a few gilded pots of what she knew to be scented massage oil, and a pile of soft silk scarves.

Her furious blush didn't go unnoticed. Harrow laid a calming hand on her shoulder. "He will be expecting such items to be present. That does not mean they must be used. Before he comes up, I intend to have a word with him concerning consent."

All she needed to become aroused was the idea of Blackthorn's hands on her bare skin. Adding these items to the mental picture she'd already built was like throwing whiskey on a fire, though she could hardly say so to Harrow. He had, of course, schooled her in the use of all these items. Her massage skills had been learned from a woman he'd hired from a salon specializing in the art. Binding had been taught by watching Harrow truss a fully-clothed René followed by submitting himself as a test subject—also fully clothed—to see that she'd learned properly. It had been beyond her ability to secure his limbs without bursting into a fit of giggles for nearly a week. He'd even made her practice feather play under his watchful eye—first on his bared forearms to demonstrate technique and pressure, and then on a pillow.

That had elicited even more laughter.

There had been other things, too, but nearly all of *those* lessons had been restricted to verbal explanations accompanied by shockingly detailed illustrations from an ancient Hindu text Harrow had brought back from India. When she'd asked him why he'd wanted her to learn these things if she was never meant to actually touch him, his reasoning was logical: experience lent one's voice a quality that couldn't be faked among those who'd experienced such things. Should his less inhibited associates inquire of her concerning her repertoire, she must be able to with utter confidence speak of and even banter about such acts as if she'd truly committed them.

His foresight had proven both accurate and valuable within only a few months of her debut as his mistress. Men *so* enjoyed discussing their sexual vices with one they thought to be an expert. She'd quickly tired of their probing questions and lewd commentary, and this, too, had worked to her benefit. When she spoke of such things now, it was with a truly jaded air of supreme boredom.

However, thinking of them with Blackthorn in mind was anything but boring. Her face felt hot all over again at the thought. "If it's what he'll be expecting, then it's perfect," she said, beginning to back out of the room.

Harrow blessedly allowed her to pass before he continued. "I wanted you to see it now so you won't be shocked or overly nervous later."

"I thank you for the warning," she said, embarrassed to hear the quaver in her voice.

"One more thing," he said before she could move. "When he and I were about Town together this last month, I tried to ascertain his...appetites, but I'm afraid he was quite tight-lipped. As such, I don't know what his tastes are. Before you take him upstairs tonight, you must agree on a stop word, and *you* must be the one to broach the subject. Remember what I told you concerning people and power?"

"Yes." In order to perform her role believably, she'd had to learn how to subtly gain the upper hand in any conversation and become the dominant participant without it being obvious. It was a skill that enabled her to steer the subject either in a desired direction or away from dangerous territory.

"Well, the same principles apply in the bedchamber.

Until his predilections are known to be otherwise, he must feel he is in the position of greatest power and control even if it's only an illusion. Requesting that you establish a stop word won't shock him if he's had previous intimate encounters involving that sort of thing, but it *will* cause him to respect any boundaries you decide to set. If he's inexperienced, he'll merely assume you're apprehensive and it will make him feel protective. Either path gives you inherent control over the situation."

Again, her face heated, but she nodded. "Very well, but in all honesty, I'll be astonished if we even make it to the point of requiring one," she confessed, wishing her cheeks weren't on fire. "The moment of truth will likely bring everything to an abrupt halt."

His eyes lit with gentle amusement. "It may, but I cannot imagine any recess lasting very long. I've seen the way the man looks at you, Diana."

She'd seen it, too. An involuntary shiver made her bite her lip. When she looked up, Harrow's smile had become all too knowing. "Don't say it," she muttered. Face aflame, she turned and made for the stairs, followed by his soft laughter.

. . .

Stepping down from his carriage a few minutes before seven, Lucas ascended the front steps of Diana's house determined not to show how nervous he was. *It's ridiculous that a man of my sophistication should be so on edge over this.*

In truth, he couldn't remember ever anticipating something so much. The whole afternoon had been spent in preparation. He'd bathed assiduously, spent an inordinate amount of time grooming himself, and had made his valet wait until only an hour ago to give him a proper shave. Even his clothing had been selected with her pleasure in mind. She must find him irresistible.

He was greeted with warmth by both Diana and her protector, which eased his apprehension somewhat. Yesterday, Harrow had made it perfectly clear he would brook no offense or injury against her. It should have irritated him, being constrained to such terms as had been outlined. After all, he'd won the wager; therefore, the debt ought to be fulfilled on his terms. But he couldn't bring himself to feel resentful, when he knew bloody well she could've reneged or accepted Harrow's proposal to offer him alternative compensation.

She hadn't. She was *allowing* this. Because she wanted him.

Enthusiasm returned, chasing away his anxiety. In the eyes of most of his peers, he was about to become one of only a rare, privileged few.

Pleasantries were exchanged, and the three went to the salon for aperitifs. There, they spoke comfortably, as friends, of matters unrelated to the evening's ultimate purpose. Except for an undercurrent of excitement that ran deep beneath the surface of the conversation, it was like all his previous visits.

That excitement was an electrical presence, a tension in the atmosphere like the sort one felt just before a storm broke. Every time his gaze met Diana's it spiked, and in the wake of this came a distinct tightening in his midsection. It wasn't arousal, though he hovered at its cusp. More and more, he wondered what it could mean.

Later in the evening, her look became pensive as she considered him across the dinner table, and he grew curious to know if she was experiencing the same sort of reaction. The world seemed to move around them like water around an island amid a fast-flowing river.

His mind acknowledged the table conversation as lively, but he couldn't have related its precise content if asked. His mouth recognized the meal served as being delicious, but he couldn't have told anyone what he ate. All his focus was trained on her. Everything else simply faded into insignificance.

Harrow excused himself for a moment but then returned to escort them to the drawing room for sherry and some light entertainment.

On approaching, Lucas stiffened at the sound of scales being practiced on a pianoforte. Mentally, he kicked himself for the reaction when Diana, who was walking beside him, shot him a quizzical glance. Anxious to account for his reaction, he patted her hand on his arm. "I was not anticipating the presence of additional guests tonight."

Her smile was easy as she guided him on into the room and over to its occupant, who stood to greet them. "This is not a guest, but rather my music instructor. Please allow me to introduce Monsieur Laurent, who has graciously agreed to play a little for us this evening. Monsieur Laurent, this is Lord Blackthorn, my neighbor."

It was Lucas's first good look at his rival. Laurent was a slender man of middling height who appeared to be in his mid-to-late twenties, with dark brown hair, laughing blue eyes, and a bright smile. To Lucas's shock, the fellow seemed genuinely delighted to meet him, his smile broadening as they shook hands. He seemed even more pleased as he then kissed the back of Diana's hand and said something to her briefly in his native tongue.

Lucas hid his jealousy and irritation behind a practiced smile. *If he thinks he's going to seduce me the way he did Harrow, he's in for a disappointment.* "I think I may have heard you play before while I was out in my garden, or was that you, Diana?"

"She is quite accomplished," Laurent answered for her with shining eyes. "There is so little I can teach her anymore. I hardly know why she keeps me," he added, winking at her.

There was a subtle, telltale shift in both Harrow's and her

expressions as their eyes met, and Lucas knew they were both worried for their secret—for *him*. Again, he tamped down his jealousy.

Then Diana answered smoothly, "These days I confess I'm more a patroness than an employer. Your gifts would be too keenly missed, were I to relinquish you."

Nausea twisted in Lucas's stomach as the musician's cheeks pinked and he looked down as though embarrassed. Eager to get this part of the evening over with, he cleared his throat and asked what piece the man would play.

Thankfully, this seemed to prompt everyone to action. The pianist spoke about the music, a piece of his own composition, while Harrow poured drinks. When all was ready, Diana led Lucas to a couch so they could sit and listen.

The piece he'd heard from his terrace was nothing compared to the one the man played now. Despite his raging envy, Lucas couldn't help being impressed. *Gifts, indeed.* He couldn't see the fellow's hands from this vantage, but he could only imagine how they must dance across the ivory and ebony keys.

Sweet music washed over and through him, soft and seductive, caressing his senses in a gentle ebb and flow that felt as easy as breathing. The woman beside him rested her head against the back of the couch, eyes closed in bliss as she listened, clearly transported.

Now the melody began to subtly alter, growing more suspenseful. Lucas found his heart beating faster and realized with a start that his breath now matched the music's tempo. On it went, climbing, then reaching a plateau, and then climbing again, the tension mounting. Gone was the soft seduction, replaced by passion's immutable fire.

Lucas had never been one to get too caught up in music, but this...*this* was music such as he'd never experienced before. It rolled over him in great waves, carrying him along with it. He felt powerless to resist its pull on his emotions as it rose to a crescendo, filling the room.

Glancing over at Harrow, he saw the man's eyes were also shut. But unlike Diana, who appeared enraptured, Harrow's face looked almost pained. As he watched, tears began to seep from beneath the other man's closed lids. When he opened them a second later, his gaze was fixed on the pianist at play, and the affection in his visage was so raw and thirst-laden it brought a flush to Lucas's own face.

He loves him. Deeply. Lucas had known this, but until now he hadn't witnessed its expression firsthand. Afraid to be caught observing such an intimate moment, he looked to Diana, only to find she, too, was watching Harrow. But there was nothing whatsoever of jealousy in her regard. Instead, he saw only love. Not the sort Harrow so obviously felt for the pianist, but another kind. As strong, yet utterly devoid of carnality.

Again, it struck Lucas what a strange relationship these three had. When Diana's gaze shifted to him, it coincided with the music's exhilarating peak, and he saw its passion reflected in her jewel-like eyes.

Directed at *him*.

Her sea-green irises had darkened to a shade resembling the ocean just after dawn, and her pupils were blown wide.

Suddenly Lucas knew the musician was no threat. Even if she desired the man now, she would no longer do so after tonight. He would make certain of it.

The music slowed and softened, and in the relative calm that ensued as it wound to a close, he realized his heart was pounding. Blood rushed throughout his body as a result, gathering in certain places. Never had he felt as aroused as he did in that moment.

Harrow broke the silence that had fallen. "Thank you, Monsieur Laurent, for gracing us with your talent." His eyes glowed with praise and something more. The result was the other man's deep flush of pleasure as he excused himself.

Turning, Harrow now addressed Lucas. "Before I bid you goodnight, allow me to again express my pleasure in our friendship. I wish you great joy tonight." His glance flicked to Diana, and a soft smile curved his mouth. "Both of you."

Lucas found his tongue suddenly thick and unwieldy, but he was saved from having to respond.

Diana held up a hand, halting the other man's departure. "Before you leave, there is one small matter I would like to discuss with you present. Lord Blackthorn, are you familiar with the concept of a stop word?"

A frown furrowed his brow at the random-seeming question. "It seems intuitive," he began lightly, but broke off on seeing an indulgent smile form on Harrow's face.

"In terms of love play, I mean," Diana clarified.

"I've heard of it in passing," he answered carefully. "If indeed we are referring to the same thing."

Harrow spoke now, his manner gentle yet firm. "It's simply a word agreed upon by both participants that when spoken by either brings about an immediate halt to all activity."

Lucas looked to Diana, noting that although her gaze was still heated, there was wariness in her eyes. "I assume you wish to establish such a word for tonight?"

"I do," she husked. "And we must both vow to, without hesitation, honor that word's intent should it be spoken."

For some reason, rather than dampening his excitement, this idea sent a thrill through him, a pang of carnal hunger so sharp it was almost painful. "Very well. What word would you like?"

"I would prefer you choose the word."

His excitement rose another increment. Did she think he'd be the one to use it? He decided to play along. "Eden."

A slow smile curled the corners of her mouth. "*Mm.* The

garden in which sin was born," she said, proving she'd not missed the reference. "Eden it is. I vow to stop whatever I'm doing should you say this word."

His vision seemed to narrow, until all he saw was her face. "As do I."

Again, he heard Harrow's voice, but it was as if he spoke from far away. "Then it is settled. Until morning, dear friends."

By the time Lucas managed to tear his gaze away from her, his host was long gone.

Diana stepped close and held out her hand.

Taking her outstretched fingers, he let her lead him from the room. He barely felt his legs moving as he followed her out and up the staircase. His pulse thumped in his ears when they finally halted before a door at the hallway's end. Within, he expected to see the pastel pinks of her suite. Instead, what lay beyond the door was a boudoir meant solely for passion. A large mirror reflected the bed in its entirety, ubiquitous candlelight left no shadows to hide their coming together, and a most interesting assortment of items had been laid out on the bedside table.

This would indeed be a night to remember.

Her hands trembled as she reached back to remove her necklace.

Nerves or excitement? "Here, allow me." Carefully, he helped divest her of her jewelry and then assisted her in disrobing.

Each ribbon pulled loose brought him a step closer to finally seeing her perfection up close. Each layer of clothing that fell to the floor served to further enflame his arousal. Every time the backs of his fingers made contact with her bare skin, a spark caught in his own flesh and sent desire rocketing through his veins.

He'd been vacillating between various degrees of stiffness

since before dinner, but his erection had been constant since the concert in the drawing room. Now, his cock twitched and strained in protest against confinement as blood rushed to fill it even further. He'd never been so hard in all his life and wanted nothing more than to free himself of his trousers, but it could wait. They had all night, and he wanted to savor his prize.

At last, he lifted her chemise over her head. Only her stockings, lacy garters, and dainty slippers remained. He feasted his eyes for a moment on creamy skin and a body to make a man weep with want. "You are, without a doubt, the most beautiful woman I've ever seen," he said, meaning every word.

The blush that stole over her cheeks as she lowered her lashes was simply enchanting. And puzzling. *Does not that Laurent fellow ever pay her such compliments?*

Looking up, she met his stare. Seemingly emboldened by what she saw there, she reached out and fingered the end of his cravat. "May I return the favor?"

"You may do with me whatever pleases you," he answered with a slow smile. He sobered as her gaze sharpened, and she gave the cravat a sharp tug, causing him to stumble and take a step closer. With a few more gentle tugs, the cloth fell away. As soon as it hit the floor, she stepped close and pressed an open-mouthed kiss to the base of his now-bare throat, following with a little nip and lick before stepping back and pushing his coat back off his shoulders.

The fire that had been slowly building inside him instantly flared white hot. But he maintained self-discipline and after shrugging off his jacket remained still, curious to see what she had planned. If there was anything he'd learned about pleasure, it was that delayed gratification was often the best kind.

Mesmerized, he watched as her nimble fingers made

short work of the buttons on his waistcoat. That, too, fell to the floor. When her hands slid beneath his shirt and she ran her palms up along his abdomen to skim across his nipples, however, he decided enough was enough.

Bending, he pressed his lips against the sensitive joint of her neck and heard a trembling sigh escape her lips. He smiled against her skin as she tilted her head, granting him better access, and rewarded her by continuing upward in a trail of small kisses, mirroring her earlier action with little nips and flicks of his tongue.

One by one, he pulled the jeweled pins from her hair, and soon his hands were buried in a wavy flow of honey-gold strands that caught the candlelight and held it prisoner. Working his fingers beneath it at the nape of her neck, he massaged her scalp and was rewarded by a soft, broken groan. Desire speared straight down through his vitals to pool in his pelvis.

I'm just getting started.

Not all touch had to be sexual in nature to give pleasure. This was evident as she leaned close and melted against him. Her warmth seeped through his fine linen shirt and sank into him like summer sunlight. Moving his fingertips in small circles, he worked his way over the back of her head and then forward to her temples.

Her eyes drifted shut. Framing her face between his palms, he at last brought their mouths together. The first contact was electric, eliciting an all but unbearable ache in his groin, as though the two places were directly connected by a single, raw nerve. Ghosting his lips across hers, he licked the seam where those rosy petals met, begging entrance. It was granted on a sigh, and he reveled in the catch and slide of their mouths as he gently angled her head so they slotted together perfectly. The sweetness of sherry and the cake they'd had for dessert erupted across his tongue, along with something he'd never tasted before, something uniquely *her.*

She pressed into him, deepening the contact, and now the groan he heard was his own. A tremor wracked his whole body as multiple sensations ran riot through it at once, reverberating back and forth like ripples crossing each other on the surface of a pond until he couldn't take any more and had to pull back to catch his breath.

He kissed the curve of her neck to hide his face, afraid of what it might reveal. The impatient nudging of her lips at the tender flesh just below his ear urged him on.

Closing his eyes against the sight of her, lest he lose control, he kissed her again, pouring all of himself into it. Kissing wasn't something he'd often indulged in, feeling it was too intimate for casual encounters. But he couldn't seem to stop himself now.

She responded with renewed fervor, and their breaths mingled in a series of soft gasps as her frenzied fingers pulled at his shirt. Breaking away, he yanked it off over his head and tossed it, not caring where it landed, such was his eagerness to feel her velvet skin, to learn the shape of her with his palms and explore every lush curve.

Her hands were busy again, fumbling with the buttons on his trousers. He batted them away. If that barrier were removed, it would be the undoing of him, and he wanted to draw out this feast and make it last as long as possible. To ease the sting of his reprisal, he brought her hands up and pressed a kiss into each palm before continuing his way upward.

The shudder that ran through her at the gentle touch of his lips against the inside of her wrist brought a smile to his face. He flicked his tongue across the delicious inch of skin, delighted to hear her breath catch. Slowly, he worked his way up that arm, over her shoulder, and the wings of her collarbone, not forgetting the charming dip between before treating the other arm to the same attention. She was pliant, like clay waiting to be sculpted by his hands as he drew back to contemplate his next move.

When he looked at her face, he expected her eyes to be closed and was surprised to find them open and ablaze with naked hunger.

Chapter Fourteen

So this is what it's like. Diana stared at Blackthorn as arousal melted through her, leaving her hot and aching. And he'd done nothing more than kiss her.

Oh, but those kisses. Tender, yet ferocious. Gentle, yet full of fire. Based on those kisses, it would be easy to believe there was more to this than lust. But she knew Blackthorn was here for one thing only. He would get it, but she'd have her desire of him, as well.

Stepping back, she looked him up and down, drinking in the sight of his broad chest, letting her gaze fall to the trail of dark hair that disappeared beneath the waist of his trousers. Just below that, she marked the distinct bulge where his cock strained against the cloth. She cupped it with a bold palm and was gratified to hear a low, animal groan torn from his throat just before he took her lips in a bruising kiss that was far more aggressive than its predecessors.

Lust rose to the challenge, and she met him with equal force until they were both gasping for breath. She thought she'd faint when his palms grazed the sensitive sides of her breasts, and the noise she let out when his thumbs began to circle her areolas was shockingly primitive.

It was nothing compared to the sound she made when he dipped his head and took a nipple into his mouth—*that* was obscene. Her cheeks heated, but her embarrassment was short-lived in the face of the maddening sensations running riot throughout her body. Lightning seemed to strike in the agonizingly empty place between her legs every time his tongue flicked, every time he grazed it with his teeth or pinched it between his lips. It was absolute torment, yet the instant he stopped, she found her fingers diving into his hair, drawing his head back.

A soft huff of laughter followed her silent command, and he gave one last flick before moving to the other breast.

If the first had been a trial, this one ought to have killed her. The sounds she made as he treated it to the same torment as the other were those of an absolute savage. It was a shock to hear herself reduced to such an uncivilized level.

He didn't seem to mind. If anything, it spurred his efforts and seemed to be wringing similarly wordless utterances from him, as well. With every tug of his hair, every moan ripped from her throat, his efforts increased. After a little while, he would leave one breast for its twin, but the relief the abandoned one felt was short-lived. This pleasurable agony continued until she felt her knees begin to weaken and the muscles in her legs begin to shake.

At which point he drew sharply on her nipple, sending an electric bolt of pure need straight down into the core of her. He released it with a soft, wet *pop* just as her knees buckled.

A squeak of protest escaped her as he picked her up, hauled her over to the bed, and deposited her on it sitting upright with her legs dangling over the side. Before she could even begin to imagine what he might do next, he spread her knees apart and knelt between them, putting him at eye level with her most intimate place. Mortification sent heat flooding into her face, but he gave her no time to protest before his hot mouth was on her, his tongue laving the sensitive flesh, stroking it, teasing at the folds before its searing hot tip darted between to dip *into* her as a butterfly sips at a flower.

She nearly shot off the bed, releasing a keening cry into the air as sensation rolled through her in a great wave of heat followed by gooseflesh that spread across the entire expanse of her skin, robbing her of breath. Where her hands had at first flown to his shoulders to push him away, they now gripped him tight, holding him to her as he subjected her to a torment ten times as acute as before.

White spots swam before her eyes. Just when she felt herself on the verge of flying apart, he slowed to languorous swirls and comforting laps against her outer folds with the flat of his tongue until she was able to slow her breathing to something that didn't threaten to make her pass out. Soft kisses were pressed against her inner thighs, which shook as though she'd run a footrace.

When he rose, there was a look on his face unlike anything she'd ever seen. Tender, yet possessive, and oh, so dangerous, if the thundering of her heart inside its cage was any warning.

Control. You must gain the upper hand.

She refused to close her eyes, forcing herself to hold his stare as he stood, his intent clearly visible in his smoky gray eyes. His hands moved to his trousers, and he began slowly unbuttoning them. The long, thick rod of his manhood pressed against the material in front, tenting it. He'd have it out in a moment, and then she would have to make her move or simply surrender to whatever he had in mind.

Again, the stubborn part of her rose up inside. Scooting back, she made room for him on the bed and let a tiny smile curl one corner of her mouth in invitation.

His gray gaze sharpened further with pure lust, and he all but shoved his trousers down to kick them off.

Want warred with trepidation, but she wouldn't let fear get the better of her. Focusing on his face, she avoided looking directly at the part of him that would well and truly ruin her tonight. She could see it jutting out from his body, flush and dark with blood and desire.

Her every muscle trembled, her every breath was ragged as he crawled up after her, angling his long body over her legs. She inched back a little more, a frisson of apprehension working its way up her spine at the unholy look in his eyes, a look that said he would as soon devour her in an instant as take his sweet time the way he'd been doing.

Curious, she put out her hands and braced them against his shoulders. He could easily have pressed on, but he didn't. Lowering her lashes, she dragged one hand down a few inches, caressing his chest and collarbone. Her voice, when it came out, was deep and husky with thirst, but not for water. "Your turn."

Surprise flitted across his features but was soon replaced by a faint smirk as he retreated to sit facing her. "How do you want me?"

Fire kissed her cheeks anew at the blunt request for direction. She ignored it in favor of glancing at the bedside table. "Lie face down on the bed."

A raven brow quirked up, but he did as he was told—an act which sent a rush of foreign excitement through her. She'd never put her knowledge to practical use. The thought of doing so now was...provocative. Crawling to the edge of the bed, she took up a pot of oil, several feathers, and three of the silk scarves.

Blackthorn's eyes were twin pools of heat as he watched her over his shoulder while she laid these items out on the bed. "What do you intend to do to me?" he murmured, a smile in his gravelly voice.

Thankful for having calmed down a little, she tossed him a mischievous look. It wasn't fear that had stopped her letting him go ahead and have what he so clearly wanted, but the desire to draw this out as long as possible, to gain as much pleasure as she could now, before the inevitable pain to come. "Surprise you," she whispered, taking up one of the scarves.

When he saw she meant to blindfold him, his eyes narrowed, but he made no protest as she bound his eyes and tied the scarf securely around his head, checking to make certain he couldn't see.

As she straightened, movement caught her eye, and she looked up to see...herself. The mirror she'd puzzled about earlier today reflected almost the entire bed, including her kneeling on it beside the prone man she'd chosen to become her first lover. A furious blush heated her face, and she looked down to help reclaim her composure.

She picked up the pot of oil she'd selected and, pouring out a little, warmed it between her palms as she shifted to straddle the backs of his thighs. It was lightly scented with sandalwood and smelled like heaven.

Unable to help herself, she peeked at the mirror again. All embarrassment fled as she gazed upon the most erotic thing she'd ever seen, replaced by exhilaration at the sight of herself, lips parted, cheeks flushed, astride this powerful man who'd made himself vulnerable for her pleasure. She stared, knowing she'd never forget that moment as it was seared into her memory.

A muffled sigh from below dragged her attention back to the man beneath her. The backside view provided by her new vantage was an impressive one, too. Blackthorn's arse was, like the rest of him, lean and muscular. Leaning across it, she began spreading the oil across his shoulders, slowly working her way down, the heels of her hands pressing in, her fingers kneading warm, solid flesh. Her naked pelvis pressed against his rear every time she moved upward, and the sensation made her bite her lower lip.

By the time she'd covered his entire back and buttocks, she felt almost feverish. But she still wasn't ready for the endgame quite yet. Her own desire was a sinful ache, but she was patient. This might be her only time with him, and she wanted it to be memorable in the best way.

Now that her hands had touched him, had felt the velvet-over-granite of his shoulders and back, they wanted to feel so much more. Tingling palms longed to run over his entire body. Rising up, she again moved to his side.

"Turn over onto your back," she whispered. Again, he obeyed, sending another twinge of excitement through her. She checked to be sure his eyes remained securely covered. "Now bring your hands up beside your head." When he'd done this, she took the two remaining scarves and used them to tie his wrists to the thick wooden pillars carved into the bed's sturdy oaken headboard, remembering to knot them the way Harrow had shown her.

The faint smile twitching the corners of Blackthorn's mouth told her he was enjoying this. Again, she plied his body with the scented oil, careful to avoid his more sensitive areas. Once the oil had been worked in, she selected from the little pile of feathers a long goose quill.

The instant its tip touched his face, he stiffened. Muscles bunched and slowly released.

"Good," she encouraged softly. "This is not meant to tickle. If it does, you must tell me and I'll stop."

A hard breath huffed from him before he nodded, and she marked with satisfaction that his smirk had fled. She ran the feather's edge across his cheekbones and forehead, and then dragged it across his lips, watching them part slightly. Bending, she dropped a lingering kiss there to reward him for his tolerance.

Next came the strong cords of his neck and his finely sculpted collarbone. Her own arousal mounted when she moved the feather lower and slowly circled one of his nipples with its tip. His breath hitched, and he stiffened—in more than one place. Not only did his back arch slightly, but his cock leapt a little, as if begging to be touched.

Soon. Smiling, she again dragged the feather across his nipples, circling them until his breathing grew rough, and she could see he was growing impatient with her playing. This time when she resumed tormenting the most recently neglected nipple, she stopped after only a few circles and covered it with her mouth.

A long hiss exploded from between Blackthorn's clenched teeth as he jerked hard. His hands pulled reflexively at the bindings but remained secure as she did to him what he'd done to her earlier, with little flicks, long licks, and delicate pinches.

Small, strangled sounds came from between his lips, as though they were escaping against his will. She paused, but he didn't utter the stop word. This time when she repeated her actions, he let out a long, filthy moan. When his exhalations were nothing more than ragged gasps, his wrists pulling almost rhythmically at the silken restraints, his hips bucking up a little with each pull, *then* she stopped.

Straightening, she licked a fingertip and circled it around one abused nipple. From the corner of her eye, she saw his cock jerk. Feeling brave, she looked at the instrument of her planned undoing, fascinated. Long and turgid, it curved up from its thick base to rise up off him, its rounded head hovering just above his taut belly. Afraid yet to actually touch it, she again took up her feather and tentatively ran it up its length to gently circle the head.

Another profane groan issued forth from Blackthorn,

sounding as if torn from the very root of his soul, and she saw a bead of clear liquid form at the very tip of his rod, which, amazingly, seemed to thicken further before her eyes. Mesmerized, she dragged the tip of the feather through the pearl and drew it down to the base of his cock, leaving a long, wet line.

"I'm a patient man," rasped Blackthorn, startling her. He sounded wrecked. "But if you don't touch me soon, I won't be responsible for my reaction."

Triumph surged through her in a heady rush, along with a frisson of trepidation. *I must maintain control.* Focusing, she hardened her voice. "Would you have me curtail your pleasure?"

An animal sound lodged in his throat, and she watched the bob of his Adam's apple as he swallowed it. "Of course not. But I should tell you, the disappointment won't be solely mine if it happens too soon."

Oh! She smiled and softened her tone. "You have but to say the word, and I'll stop."

His low, crushed-gravel chuckle was an almost tangible thing. "If you think I'll break first, you'll be waiting until dawn."

We'll see about that. Emboldened by the challenge, she leaned over him and, just as she'd heard René say once when the door hadn't quite shut properly between their rooms, whispered against his lips, "Be a good lad now, and spread your legs for me."

The flush across his chest deepened to scarlet, and she saw a muscle work in his jaw as he doubtless bit back a curse—but he did it. By George, he *did* it.

Repositioning, she knelt between his long, strong legs, running her hands up and down them to learn their shape. Staring up at him, she decided she quite liked the view from here. She could see almost all of him, from the secret, dusky flesh just below his sack to the underside of his clean-shaven jaw and chin.

Determined not to be a coward, she scrunched her eyes shut, then reached out and firmly grasped the base of his cock in one hand, getting her first feel of what would soon be inside her. At its owner's hard flinch and soft, relieved groan, she cracked open first one eye, then the other, and grinned. "*Shhh*, quiet now," she softly admonished, inordinately proud of herself for not backing away from this.

He stiffened but kept silent as she slowly stroked him up and down, exploring his flesh with her palm and fingers. It was a strange amalgam of hard and soft, like hot stone sheathed in fine silk.

Do I dare? Leaning forward slowly, she released him to run her hands over his abdomen and up across his chest and shoulders while contemplating her course. It was something she'd been told men absolutely loved. Certainly, Harrow and René had both professed to enjoy it immensely. But would she? Only one way to find out. Without preamble, she slid backward, dipped low, and took the head of his cock into her mouth at the same time as she again gripped its base with her free hand.

"*Mmngahhh!*" The hoarse outcry was torn from Blackthorn's chest, and his back arched so hard it lifted his shoulder blades up off the bed.

Releasing him, she braced her hands on his hips and shoved, using her body's weight to push him back into the mattress. The taste of his hot, firm flesh lingered on her tongue, slightly salty with a faint underlying tang that was not unpleasant. This time when she went back down, she dipped lower to lick a broad, wet stripe from the underside of his cock all the way to its tip before again taking the head into her mouth.

Blackthorn positively writhed beneath her hands, his

hips jerking upward in little involuntary thrusts.

Again, she released him. This was going to get uncomfortable if he kept doing that. There had to be a way to make him stay down. A memory arose, something she'd seen in Harrow's Hindu text. Smiling, she began slowly working one hand up and down his rigid length, granting him some small relief. When a large bead of liquid formed at its tip and began to slowly drip down the side, she stopped it with a swipe of her index finger instead of using it to ease the friction as she continued to slowly pump him.

She had a better use for it.

Blackthorn yelped, actually *yelped* when she touched that slicked-up fingertip to the soft patch of flesh Harrow had identified as the "perineum" on the drawing he'd shown her. She paused, but though Blackthorn's breathing caught and hitched, he didn't say the stop word, so she continued, sliding that finger down a fraction of an inch at a time, down, down, until she was able to ever-so-gently circle his opening.

· · ·

Lucas had thought he was prepared for this, that he'd known what to expect.

This wasn't it.

He'd been with women of every class—tavern wenches, farmers' daughters, whores, and more than a dozen ladies (mostly married, a few widows) from his own stratum—but none had managed to unravel him.

Until now.

He'd expected her to pleasure him with her mouth, but not like this. Not as if he were a banquet set out for her delectation. Not as if she was actually *enjoying* herself. The women he'd lain with to date had all made it very plain they loathed the act of giving fellatio. He couldn't see Diana's face, but he could tell by the smile in her voice when she spoke, the little humming sounds she occasionally made, and the way she was touching him—almost *lovingly*—that she was pleased with what she was doing.

That thought alone made him even harder.

And now that she'd released him, she'd taken his own slick and was using it to stimulate him down...*there*. For one terrible moment, he'd worried she might be thinking to prepare him for something he truly didn't want to do—and wouldn't—but she'd done nothing more than touch him in gentle circles.

It felt different, but not bad.

In fact, it was starting to feel pretty damned good, actually.

He revised this opinion when she abandoned his hole to press two fingers firmly into the spongy flesh between it and his bollocks and began moving them from side to side, wringing an involuntary grunt of pleasure from him as a rush of tingly fire raced from that point straight up his cock, which was now leaking copiously, and back down to settle deep beneath its root. A sweet ache had taken up residence there, pulsing in time to the long, firm strokes she was now giving his rod with her other hand.

No. This went beyond pretty damned good—this was bloody *amazing*, that's what it was. As much as he wasn't attracted to the fellow, in that particular moment he could have kissed Harrow out of sheer gratitude for having shaped a timid little debutante into this glorious, sensual creature.

Her hot mouth closed once more over the tip of his cock, her tongue swirling across its head, tasting him as if he were some sort of delicious confection. The air burst from his lungs again, pulling with it another long groan from somewhere deep down within his vitals. He'd wanted so badly to taste her sweetness when he'd taken Cupid's feast, but hadn't expected her to want to reciprocate, and certainly not with such... enthusiasm.

And there, my lad, is the difference between a high-class courtesan and a common harlot. Duly noted.

Right then he decided it was going to be worth every penny he was going to have to pay for her doubtless expensive upkeep. He'd support her in whatever style she demanded until the gold either ran out or he grew too old and feeble to get it up anymore.

Another blue curse clawed its way out of his throat on a gasp as she suddenly sucked hard on his head and simultaneously pressed a slick digit against his opening—just *held* it there at the same time as she bore down with the pad of her thumb just above it and wiggled it from side to side—and the river of tingles intensified.

Just when he thought he was going to lose control, she eased off with a soft *pop* and lifted her hand away. He drifted back from the edge of the precipice, gulping air like he'd been drowning. Then, with a siren's chuckle, she was at it again with that fingertip, circling, circling.

She was going to drive him insane. For the second time that evening he'd nearly come undone, and he needed to be inside her before that happened. The last thing he wanted was to shame himself by not bringing her to peak first. Or worse. If she took him in her mouth and did that *thing* again, there was a real danger of him coming untouched the moment she pulled off. He anticipated going several rounds before the night was done, but first impressions mattered to him.

Enough. He wanted to see her, to verify that she was truly enjoying this as much as he suspected, and then get down to the happy business of plowing her like a fallow field.

He balked at making the request, but then reminded himself that asking wasn't the same as begging. "The blindfold—" Bloody hell, his throat was dry!

She tenderly cupped his firm, aching sack and began to gently massage there. It felt wonderful. But he couldn't afford to let himself be distracted. "Take it off."

Yet another gasp was wrung from him as she ignored his request and slid her other thumb up through the slickness coating the head of his cock and pressed down, covering the slit.

Remembering the approval that had warmed her eyes when he'd meekly complied with her commands before being rendered blind, he added a polite, "Please?"

"You want to see me?" She sounded almost shy, which he knew was a damned lie.

"Yes, I want to see you," he said, doing his level best not to let any of his desperation come through in his voice. His pulse thundered in his ears, thumping so hard he could feel his heartbeat in every one of his extremities. *See you, touch you, take you, make you mine...*

The mattress shifted beneath him as she changed position. Then her fingers were sliding through his hair and removing the silk that had obstructed his vision.

What he saw when his eyes finally focused had to be a figment of his imagination. No woman who'd just done what she'd done to him could look that ingenuous. Her jewel-like eyes held none of the sultry teasing he'd heard in her voice. Nor did they hold the demanding woman who'd told him to shush. She looked entirely unspoiled. Yet he knew better. He saw the swollen lips, the blown pupils, the flushed cheeks. She was the best kind of contradiction.

He couldn't help smiling just a little as he asked, "Untie me?" Had he truly been inclined, he could've torn free of the flimsy silk, but it was more fun this way.

Twin crescents of thick, burnished gold lashes lowered demurely, and she nodded.

He stared up at her as she stretched across him to unbind

the far hand first. Once untethered, still he held back, denying himself the pleasure of touching her for just a little longer while he mastered himself. "You're still wearing stockings," he observed, holding her unwavering gaze as she settled back on her knees. "Take them off?"

Rising, she backed off the bed and stood to oblige.

His cock grew impossibly hard as he watched her bend to untie the garters and peel the silk sheaths off one at a time. "Come here," he rasped when she was done, holding out his hand.

Chapter Fifteen

Diana's insides shook as she took the final step and joined him on the bed. He drew her close for a breath-stealing kiss that made her feel boneless, and then she found herself pressed beneath his nakedness from shoulders to toes, their legs entwined. She stroked her fingertips down his long back, squeezed his taut buttocks, then dragged her nails lightly back up his flanks to wrap her arms around his neck and hold on for dear life as he continued to kiss her senseless.

She was drowning in desire. The rigid length of him lay caught between their bodies, digging into her pelvis, thick and heavy. He shifted a little, and the pressure changed. It was no longer nudging at her middle, but sliding against the swollen, heated flesh below.

His voice at her ear was thick with passion. "Lady's choice the first time. Tell me how you want me."

When she failed to answer immediately, he drew back a little and peered down at her, the question in his smoke-colored eyes. "You've brought me such pleasure," he murmured. "But I want to please you, too, you know. It's a point of pride with me that my bedpartner should take equal enjoyment."

Warmth blossomed in her chest. "I like the way we are now," she whispered, feeling suddenly insecure. Would he think it too ordinary?

The smile that broke across his face was the most endearing she'd ever seen on any man. "As do I. And we'll still have plenty of time for more adventurous games before the sun rises." With that, he rose up on his haunches between her legs, propped her legs up to bracket his waist, and reached down between them.

She expected to feel him positioning the blunt head of his cock at her entrance, but instead felt the light caress of his fingertips bathing in her slickness, dipping in and teasing the sensitive little nub concealed within her innermost folds. Sighing, she gave herself up to the happy sensation, letting him build her back up to fever pitch.

Only when she began to wriggle her hips in mindless frustration did he stop.

Now she closed her eyes, willing herself not to tense up as he reached beneath her bottom and slid her a little closer until she felt his manhood bump against her thigh, and then as something hard, hot, and silky smooth touched her core.

The expected pain didn't come when he leaned into the cradle between her thighs to bring his head up to her breasts and suckle first one and then the other, making her gasp as the lightning connection between nipples and core sizzled back to life. Or as he then shifted farther up and pressed his cock snugly against her slick opening.

She buried her face in the curve of his neck as he began to enter her. There was only a little discomfort as she felt him nudge against something a little way in. It didn't exactly hurt, but it also didn't really seem to want to easily yield.

The man above her suddenly stilled. "Diana..."

Her heart slammed against her ribcage, and panic won out. Wrapping her legs around his waist, she pulled their bodies together in one quick motion, unbalancing him so that his full weight fell against her.

The result was a sharp, burning sensation where they were joined that made her clench her teeth to keep from crying out. She prayed he would simply continue on until he found release. *If he does not notice, I might not have to tell him about René, and then this whole debacle can be easily—*

"George's bollocks!" gasped the man above her, clumsily shifting up onto his elbows to peer down into her face with an expression of utter dismay. "Are you…? You were a *virgin*?" Scrambling back, he withdrew and looked down at himself in horror.

"I can explain—" she began, trying to inject a sense of calm in spite of the sick feeling in her stomach.

Gray eyes snapped up to meet hers, and now she saw fury slowly replace the shock as he held up his hand, on which there was a smear of blood. "Damned right, you will!" he rumbled menacingly. "Is this some sort of sick jest? Are you and your friends—or should I say '*lovers*'—having a laugh at my expense?" His face went blank for a moment before the anger returned, and along with it a new wariness. "Is this a trick? Are you—are you trying to *entrap* me?"

"No," she answered glumly. "As if anyone would ever believe me still a virgin after living openly as someone's mistress—even if it *is* true." She hadn't intended to come off that sarcastic, but it felt damned good to see him flinch back as she spat the words.

His expression went from angry to incredulous. "If it *is* true then—" Breaking off, he again looked down at himself, clearly trying to discern whether there really wasn't some trickery involved.

"I assure you it most certainly *is*," Diana hadn't thought

it possible for one's ears to be this hot without melting right off the sides of their head.

"But if you were a virgin, then..." He gestured wildly around the room and then stabbed a finger at the incriminating feathers and scarves scattered across the bed. "What of all this, and the...*things* you did to me? How could a virgin know how to—"

"Harrow taught me—using books and drawings, obviously," she added when his eyes widened. "Before you, no one had ever touched me. It has all been an act."

He blinked, clearly flummoxed as he tried to process this information. Then his gaze again narrowed in suspicion. "Why did you agree to honor the forfeit when I *know* you had plans to start over anew once your agreement with Harrow was fulfilled? Yes, he told me all about it. As a virgin, you could have one day married."

"I still can, if indeed the prospect of forever binding myself to any man ever appeals," she shot back, irritated. She hadn't thought it would end this way. It wasn't supposed to be like this. She'd thought she could hide it or that he'd be so impassioned he wouldn't notice or possibly even care until after he'd found his pleasure, if at all. "Diana Haversham was ruined long before now. I can move, take a new name, claim to be a widow or—"

"You idiot," he cut in, his soft tone stunning her into silence. "You did not have to do this. *Why* did you do it?"

Her temper flared at the regret she saw reflected in his face. She didn't want his sympathy! "Harrow asked me if I wanted him to offer you alternate compensation to discharge the forfeit, and I told him no. Because I *wanted* this. The choice was mine. I wanted to know passion before enduring what might be a lifetime without it." Her eyes brimmed, and she swiped at them angrily. "I'm *owed* that much by Fate!"

They sat staring at each other in silence for several

heartbeats before he spoke. "I have questions."

"No doubt," she said bitterly.

"Will you answer them truthfully?"

She refused to dignify that and told him so with a furious glare.

He sighed. "Why did you become Harrow's mistress?"

"Because I've yet to hear of a tree that produces lumps of gold, why else? I was cast out—"

"In error, obviously," he interjected wryly.

"Yes, and through no fault of my own, save that of trusting the wrong people," she added pointedly. "I had neither friends nor prospects when my uncle threw me out. It was this, sell myself at the docks, become an indentured servant, or starvation. I consider myself fortunate to have avoided my other choices." Her already frayed nerves unraveled a little more, and she prayed he would leave it at that.

He didn't. "I'll spare you the trouble of lying in answer to my next question, which is why Harrow took you in the first place. I think your function is to provide a plausible alternative to, and therefore a distraction from, his true affair with that Laurent fellow."

Diana felt the blood rush from her head and was glad she was sitting.

A sly look of amusement entered his eyes. "I see I've struck gold with that supposition." He chuckled softly. "I'll admit my mind ran wild with conjecture when I saw you three. I imagined your pianist friend being the man who ruined you for Grenville, and that you'd introduced him to Harrow and that you, he, and Laurent had become a love triangle."

Shock brought the blood flooding right back into her face. "*What?* And what do you mean, you *saw* us?" And just how much had he seen?

His gaze slid away, as if he couldn't bear to look at her. "I happened to see you all together one morning and witnessed them kiss, immediately after which I watched Laurent handle you in what I felt was a most...*familiar* manner. Naturally, I made some assumptions."

Confusion made her frown. "In the morning? But our little act was put on at nigh—" She suddenly remembered the duet in the drawing room and Harrow surprising them with an early visit. "Oh. *That* morning. But René has never touched me inappropriately—he's like my brother."

Now he looked at her again, skepticism written all over his face.

"This is ridiculous!" she scoffed. "Harrow and René have been in love with each other for years—*exclusively.*" Fear gripped her anew at the admission. "Every word of what I told you about Harrow's wife, Minerva, is true—by my own life, I swear it. His love for René harms no one. Indeed, if not for that love, I myself would have been lost." She caught herself reaching out and pulled back her hand, unsure how he'd react to her touch now. "You...you won't tell anyone? Will you?"

Skepticism was replaced with wry cynicism. "Harrow is not the first man of his kind I've met," he told her. "Even if what such people do defies the edicts of both church and state, it's not my place to judge a man for what he does in private with another consenting adult. Besides, I believe you've made it all but impossible for me to incriminate anyone without also incriminating myself. Or was that not your plan from the start?"

Guilt assaulted her, but it was tempered by resolve. "Everything was perfect until you came along," she accused, again glaring at him, but without any real heat. "Other men had made nuisances of themselves, but you were different. More persistent. And when you took the house behind mine...well, it frightened me." She'd meant to say "us," but the truth was it had been her fear that had spurred Harrow to act.

"I never intended to make you afraid."

The gentleness of the admission did something to her. Something dangerous. *No. I cannot afford to be soft.* "I knew there was a chance you'd learn the truth. I tried to convince Harrow to move me again, but he..." She felt herself flush. "He refused, as he thought it would look too suspicious."

A slanted smile twisted his lips. "So instead of running away or giving me the cold shoulder, you decided to draw me in close enough to make certain I could not escape the honey trap without damning myself."

It was difficult to meet his eyes, but she made herself do it. "Yes."

Soft laughter followed her answer. "It surprises me that a gently raised female from a morally upright family would be so devoted to someone like Harrow—and it *is* devotion," he said before she could offer any lame excuses about being paid for her loyalty. "You care for him. For them both—you said Laurent is like a brother to you. I assume you must feel the same way about Harrow."

Diana had no qualms about answering this time and did so with her head held high. "Society might condemn them, but I won't—not when so many of the supposedly righteous members of the *Ton* have proven themselves anything *but* virtuous. Most of them are no better than snakes."

Like my uncle.

It was hard not to be bitter. Too hard. And now, with all that had happened, she decided the time for holding back was done. "Throughout my time with Harrow, I've become privy to a great many of the *Ton's* dirty secrets. Their hypocrisy disgusts me, but his steadfast kindness has proven him a better man than most. Better than my own kin, who robbed and abandoned me without just cause. Harrow took me in when I had no one. He gave me a new life and a chance for a fresh start."

"At great cost to you," he interjected, arching a brow.

The smile she gave him was broken, but she didn't care. "I was already ruined. He saw my need and an opportunity to help himself while helping me. That is no sin. Our friendship may have been born of mutual necessity, but I now consider both him and René—as well as Lady Harrow and her son—my family, and I know they feel likewise. There is nothing I would not do to protect them."

His expression when she said it told her she'd made her point. "Including ruin me," he confirmed flatly.

"If necessary, yes." Shame filled her at how her voice wobbled, but her resolve was adamant. "You said you don't judge your fellow man. Would you judge me? I only wanted to keep my family safe. You know the punishment they face for their love if they are discovered."

. . .

Though being fooled sat ill with Lucas, he couldn't find it in himself to remain angry. *This is my fault.* He knew it with certainty. Had he let her alone when she'd first tried to fend him off, none of this would be happening. Instead, he'd pushed.

She'd merely pushed back harder.

He also believed with absolute certainty that her interest in shielding her friends—or family, rather—wasn't rooted in self-preservation or mercenary ambition. She truly was willing to give up everything to protect them. Such loyalty was both commendable and dangerous.

Not loyalty—love. She loved them. Fiercely. And he knew they loved her. He'd seen firsthand the genuine affection in their eyes when they looked at her—*all* of them, including Lady Harrow. Their love hadn't been bought. It had been earned through merit and sacrifice.

"No," he finally answered. "I won't judge you. In your place, I would likely have done the same."

Her shoulders dropped in evident relief, and suddenly he realized they were both still quite naked. The instant his gaze fell to her bare breasts, she apparently realized it, too. He fought back laughter as she snatched up a pillow and covered herself with it, her face turning beet red.

"I think by now we must be past the point of modesty, you and I," he drawled, deliberately stretching.

Her gaze had fixed on something just above his head. "Yes, of course," she mumbled, still clutching the pillow. "But in light of—"

"This changes nothing, you know," he said over whatever excuse she'd been about to toss his way. "I still won the wager. And the night is still quite young."

She flinched, her gaze lowering to meet his. "You still want me? Even after...?"

Especially after. The internal confession was more than a little shocking. When he looked at her, an odd mixture of emotions rose to the surface. Some he identified, like admiration, lust, and longing, but there were many others which he couldn't or didn't want to pin down. The chaos within quite frankly terrified him.

One thing he did know for certain was that his desire for her hadn't diminished one whit. "Of course I still want you. And there is also the matter of that first impression I spoke of. I made a terrible one."

"The fault for that is mine," she said softly. "I let you believe I was something I'm not."

"But you are," he insisted, reaching out to take one of her hands. "You're amazing, Diana." He let out a laugh and brought her hand up to kiss her palm. "At one point, I actually contemplated kissing Harrow in gratitude for training you so well."

It elicited the smile he'd been looking for. "I won't tell him—I don't wish to put ideas into his head." She sobered. "Please promise you'll keep our secret?"

"Of course I will," he vowed without hesitation. "Even if it means people start calling me a molly." Brave words, but for her sake, he'd suffer it—and then run the offender through for saying such a thing. Harrow had been doing it for years.

And what of my parents? He pushed aside his conscience's unwelcome intrusion. "I accepted the consequences of coming here tonight in full knowledge of what they might entail." Scooting closer, he took a corner of the pillow she held, but didn't attempt to pull it back. "As did you," he added very softly.

After a moment, she let the pillow go and he set it aside. Holding out his hand, he waited. When she put her fingers in his palm, he pulled her toward him and just held her, reveling in the trust granted him.

The desire that had been snuffed by the shock of learning the truth flared back to life. But it was nowhere near as urgent as before. He ran his palms up and down her long back, warming skin that had grown cool. "Do you still wish to taste of passion with me?" he murmured at her ear.

Her whispered "yes" was accompanied by a little shiver he felt run through her as he held her close. She was the most physically responsive woman he'd ever known. Burying his nose in the tumble of caramel locks that had fallen over one shoulder, he kissed the curve of her neck and felt another tremor. "Then tell me what you want me to do, Diana."

Chapter Sixteen

Diana had expected there would be pain the first time. She hadn't been wrong. But it had been short-lived. Blackthorn— Lucas—was a skilled lover, and he soon made her forget any discomfort. With surprising tenderness, she was again brought to the height of frustration and then the lofty peak of ecstasy. Because of his diligent preparation, the ache of stretching around his girth for the second time had been exquisite rather than excruciating.

The soreness between her legs as she stretched them out in the warm water of her tub was already easing away. A little groan of relief fought its way from her throat as she shifted.

Lucas, who was soaking in a second tub which had been placed beside hers, shot her a knowing grin. "I think your servants have been scandalized tonight. First by all the noise we made, and again when they brought the water in and witnessed the wreckage."

"They are accustomed to such things here," she said, in fact not at all concerned with what they thought. "But I imagine they will be a bit surprised when they have to come again in the morning with a second bath."

His eyebrows shot up. "You intend us to make love again before morning?"

"You don't?" She waited until after he stopped chuckling before broaching a sensitive issue. It was going to come up anyway. Better to address it now while he was relaxed than in the morning when his mood might be altered. "I don't know what your plans are concerning us, but I do know I'm not opposed to doing this again. On another night, I mean," she amended, lest he misunderstand.

His gray eyes held hers, their expression open and frank. "I want that, too—only I want it every night."

The breath stilled in her lungs, and a pain blossomed in her chest briefly before she quashed it. He wasn't asking her *that*, of course. Even if he was, the answer must be no. "I cannot leave him. I cannot leave *them*," she corrected.

"Why not? It's not as if Harrow cannot find another to do for him what you do now. He found you, after all."

"Perhaps he could find another to take my place, but that would require time." *And what if she's not as trustworthy or loyal?* She didn't voice the question aloud. He wouldn't understand. "It took a great investment of time to shape me into what I am now, and I promised him five years."

Frustration pinched his brows. "I know you consider them your family. I'm not asking you to give that up."

"Oh?" She pursed her lips and, sitting up, propped her chin atop her folded arms on the lip of the tub, facing him. "You propose making yourself our 'special companion' as far as the public is concerned, then? Because that's what they will think. And at that point, they *will* start calling you a molly."

"Bloody hell," he sighed, sinking back a little deeper into the water. "I don't *want* to do it that way, but if it's what I *must* do, then…"

She sat up so abruptly that it splashed water over the side

of the tub, wetting the rug beneath. "You're serious?" She'd assumed the very idea would be off-putting enough to make him drop it.

"I'd really rather not, but yes." He too sat up. "Why can we not simply see each other secretly? Our gardens share a gate. It would be a simple thing to keep it quiet."

A snort broke free before she could stop it. "So you say. But I'd wager it would be out within only a day or two."

"I think we can do better than that. But even if it does get out, what harm is there in it for you?"

"Not me. *Harrow*. If I'm seen having a clandestine affair with you, it will make him look bad."

"You mean worse than if people think the three of us are in bed together every time I come to pay a neighborly call?" he said with a chuckle. "I should think that far worse than you leaving him for me."

She shook her head. "You don't understand. Even if you were truly amenable to becoming our 'third', we've never—to all appearances, thanks to René's talent with disguises—had the same 'gentleman friend' overnight with us more than two or three times within the same year. As long as it's an occasional event, people generally don't make assumptions about Harrow other than that he's got a penchant for voyeurism—a perception I support as often as occasion provides."

"So we continue to perpetuate that assumption, only with *me* being the regular 'entertainment'."

"And how long do you think that will last before people start presuming you and he are *also*...involved? You're already known to be good friends, and he's 'sharing' me with you tonight. You must consider how it would look."

"As long as we are discreet, stick to our story, and no one can prove otherwise, people can speculate all they like."

"That's a reckless way of thinking, and it leaves too much

to chance."

"*You* were the one who suggested it as a possible solution."

"Only because I thought you would never actually consider it," she confessed, frowning.

A smug grin spread across his face. "I guess I'm more open-minded than some people assume. Why would it be any more reckless than what you currently have in place?"

Sighing, she rose from the bath. It was growing tepid anyway. "To date, there has been no one person people can point to and say, 'there he is, the man who shares their bed.' As of now, it's just something people whisper of and snicker over in dark corners at balls. As I said, a titillating bit of gossip. But if you become *that* man, it gives people a target for their curiosity *and* their disapproval. From there, it will progress to persecution, and that risks engulfing us all. I cannot allow that to happen. Too many people could be hurt."

"Then the only solution *is* to become my mistress outright," he said, following suit and stepping from his bath. "We'll think of a way to make the transfer that won't damage people's perception of him as a man."

She was already shaking her head in denial. "No. I made a promise, and I intend to honor it. If you wish to engage in the occasional rendezvous with me, we will need to arrange it with Harrow, and it cannot be so often as to give rise to the aforementioned consequences."

"That's not going to work for me, Diana." Coming up behind her, he wrapped his arms around her waist and rested his chin on her shoulder. "I can tell you now I'm going to want to see you more often than what you're suggesting."

Part of her was thrilled to hear him say it, but she knew it wasn't safe to let that part overrule good sense. "I feel the same way, but we must be prudent about this." It was difficult, but she clamped down on the longing that rose up within her, wrestling it under control. Emotions—especially ones without any chance of reciprocation—couldn't be allowed to get in the way of her purpose.

He kissed the damp curls at the nape of her neck. "If you give me the key to the gate, I could slip in under cover of darkness and no one would be the wiser. We could even plan ahead for it." His lips nuzzled her ear. "I could come every Tuesday, Thursday, and Sunday."

Laughing, she turned in his arms. "Lucas—"

"I love the way my name sounds when you say it." He dropped a kiss on her upturned lips.

She pulled back before he could deepen it, but didn't break the circle of his arms. "I cannot be persuaded," she said on a laugh, which was wrung out of her despite the intention to sound stern by the sight of his pursed lips chasing hers.

"Care to wager on that?" he taunted, waggling his brows. When she didn't answer immediately, he moved to her neglected ear to nuzzle it, too. "You should reconsider your response to either option. I believe a clean break would be better, but I'm willing to risk a quick run through our gardens during the wee hours if it means I get to do this several times a week." His lips trailed across her collarbone.

Damn him. After what they'd done tonight, she knew she'd be unable to resist the temptation he represented. She needed to talk to Harrow about this. Unlike her, he would have a clear head and be able to look at it objectively. Well, more objectively than her, at least at the moment. "I'll think about it," she said noncommittally, bending her neck to give him better access.

• • •

The following day after Lucas left, Diana told Harrow about his offer and watched with utter confusion as he smiled and then softly chuckled. But he agreed with her that it was too soon to consider such an abrupt change. He also agreed to plan more rendezvous for them—not frequently enough to raise any dangerous suspicions, but often enough she knew people would begin to wonder about the men's friendship. It worried her.

He waved away her concerns. "They already think we are closer than we ought to be. It won't make a jot of difference one way or another."

Reluctantly, she also told him of Lucas's idea to visit her in secrecy via their garden gate.

A smile creased his face. "I've already had a copy of the key made for you to give to him, as well as one for the back door."

It was several seconds before she could force her mouth, which had fallen open in shock, to form coherent speech. "I—I beg your pardon?"

"It's ridiculous to imagine him staying away, Diana," said her friend, frowning at her as if she were being deliberately obtuse. "He'll be scaling the damned wall and making an enormous racket trying to get you to let him in if you don't grant him a quieter means of access. I leave it to your discretion, of course, but unless you prefer to be the one sneaking about at night outdoors, you had better leave it to him. Then if he's caught, it lands on his head and not yours."

"As if I would ever do so foolish a thing as sneak about at night to meet with him!" she snapped, indignant. Her ire only increased when he gave her a sidelong look full of doubt. "I'm in love, but I'm not stupid!"

Horrified, she clapped her hands over her traitorous mouth, but it was too late. The words, formed without forethought, had already escaped. A low moan escaped from between her fingers as she met Harrow's now smug gaze. Her hands shot back down to her sides, clenched in fists of outrage. "You *planned* for this to happen!"

"No, my dear," he replied, his complacent look transforming into one of utmost sobriety. "But a good tactician always prepares for every contingency. I knew it *might* happen, but I could not have predicted when or with whom."

"How can you be so calm about this?" her voice wobbled, and she knew she was dangerously close to tears. "Everything, all our plans, they are falling apart!"

Coming over to her, he gently grasped her shoulders. "Plans can be changed."

• • •

The following day Lucas turned the key to the garden gate over in his hand, astonished beyond words. She'd sent it and another, smaller key wrapped in a parcel via one of her footmen. The note that accompanied them simply read:

Mondays and Wednesdays at the second hour.
L.D.H.

Happiness welled up in a rush, making his skin tingle in anticipation.

Later that same day, a letter also arrived from Harrow inviting him to again join them the following Tuesday and Thursday for cards and musical entertainments, additionally informing him that his good friend Westing had also been invited.

However, Westing, he learned that evening at their club, hadn't been as pleased to receive the invitation.

"I'm afraid I had to politely decline," said the other man, frowning over his brandy.

Perplexed at his friend's sudden change of demeanor, Lucas leaned forward and lowered his voice. "Why? Has he done something to offend?"

"Not exactly." Westing looked distinctly uncomfortable. "Perhaps we ought to retire to somewhere more private to have this discussion."

Once they were in Lucas's carriage, it came out.

"I'm afraid Charlotte's parents are displeased by my association with Harrow. I cannot join you without risking their disapproval and possibly the withdrawal of their permission to court their daughter."

"Damn," Lucas muttered. He'd not thought the stain would set in so quickly. "Tell me this does not extend to *our* friendship?"

"No, of course not. Although…"

A trickle of dread ran between Lucas's shoulder blades. "Although *what*?"

Westing heaved a sigh. "The wager was one thing, but your deepening friendship—or whatever it is—with Harrow could become a concern. Her family is highly adverse to anything that smacks of immorality, and they firmly believe in guilt by association."

Snorting, Lucas eyed him. "If that's true, then I'm surprised they saw fit to allow *you* anywhere near their daughter in the first place. And what do you mean 'or whatever it is'?"

The look Westing gave him was penetrating. "Everyone knows you claimed the forfeit. They also know Harrow stayed at her house that same night. I'm sure you can guess what's being said about that."

"I spent the night with *her*, Westie." He debated his next words carefully, but was sure they wouldn't contravene his agreement with Harrow. "No one else was in that room with the two of us, I assure you. Harrow remained there overnight because he was uncomfortable leaving her there alone with me. It was a matter of his ensuring her safety."

Westing raised his palms in surrender. "I believe you, but

surely you must know that not everyone will. You know how determined some people are to believe the worst of others."

"I assume Charlotte's parents are of said ilk?"

"You assume correctly," replied Westing, his voice flat as a crepe. "I'm going to have to become a damned altar boy if I want to marry her—and I *do* want to marry her," he added softly.

"Are you certain you've selected the right bride for a man of your particular moral fiber?" Lucas asked, giving him a sidelong look. "There are plenty of women out there, old boy. You need not burden yourself with one who does not suit."

"But she does," insisted his friend. "She's perfect for me. I adore her in every possible way."

The quiet admission set Lucas back on his heels. "I must applaud the lady on her efficacy. To have set her hook in so quickly no doubt requires great skill."

"You're one to talk," drawled Westing with a smirk. "I'm not the only one with a hook in his cheek. You've been reeled in with just as much skill as I, my friend."

His words drew a flush up Lucas's neck, but he laughed it off. "I'm not the one who just confessed he's in love. I may enjoy Diana's charms, but you don't see me setting aside my friendships in order to win anyone's approval."

"Not yet. But you may find yourself dancing a different jig when your father hears about you and Harrow," his friend muttered back.

The way he said "you and Harrow" made Lucas's hackles rise. She'd warned him, but he hadn't expected his best friend to be the first to jump aboard that coach. "Just to be perfectly clear, my 'interest' is in Diana, *not* her protector," he growled, glaring. "That you of all people would even imply otherwise is an intolerable affront."

Westing's expression became unreadable. "It was not my intent to imply anything of the sort," he said quietly. "Any such interpretation was purely your own."

Lucas's heart slowed, and the anger that had begun to boil in his veins ebbed away. "Your pardon. I suppose I may indeed be a bit anxious over the prospect of what people might say, after all."

"Forgiven," his friend murmured a moment later. "Considering what just occurred, I do hope you know what you're doing and are prepared for the ramifications should this continue down its current path. This is not the same as tupping other men's neglected wives. People are willing to overlook *that* sin."

"I'm well aware of the situation into which I've put myself," he answered. Drawing up his courage, he looked his friend squarely in the eye. "I knew the possible consequences when I began pursuing her and accepted them. Having said it, I don't wish to lose your friendship over this."

Westing's usual irreverent expression returned. "That won't happen, I can assure you. I may not be around as much until after the wedding, but once my ring is on Charlotte's dainty little finger, her parents will have no more leverage over me. They certainly won't be dictating my friendships or pruning my circle."

"I'm glad to hear it."

Westing leaned closer, his expression avid. "So, what was she like?"

Lucas laughed.

· · ·

The first night Lucas used the keys, he nearly worried himself an ulcer. Just traversing their gardens unseen—and unheard, considering he tripped over what felt like every rock and root in Christendom while fumbling in the dark—seemed an impossible challenge. Cursing beneath his breath the entire way, he questioned his own sanity.

On reaching the house, he waited in deepest shadow several long minutes to be sure all was clear and quiet before venturing within. He tiptoed down the dimly lit halls, keeping to the thick runners to deaden his footsteps, praying he encountered no stray servants. His trepidation evaporated, however, upon entering his amour's boudoir and finding her waiting for him—naked.

Their second night of passion was well worth his nerve-wracking journey. As was their third.

Days slid by, becoming weeks, during which Lucas saw more of Diana than he'd dreamed possible. Evenings spent playing cards with her and Harrow actually worked to stave off the ugliest of rumors, as there were always servants—or, as he now liked to call them, *spy eyes*—present, and he always returned home before it grew too late.

The keys were a godsend, allowing him to come to her on their appointed nights, which changed from week to week to avoid establishing a pattern. There were a few close calls where he nearly ran into a servant either at his house or hers, but he managed to evade detection.

Between these clandestine visits, Harrow arranged more "official" ones, providing just enough grist for gossip's mill to perpetuate the myth of his own voyeurism. But Diana had been right in predicting that the longer these went on, the more people would begin to suspect the men's friendship of being something else.

And indeed, no one dared say anything to his face, but Lucas began to feel it hanging in the air like a foul miasma whenever he went to the club to meet up with Westing or other friends. A few of these became increasingly absent during the times they usually met, and when he subsequently ran into them about Town, there was an awkwardness present that hadn't been there before.

It stung. He felt the weight of their judgment on his shoulders as tangibly as if someone had settled a cloak about them. And it made him wroth. Such fair-weather friends were well shed, as far as he was concerned—and easily replaced, he soon discovered.

Harrow had many friends, all of whom Lucas quite liked. They were no different than the people he'd known most of his life save in one area: they were, in general, far more easygoing and a great deal less judgmental. And because Harrow was a marquess, many of these friends were part of a much higher circle than the one he'd been privileged to inhabit prior.

This was a thought that warmed him whenever he was forced to endure parental disgruntlement—which was no laughing matter—or bear the slights of certain former comrades.

Meanwhile, the time he spent with Diana was something he found himself anticipating more and more. It wasn't even the prospect of engaging in carnality the likes of which he imagined few men *ever* enjoyed—she had, he'd determined, almost no inhibition regarding *any*thing he wanted to try and had even surprised him with a few shocking suggestions herself—but rather the time they spent talking and laughing together.

At random moments, he often found himself wishing she was with him to share news with or ask an opinion. Nights when they couldn't be together were the worst. His arms felt empty, his bed cold. On the nights he did spend with her, their time together was far too brief for his liking. More and more, he wished he could wake up in her arms with the dawn, as they did on those special occasions when Harrow extended an invitation to overnight as their guest, instead of having to arrive and depart like a thief under cover of darkness.

There were several flies in the inkwell when it came to their relationship. For one, the stealthy nocturnal visits were both nerve-wracking and exhausting. The possibility of being caught lent a certain excitement to the endeavor, but it was also worrisome. The loss of old friends and the increasingly emphatic disapproval of his family were both ticks in the negative column. Being called a molly behind his back—and he *knew* it was happening—was yet another.

But there was one inky fly that bothered him more than all the rest combined. Though he and Diana had shared many personal secrets with each other over the feather mattress, she steadfastly refused to discuss the circumstances which had led to her being disowned by her family.

If Lucas had one grave fault, it was the same insatiable curiosity that had led him to Diana in the first place. He knew the same story everyone else did, that Viscount Grenville had abandoned his fiancé and eloped with her closest friend, telling everyone it was because Diana had been compromised by another and thereby ruining her. Well, Lucas knew *that* for an outright lie, which meant there had to have been some other reason why he'd done it.

One night as he was coming home after an evening of cards and music with his new friends, Lucas had a clever thought. If she wouldn't tell him, perhaps Grenville would.

He didn't request an appointment. He didn't send ahead to tell the blackguard of his intent to call. He simply showed up on the man's doorstep the following morning claiming to have business with his lordship.

Unfortunately, Grenville wasn't at home, but Lady Grenville was. As Lucas was of equal rank with her husband, he was permitted to come inside to leave a message with her on his behalf.

Knowing this woman had once been Diana's best friend made him fairly itch to meet her. She was a piece of Diana's past, and part of the puzzle he'd as yet been unable to complete. He was uncertain of her culpability in the affair, but instinct told him one didn't marry a beau belonging to one's best friend without there being an element of betrayal involved.

The lady, when she came to greet him, was pretty enough, if a bit wan and tired-looking. *Grenville chose a candle for his bride when he could have had the sun.* "Madam, I'm pleased to make your acquaintance and must apologize for my unannounced presence here today."

"What may I do for you, Lord Blackthorn?"

He eyed her and made a snap decision. "I came because I wished to speak with your husband concerning Lady Diana Haversham. Specifically relating to the incident which caused her uncle to disown her."

The lady's face went white, and for a moment he feared she might faint dead away. Instead, she turned and went to the drawing room doors to close them before addressing him in a hushed voice. "When I was told of your arrival, I wondered if that was what brought you here," she said, bidding him sit. "I almost refused to receive you, but to be perfectly honest I've been wanting to unburden myself for years. I'm sure she has already told you the truth of what happened."

Lucas couldn't believe his good fortune but managed to keep his surprise and excitement hidden. "She has not told me anything," he said slowly. "But yes, that is why I've come. I wanted to know why…" He stopped himself just in time—he couldn't tell her he'd discovered proof the excuse Grenville had given for abandoning Diana was a lie without exposing Harrow for a fraud. And he couldn't tell her he was trying to persuade Diana to leave Harrow without sabotaging the ruse they had in place. *Damn it all!* Why hadn't he thought this through more carefully?

You must tell her something…think!

His hostess, however, saved him the trouble of concocting a plausible excuse. "It was wrong of us, but we could not help ourselves," she whispered through trembling lips. "Grenville and I realized we were in love *after* he asked Diana to marry him." The lady's fingers twisted the fabric of her skirts. "My husband invented the story that ruined her to justify our elopement and preserve his honor."

Sniffling, she looked at the ceiling as if seeking absolution, and he saw her eyes were brimming with unshed tears. When she looked back at him, it was with a brief, shaky smile. "I thought the scandal would blow over once Diana refuted the claim. I was *horrified* to learn she'd been disowned over it. I wanted to come out with the truth at once, but my husband forbade it. And then…it no longer mattered, because Diana became Harrow's mistress."

Tears ran unhindered down her face. Lucas knew he should offer his kerchief, but instinct told him to be still, that there was more to come. As usual, instinct proved right.

"I learned afterward that her uncle had been depending on funds tied to her marriage contract to pay off a large debt," she continued, her voice thick. "As part of a sealed addendum to her father's will, Diana's guardian—which the duke presumed would be her mother—was to receive a tidy sum separate from her jointure in order to care for them both. In the event Diana was orphaned, that sum would be awarded to her uncle upon her marriage in return for caring for her in his stead. I doubt she ever knew about it. I only know because I overheard my husband talking to one of his friends about how Bolingbroke had confronted him in a drunken rage at their club and revealed it."

Lucas remembered Diana saying Bolingbroke had robbed her. She couldn't have meant this, since the money wouldn't have gone to her. She must have been referring to something else.

"When my husband lied, Diana's uncle believed him," Lady Grenville went on, her voice breaking. "He thought that money forever out of his reach, and that was what drove him to disown her. By the time he came to his senses, it was too late. She'd run away and taken up with Harrow, making her truly unmarriageable."

Hoisted by his own petard. He couldn't bring himself to feel any pity for the bastard. In fact, he hoped that mistake haunted the man and gave him regret and sleepless nights for the rest of his life. He, not this woman's foolish husband, had condemned his niece. "Thank you for telling me."

"Will you...will you tell Diana I've never stopped regretting my part in what happened to her?" She covered her face with her hands as a sob broke free.

"I will," he promised. *Someday.*

He watched as she struggled to regain composure. "I've had to live with my guilt, with knowing my foolish heart led to my best friend's undeserved ruin." Her voice hardened. "Grenville, however, absolved himself by pointing out how quickly Diana took up with Harrow. He told himself and anyone who would listen that he'd narrowly avoided marrying a harlot. But I *knew* her," she said with fervor, "and she was *not* what he said she was. I've never forgiven myself or him for what we did to her. He knows it, and it has made him hate me. What began with love and a lie has ended in misery."

Lucas had been ready to condemn her along with her husband, but now he found he couldn't. Grenville was partly to blame, but Bolingbroke was the one ultimately responsible for what had happened to Diana. His greed had been her undoing.

The sobbing woman across from him demanded his sympathy. When he at last addressed her, it was with as much gentleness as he could manage through his simmering anger and mounting disquiet. "I cannot forgive you because the forgiveness you desire is not mine to grant. But what you did, though it was wrong, was for love, and I'm truly sorry for your disappointment." Discomfort spiked as his hostess broke into a fresh round of sobs, and he rose. "If you will please excuse me, I'll leave you now." He paused at the door before letting himself out. "I hope you find peace, Lady Grenville."

His mind raced as he boarded his carriage for the return home. Now he finally had the whole story, and it hadn't been at all what he'd expected. Not one, but three people had engineered Diana's downfall. She'd been utterly undeserving of her fate.

Lady Grenville's words echoed in his thoughts: *But I knew her, and she was not what he said she was.* Greed and deception had robbed Diana of the life she could have had.

And now he'd taken her virginity, robbing her of yet another possible future, one where she wouldn't have to lie to the man she one day married.

She could have refused. But she'd chosen not to. Why had she really done it? And why had she continued seeing him?

Can it possibly be that she loves me?

Something huge and scary swelled in his chest until it throbbed with an almost physical pain. He'd vowed never to become emotionally attached to any woman, but that pain forced him to acknowledge that it had happened. It had happened without him even knowing it. He stared out through his carriage window with unseeing eyes.

She's in love with me. And oh, God, I'm in love with her.

Trepidation transformed into sheer terror. Even if she *was* in love with him, it was unlikely to last, at least on her part. He could never tell her the truth. To do so would be to abandon all pride and open himself up for every indignity a man could suffer. She'd only use it against him, just as his mother had against his father. His poor, miserable father, who to this day still mourned the loss of his heart to the unworthy woman who'd deceived him.

A wise man would cut bait and run as fast and as far away

from this disaster as possible. But he wasn't feeling wise. Though it be the height of foolishness, he wanted Diana—more than anything he'd ever desired in his entire life. And he meant to have her. He'd just have to be careful to hide the true depth of his folly and find a way to make her his without exposing himself for a fool and her for a fraud.

Chapter Seventeen

Something had changed. Diana didn't know why, but in spite of successfully evading discovery and despite them having found a happy compromise that allowed them to see each other on an almost daily basis, Lucas had renewed his attempts to persuade her to leave Harrow.

She'd asked him why he was suddenly so keen to alter what they'd put in place, but he'd avoided answering her, instead leading her off topic or misdirecting her attentions elsewhere. There was something he wasn't telling her, and no matter how she tried to get it out of him, he kept it securely behind his teeth.

A fortnight after she noticed this shift in his behavior, the gates of Hell opened and unleashed its demons in the form of a damning article in *The Tattler*. Five lines. Five lines was all it took to expose her 'ongoing affair' with Lucas, firing off London's gossip grapevine, tearing apart the careful facade she and Harrow had built.

"I'm going to stop seeing him," she told Harrow, who'd come over within an hour of receiving her frantic note.

"I won't let you do that."

"You cannot make me do otherwise," she said crisply, sticking out her chin.

He passed a hand over his face, which was pale and drawn. "It won't matter. The damage is done. What I want to know is *how*. How did this happen?"

"One of the servants must have seen him," she reasoned. "Ours know to keep quiet about anything that happens here, but it could have been one of them. There is no way to know who is responsible. But that's not what troubles me most. What worries me more than anything is what else they might discover—or worse, already know, concerning you and René."

"No. If they knew about us, it would be here," said Harrow, tossing the mangled paper he'd been holding onto the table.

"We cannot risk them finding out. What are we going to do?" She watched as he paced the room, afraid to speak lest she disturb his thoughts. Harrow was brilliant. He would think of something.

"We are going to have a row."

She felt the blood leave her face. "You're going to call him out?"

He looked at her with incredulity. "He's my friend and your lover—of course I'm not going to call him out. No, *you and I* are going to pretend to have a fight. Then you are going to play at contrition, and I, anger at your betrayal. Give it a fortnight, and we'll put on the appearance that we've 'patched things up' until I can think of a more permanent solution to the problem."

But there was no permanent solution that would allow her to keep her friends safe and continue seeing Lucas, and she knew it. *This is it. This is the end of it.* She'd known it was inevitable, but for some reason it was still a shock to realize it was actually happening. *We had so little time...* "What of Lucas?" she forced herself to ask.

"I've asked him to call at my residence later this evening where we will discuss the matter in guaranteed privacy. None of my contemporaries will dare inquire of me concerning this matter, but his friends might ask him, and he must know how to answer."

"And that answer is?"

"That he made the mistake of thinking you meant more to him than he should have."

It sounded so cold. "I assume that means your friendship must appear to be at an end, as well?"

"Yes."

At least that will put him back in his family's good graces. "You know what they'll say about you when you don't call him out. Better to call him out and simply make certain your aim is poor—"

"I *cannot* call him out, Diana," he said, his face finally betraying his upset. "We are both too skilled with pistols and blades to make it believable without grievously wounding each other. Ending our public association will have the same result. It's the easiest way."

"I have a better solution." She steeled herself. "Cast me out. Publicly."

He stopped pacing, his eyes wide. "If you go to him—"

"I won't. I'll disappear. Like we originally planned. Give me a week to make arrangements, and then cast me out. Once I'm gone, you'll find another mistress and life will go on."

Coming to her, he put his hands on her shoulders and stared into her eyes. "You love him, Diana. Please, just give me a little time to figure this out, to find a way to make it work."

"There *is* no way!" she hissed, furious and wanting to shout but unable in case there were ears listening outside the door. "Not one that ends with everyone happy. We both know it. But you and René still have a chance, provided we do this right. You *must* cast me out."

"No," he said in a tone she knew meant there was no winning. "Give me two weeks. I beg you. Let me at least *try*."

Sighing, she capitulated. It would make no difference, but she would give it to him. If nothing else, it would allow her more time to get her affairs in order. The new start she'd had planned to make didn't seem even remotely appealing now, but it was all she could hope for. Some irrational part of her had wanted so much to believe that she, Lucas, Harrow, and René could continue on as they were indefinitely and be happy, free of the world's interference. But that wasn't realistic. In truth, life was painful, unfair, and utterly without mercy. Especially when it came to love.

"Fine. But I'm coming with you. I want to speak to Lucas one last time. He deserves to hear this from both of us." She held his eyes until he lowered his, and she knew she'd won the argument. There was a reason his plan wouldn't work, but he couldn't see it. Neither would Lucas. She had to make them *both* understand.

When Lucas arrived at Harrow's house that evening, it took every ounce of willpower not to throw herself into his arms.

Harrow closed the doors, shutting out the world, before addressing his guest. "We have put our foot in it, so to speak," he began quietly. "And now there is nothing for it but to attempt to salvage the situation."

"Agreed," said Lucas, his eyes on her, though he was talking to Harrow. "I assume we won't be facing each other on the field tomorrow morning, or I would not be here."

"Correct," said Harrow. "As I told Diana earlier today, I cannot call you out without us either wounding each other or making a mockery of the practice, which would be even more damning. There is a way to settle this without bloodshed."

She watched Lucas's face as Harrow laid out the plan, such as it was, knowing what he was going to say before he spoke.

"And in two weeks we'll be in the exact same place we are now," Lucas said when he finished, looking at her. "Unless you defect and become my mistress."

"No," she told him flatly. "If this were a true rivalry, the two of you would not be able to coexist in the same city if I did such a thing. Harrow would be honor bound to seek satisfaction in order to save face. No. I must do as I originally planned. It's the only way—and you *know* it is," she said to Harrow over the objections he'd begun to voice. She knew he was wroth with her for gainsaying him, but this was the only way to be sure he and René were safe and Lucas stayed alive. "Harrow and I will make a show of disagreement and strife between us over the next two weeks. It will culminate in a public argument, at the end of which he will cast me aside. Then, I disappear."

"No," said Lucas, the muscle in his jaw twitching as he shook his head. "I won't agree to that."

She pressed her lips together briefly before rebutting, knowing her heart was about to break and powerless to stop it. "I'm afraid you don't get to make that choice."

• • •

Lucas couldn't believe what he was hearing. He thought she loved him. He knew now that he was in love with her, because he hurt more than he'd ever thought possible. And there was nothing he could do but sit there, listening to their plans, and suffer in silence as everything inside him unraveled.

Because he wouldn't—*couldn't* show what he was really feeling.

Every now and again, he caught Harrow staring at him with a look of sympathy. He suspected the man knew something of what he was keeping pent up inside but thankfully said nothing. Lucas didn't want his pity. He didn't want *anyone's* pity.

The longer he sat there, the angrier he became. *I'm a bloody fool, just like my father.* He'd made the mistake of letting himself get too attached, and although he hadn't fallen into the marriage trap, he'd put his foot into a nasty snare just the same. And the pain he was feeling? It was his own damned fault.

He couldn't bear to look at Diana anymore. He knew if he did, he'd see the same unfeeling mask he now wore, only unlike his, hers would be more than skin deep.

The plans they were discussing didn't even involve him, save for the caution to stay out of their way. After today, his part in this was over and done. They didn't need him anymore. She'd never really needed him at all.

By the time they finally agreed on what was going to happen, Lucas was itching to leave. At last, the discussion ended, and he found himself standing up and shaking Harrow's hand.

"I'm truly sorry," the fellow was saying. "If either of us manages to think of a better way to solve this problem, we must send a message to the other. Until then, I think it best we sever casual communication lest we make matters even worse."

He had no problem with that at all. "I truly regret having cast your happy arrangement into chaos," he said, and he meant it. "I know the stakes for you are especially high, and I would not willingly bring tragedy down upon you or your loved ones."

Then it was Diana's turn. He took in her waxen cheeks and downcast gaze. She wouldn't even look at him. *Coward.*

Blessed wrath burned away the unmanly stinging in his eyes. "I suppose this is goodbye, then," he said, keeping his manner brisk.

No response.

As he stared down at her, the pain in his chest blossomed into an unbearable, empty ache. He filled it with cold fury. "I, for one, will be glad to put this whole disaster behind me," he said with an air of supreme indifference. Did he imagine that flinch? The idea that she might actually feel something brought him great satisfaction, and he craved more. "My father was right. It's time I set aside selfish fancies and attend to my duties. I hope your plan works as you imagine, and that you're able to put this all behind you, as well. Good day, madam, and I bid you the best of luck."

Still nothing. As far as he could tell, she wasn't even breathing. She might as well be a marble statue. His eyes burned again. Before he lost all remaining dignity, he turned on his heel and strode away.

As he approached his carriage, he realized he didn't know where to go. He couldn't go home. He couldn't bear the thought of catching a glimpse of her house from his windows. He didn't want to see the gardens he'd navigated on so many nights just to spend a few stolen hours with her. He'd just as soon burn the whole place to the ground as see it right now.

Going to the driver, he instructed the man to take him to his club. He could go to any tavern and drink himself into a stupor, but then people might think him a coward—*as well as a molly*. This thought only stoked his anger.

He'd alienated his old friends and destroyed what little reputation he'd had over a *woman*. The new friends he'd made were all Harrow's, and they all doubtless thought him a treacherous bastard for attempting to poach his ladybird.

It would take him years to rebuild what he'd lost—if it were even possible.

The club was busy when he arrived and placed a brusque order for brandy. Before the servant could turn, he grabbed the man's sleeve. "And just bring the bottle along with the glass," he added sullenly.

By his fourth glass, he was surrounded by those few of his friends he hadn't yet managed to estrange, and was parroting the line Harrow had given him, which was, ironically, all too true. "...made the foolish mistake of thinking she meant more to me than I should have. She's staying with the bastard."

"But I thought you and he were friends?" said one fellow with an altogether-too-sly look in his eye.

"So did I," Lucas said flatly, pouring himself another two fingers of brandy. "But apparently, he did not take kindly to me dipping my quill into his favorite inkwell without his express permission. The lady, however, had other ideas. It was she who gave me the key to her castle and bade me enter in. I ask you, what man would refuse such an offer? Not I."

It earned him a few laughs and a smattering of ribald jests.

"Yes, dear friends," he continued, deciding to lay it on thick. *The thicker, the better.* "Let no man—or woman, for that matter—tell you love is anything but a damned lie."

Silence greeted his pronouncement.

Unsure what had elicited this reaction, Lucas occupied himself with knocking back the remainder of his drink. Just then, he noticed Westing had joined the little gathering. "Ah! My *good* friend Westie—I was just telling everyone here that—"

"I heard," interrupted Westing with a smile that seemed just a shade too bright. "So, you're a free man once more?"

The way he said it nettled. Lucas drew out his next words for emphasis: "*I* was never *not* free." Scowling, he snatched up the bottle and poured yet more liquor into his glass. Or, rather, tried to. For some damnable reason, the precious amber fluid seemed to be pouring out all over the tray instead of where he wanted it to go. Cursing, he decided it was better to just take his painkiller straight from the bottle.

But before he could manage to get it up to his lips, Westing had gently pried it from his hand.

"I say," Lucas objected, grabbing for it. His effort was in vain, however, for his friend only moved it just out of reach again. "Can a man not drown his woes in peace among friends without some busybody interfering?"

"Certainly, he may," agreed Westing, his manner jovial. "As I'm your oldest friend, I claim the right to host the next toast. Come, let us go to my house and continue the party there."

Feeling rebellious and unwilling to be manipulated— he wasn't *that* drunk yet—Lucas merely crossed his arms and stared him down. "I should like my brandy back, if you please."

"Give the man back his liquor," said one of his other friends, snickering. "If anyone has earned the right to drink himself under the table, it's Blackthorn."

Another muttered just loud enough to be heard, "Indeed, for he's just lost the love of his life—or, 'loves' rather, as in *both* of them."

Lucas froze as soft snorts and quickly stifled snickers broke out all around him. Turning, he identified the owner of the voice that had uttered the slander. He might be drunk, but he could still throw a bloody punch.

And he did.

All hell broke loose. Fists flew indiscriminately, curses were shouted, and furniture was smashed. Lucas saw it all through a red haze, feeling—despite the pain blossoming in his jaw and nose—as if he were watching from outside himself. All the rage he'd stuffed down inside, he now poured into each meeting of knuckles with flesh. He reveled in it until all coherent thought fled.

The next thing he knew, Lucas found himself in Westing's carriage, facing his friend, who was holding a bloodstained kerchief to his nose and glaring at him. "Oh, God," he groaned as the blessed blanket of numbness that had cloaked him was abruptly ripped away when the carriage hit a rut and nausea threatened to unman him.

"Don't you dare," growled Westing, his voice sounding nasally. "If you must empty your stomach, you do it *outside* my carriage."

Too sick to feel embarrassed, Lucas lunged for the carriage door and opened it just enough to put his head out. Just in time, too. When he'd finished turning himself inside out, he shut the door and dragged himself into a sitting position on the floor beside it, leaning his head against the seat he'd just vacated. He took inventory as best he could without a mirror. He *hurt*. His lip felt split, his nose was either broken or badly bruised, and his left eye ached abominably. Several places on his body did, too. "How bad is it?"

Westing let out an indignant snort, then cursed roundly as another gout of blood ran from his nose. "If you think *I* look bad, you should see yourself. You won't be winning any prizes for beauty anytime soon, I'm afraid. Charlotte is going to kill me," he groaned. "When her parents hear about this, it will be the end of our courtship, I'm afraid."

"I'm sorry." But then his temper made another attempt to rise. "You did not have to defend me, you know."

The look Westing leveled at him was scathing. "Oh, bollocks, man. If I had not, you would be lying in the gutter right now, beaten senseless and possibly left for dead."

Quiet shame filled him. Shame for how he'd treated his truest friend. Shame for having been so stupid. "I thought they were my friends." His mind replayed the words that had broken him. Diana had been right—which made him feel no better at all.

"Broomfield is an arse, and everyone knows it," offered Westing.

"He only said what they were all thinking—what the whole of London doubtless thinks."

"I don't believe that to be true. Several of our comrades back there fought on your side."

"Wonderful. Except that I don't know who was fighting who," Lucas countered sourly. He couldn't take offense at Westing's chuckle, because it really *was* funny. "I'm such an idiot."

"That you are, my friend. But we are all fools in love."

Oh, how Lucas wished he could take it all back. Now everyone would know he'd been the world's greatest dupe. "What will you do about Charlotte?"

Westing shrugged, his expression dismal. "Throw myself upon her parents' mercy, I suppose?"

"Elope." He said it without thinking, but in truth it seemed like not such a bad idea.

"I beg your pardon?" said Westing, his eyes widening.

"You love her, correct?" He saw the other man nod a little. "Then fetch her tonight and take her to Gretna Green. Don't overthink it. Don't wait. Just do it."

"But she'll want a wedding and—"

"If she loves you, I think she'd rather have you than a fancy wedding with some other man waiting for her at the altar."

Westing's gaze narrowed. "I thought you did not believe in love?"

The only thing that kept Lucas from curling in on himself and letting out his pain was the brandy still coursing through his veins. It wasn't enough to numb him, but it was enough to let him keep a shred of dignity. "Love is for people like you, Westie. Not people like me. You are good and kind and loyal.

Me? I'm just a selfish hedonist and a gambler. I pushed to get what I wanted, and it has landed me exactly where I deserve to be."

The look on Westing's face shifted. "You want my advice? Go after your Diana. To hell with Harrow. If he calls you out, I'll second you."

Lucas tried to offer him a smile in thanks, but his swelling lip prevented it. "There are numerous reasons why that would be a terrible idea. Reasons I cannot reveal, even to you. It's over, Westie. She's gone, and I'll never get her back. In truth, she was never really mine. It's better off this way. For both of us."

Chapter Eighteen

Diana threw down her paper and tried with no appetite to nibble at the toast Francine had brought her. London was rife with scandal heaped upon scandal. A week had passed, and still all of London was talking about the terrific row in which Lucas had attacked several of his old friends.

It wasn't hard to guess why he'd been throwing his fists about.

As Harrow had predicted, no one dared directly broach the subject of his falling out with his mistress and his newest friend, but he'd reported the looks he'd been getting whenever he went out as "telling." The few people he'd confided in—purposely—about the whole unsavory affair had set about industriously spreading a tale of his anger at having been betrayed. The reason he'd given for not calling out Blackthorn was that he could hardly blame the man for having fallen prey to her skilled seduction. Thus had the blame been shifted from Blackthorn's shoulders to hers—which was exactly what she wanted.

Theirs was not the only scandalbroth brewing in London,

however. Rumor had it that Lucas's erstwhile comrade, Lord Westing, had disappeared the day after pulling his friend from the fight—as had the young lady to which he'd been paying court. They'd been missing for several days now, and it was widely accepted that they'd gone to Scotland.

Diana was glad, both for the young couple and for the much-needed distraction from her and Harrow. Now, however, the spyglass would once again focus on them, for they were due to have their first public disagreement. They'd spent the first few days after their shock sequestered in their respective houses, cancelling all appointments and calls. The two parties they'd attended together since then had been painfully awkward—deliberately so. Harrow had pretended coldness toward her, and she'd pretended resentment. Tonight would be damned uncomfortable, but it had to be done.

When they arrived at the ball it was no surprise that eyes followed them everywhere. Harrow's instructions had been clear. She was to remain glued to his arm the whole evening—and he would resolutely ignore her.

It was working beautifully until she saw Lucas staring down at her from the gallery.

"What is it?" hissed Harrow, stopping along with her involuntary pause.

"He's here."

His gaze followed hers up to where his supposed rival stood. "Come," he said tersely, pulling her back into motion. He led her out of the other man's line of sight before stopping. "Don't worry. This can only work to our advantage. Change of plans. In a little while, I'm going to leave you to talk with one of my friends. If Blackthorn comes to you, let him. I'll step in after a few moments and pull you away before anything truly untoward can occur. You must object—tell me you're not a child or something to that effect—and then we'll improvise until we can circle back to what we rehearsed."

Nodding, she agreed. Her pulse was racing, her skin felt too hot, and her head light. *Just get through this. It will all be over soon, and then you can go home.* Home. *I should not be thinking of it in such terms anymore.*

Her home was now a tiny village far to the north, almost in Scotland. Soon, she would leave everything behind. Again. Only it felt far worse this time. There would be no Harrow or René there to talk to and ease her loneliness. There would be no Lucas to share her innermost thoughts with and set her aflame with his touch.

These thoughts made her want to cry, but she couldn't afford that luxury quite yet. Stiffening her spine, she nodded. Nerves on edge, she waited.

When Lucas finally found his way to her, she gasped at the fading purple and yellow bruises on his face.

"It's not as awful as it looks," he said in greeting. "I believe the other fellow looks much worse."

"Why are you doing this?" she asked, staring at him. "Why torture us both when you know there is no other way?"

His brows pinched, but he offered her a faint, lopsided smile. "Torture? Why would I consider this torture? You're nothing to me."

She jerked as if he'd slapped her across the face, and tears sprang into her eyes. She had no words to counter the pain he'd just inflicted. None at all. She just stood there, feeling like a giant hole had been punched through her chest where her heart had once been.

Fortunately, Harrow was as good as his word and came to her rescue before it could become any more awkward. "I thought we made a gentlemen's agreement," he said to Lucas in the chilliest of tones. "You vowed to stay away from her."

"So I did," said Lucas in the same flinty manner. "I cannot help it if we are both in attendance at the same ball. We're bound to cross paths. Or perhaps you'd like to meet in private to compare our schedules so we can ensure this does not happen again?" he added sarcastically.

Diana heard his words as though from far, far away, drowned out by the blood whooshing in her ears. Dizziness swept over her in a great wave, the room tilted, and all went dark.

When she opened her eyes, it was to see Harrow bent over her, his face lined with worry.

"Here," he said, helping her sit up a little and pressing the rim of a glass to her mouth.

Cool water bathed her tongue and slid down her throat. Her head was pounding. She closed her eyes again, but her lids shot open only a moment later. "Lucas?" Her voice sounded cracked, as though she'd not used it in a week.

"Gone," he answered, again helping her drink. "He left a few minutes ago after helping me bring you in here."

Confusion made her scowl at her surroundings. They were in an unfamiliar parlor. "He helped you?"

"Indeed. Damned stupid thing to do, too, but I could not dissuade him. I think I was lucky he allowed me to carry you." At her askance look, he continued. "You fainted. I've sent for a doctor to examine you."

"A doctor?" She tried to sit up and suffered a wave of nausea. Gasping, she braced herself on the edge of the couch and bowed her head, willing the room to stop moving. "Why? I only fainted. I suppose I should have eaten something before coming here, but I was too nervous."

"No doubt, but the lump on the back of your head bears looking at," he said drily. "It probably hurts like the devil, but at least it's on the outside. I was quite worried for a while when you failed to awaken."

She muttered something like an agreement, but her thoughts, hazy as they were, were elsewhere. If she truly meant nothing to Lucas, then why had he stayed?

...

He'd regretted his ill-chosen words the instant they'd left his foolish mouth. Yes, he'd wanted to hurt her, but he'd thought it an impossible task after her lack of reaction that day at Harrow's house. Not so, apparently.

She loved him. He'd seen it in her eyes. And he'd probably just killed that love.

London's streets passed by his carriage window, but he saw nothing of them. All he could see was her face and the pain etched upon it. That had been right before Harrow had stepped in like a wrathful avenging angel to fend him off. Right before her lashes had fluttered against her white cheeks and she'd gone down.

The resounding *crack* as her head had hit the marble floor had all but stopped his heart and would haunt him forever. He'd only left once she started to show signs of coming 'round.

What a damnable mess he'd made of things. He'd probably ruined whatever plan they'd been enacting tonight. Even so, he couldn't help the tiny spark of joy that flared to life from knowing she loved him.

You're a damned fool. He knew it and didn't care. Everything he'd ever considered an absolute where women were concerned had been set on its ear. She'd sacrificed her own happiness to spare him being caught up in what would undoubtedly be the most damaging scandal in a decade. It didn't matter that she'd done it to save her friends, as well. Love—for them *and* for him—had been at the root of her actions. She'd put them all before herself when she could've simply cut and run. Her loyalty shamed him, and though it hurt to be on the wrong end of it, he couldn't help admiring her all the more.

Hot prickles stung his neck at the thought of his family's

reaction when it became clear he intended to continue their relationship. *Father may never forgive me. Mother* certainly *won't.* But he couldn't bear the thought of being without Diana. Tomorrow, he'd write Harrow and ask after her health, social consequences be damned.

On arriving home, he found his housekeeper all in a dither, requesting a private moment with him in his office. Perplexed, he ushered the woman in and bade her sit and be at ease as he closed the door.

She politely refused and at once drew from her pocket a letter—an opened letter. "I'm sorry to be disturbing you, my lord, but I felt you had better see this at once."

He took it from her, frowning. "What is this? Who is it from?"

"You should read it," she said quietly, nodding at the note in his hand. "I found it in Anne's room—she was sent to the market this morning and has yet to return. I was worried— one of the other girls said she's been seeing a beau—so I went into her room to make certain she'd not run off and left us. I found that on the floor beside her bed. I can only guess she must have dropped it."

The way her gaze slid away told him otherwise, but he let it go in favor of opening the letter to scan its contents. What he read made his blood run cold. "How long has Anne worked for me?"

"A few weeks, my lord. I hired her to replace Gertrude."

Bloody hell. He tucked the letter into his pocket. "I want to know the instant she returns. You're to say nothing to her. Just come and get me. I don't care about the hour."

Her eyes widened. "Of course, my lord."

When she left, he again pulled out the letter to read it over once more. Now he knew whose spying eyes had discovered their trysts and whose lips had told the papers about them; it'd been one of his own servants. What he didn't understand was *why*.

Lucas couldn't have slept if he'd wanted to, such was his anxiety by the time the housekeeper returned several hours later to inform him the girl, Anne, had returned and was back in her room. He dispatched the housekeeper and two footmen to escort her down.

Once she was seated and the doors closed, he came and stood before her, drawing the letter out of his pocket. The horror that filled her face on seeing it told him she knew exactly what it was.

"Who wrote this?"

She remained mute, her gaze sliding toward the closed door.

He put himself between it and her. "You will tell me what I want to know, or I'll report you for theft and have you transported to a penal colony." He let that sink in for a moment. "Now, who wrote this? Who paid you to spy on me?"

"Lord Grenville," she whispered, her voice shaking.

Shock coursed through him and made the hair on his neck rise all at once. "You will tell me everything you know. If you do so, I may find it within my heart to not have your entire family sent to separate corners of the globe. If you don't…"

Words began to flow from her lips in a steady gabble, mixed with a lot of begging and pleas for mercy. In this manner, he learned Grenville had stationed men to watch his house just days after he'd had his little chat with Lady Grenville. When Anne had been hired, he'd seen an opportunity and had one of these men bring her to meet with him. She'd been paid handsomely to report back concerning his activities— especially those involving Diana.

It's all my fault. He'd dug into Diana's past, and now Grenville was evidently afraid he'd be exposed. Lucas kicked himself mentally for not having the forethought to ask Lady Grenville to keep silent about his visit and what they'd discussed. He'd likely never know what had prompted her to confess to her husband, but in truth the motivation for her betrayal didn't matter.

All that mattered now was ending this. He wasn't going to let the same man ruin Diana's life twice.

"You have a choice before you," he told Anne. "I advise you to think this through very carefully. You can be reported for theft and transported to Australia on a prison ship...or you can tell me *everything* you've told Grenville about me and Lady Diana and take the next boat to the colonies freely with enough coin in hand to make a comfortable life there."

Two days later, Lucas stood on the docks at Liverpool as the packet ship *Albion* sailed away on the tide for Boston, with Anne safely ensconced in steerage with full amenities and a hundred pounds gold for her cooperation. He hadn't trusted her to keep her word, and for peace of mind had insisted on escorting her himself rather than simply putting her on a coach with a couple of footmen. It had been a nerve-wracking, sleepless journey made in great haste, keeping the girl under guard until he could see her safely off.

Now he must get back to London with all speed. He briefly toyed with the idea of taking a room and traveling tomorrow morning, but a sense of urgency overrode his desire for a night passed in comfort. He'd sleep as best he could in the coach.

As he sat swaying in his seat and watching the hills and fields slide by, Lucas thought about what he must do. Everything would depend on Harrow's cooperation. The letter he'd sent explaining Grenville's part in Diana's ruin and his current interference in their lives had been written with no way of knowing how far their plans had progressed. He only hoped he wouldn't be too late.

On arriving in London, Lucas didn't bother stopping at his house to bathe and change in case Grenville was still having it watched. Instead, he went directly to Harrow.

"I wondered when you would show up," the other man said, greeting him warmly. "Your letter, while it brought me no joy, gave me hope."

"I think we may be able to turn this around, if you're willing," Lucas replied. "I believe Grenville knows nothing of you and Laurent. In fact, I'm certain of it. Nothing the girl said indicated she possessed any knowledge of the goings-on in Diana's household. She only witnessed me sneaking across the gardens to see her in the night. Which means there is a chance, albeit slim, that we can make this work."

"Make what work, exactly?"

He'd arrived at his decision almost the moment he'd put Anne on that ship. He couldn't stand the thought of losing Diana, but he knew she wouldn't settle for anything less than a wedding ring. "I'm going to ask Diana to marry me."

The shock on his friend's face likely mirrored that which could be expected of all of Society. "You wish to marry her knowing everyone thinks—"

"I don't give a *damn* what everyone thinks," Lucas said with vehemence. "Not of her *or* of me. Other men have made wives of courtesans. Most of the people we know expect you to marry her when your wife dies. Why you and not me?"

"To begin, I'm in no danger of being left penniless," answered Harrow. "Your father may not be able to disinherit you, but he *can* cut off all support while he lives."

"I don't accept my father's support now, and I'm far from penniless." Lucas then shared information concerning his financial ventures and current means. "As for my family's approval, I've lived without it for a long time. And who knows? In a few years, after things settle a bit, we might reconcile."

Harrow peered at him with an inscrutable gaze. "You'll be ostracized. Those in your old circle who have yet to abandon you will turn their faces from you. Those in mine currently believe you a poacher and besmirch your name at every turn. You'll have no social standing."

"I can live without social standing. I *cannot* live without her."

Their eyes met and held.

"You love her," murmured Harrow.

"I do," he replied with conviction. "And I need your help to win her back." Lucas had never really been one for praying, but he sent one winging to heaven now. *Please…*

"Indeed, I think it could work," said Harrow with a dark chuckle. "But I have a few changes to make to this plan of yours."

"Go on," Lucas prompted, wondering what he had in mind.

"I think it might be time for me to make a strategic retreat from Society—with René, of course. I've been thinking of taking an extended trip abroad. Minerva—my wife—has expressed a desire to leave London altogether and remove our son from its toxic environs. I agree. She's always been happier out in the country, and since the recent scandal broke, her pleasure in Town has been greatly diminished."

Hope flared in Lucas's heart.

"The public dispute we'd planned for tomorrow's ball will take place," continued Harrow, pulling at his chin with a pensive look. "But instead of casting her out in anger, I'll play it differently. Instead, I'll act as if her betrayal has broken me, which will justify my leaving England for a while. René and I will disappear for a few years. When we return, he will have a new name, and my lingering 'heartbreak' over Diana will provide cover enough to keep us safe."

"You would leave England for our sake?"

"For *her* sake," the other man clarified, shooting a hard glare at him. "Diana was—*is*—willing to give up everything for me. How can I not reciprocate in kind? She's part of my heart, my family. If you can make her happy, *then* I shall consider you truly my friend—indeed, if you can give her the life she deserves, I'll consider you as dear as any brother."

Lucas met his steady gaze and nodded solemnly. "Upon my honor, I'll do everything in my power to make that happen."

"One more thing," said his host. "I want her married before my ship leaves port. I won't sail until I know she's safe."

"Agreed." They talked a few minutes more, and then Lucas was on his way to obtain a special license before returning home to make the necessary preparations.

Chapter Nineteen

Everyone was in attendance at the Season's largest ball, which made Diana even more nervous about what she and Harrow were planning to do. She'd already spotted Grenville, as well as her treacherous uncle. When all was said and done, her humiliation would be complete in their eyes. She would endure it, knowing she'd have the last laugh as a free woman of independent means.

Unfortunately, the price of attaining that long-desired goal was too high to allow her to take true joy in it anymore.

The papers had been diligent in reporting her quarrels with Harrow, and their entrance at the ball had drawn much attention. They'd parted, agreeing to meet again for the first dance, and since that moment, she'd drifted through a crowd seemingly determined to pretend she didn't exist—at least until they thought her out of earshot.

She'd anticipated as much.

An announcement was made calling everyone for the first dance. She cast about, looking for Harrow.

To her shock, however, it was *Lucas* who came to claim

her. She balked as he reached for her hand, but he was too quick and drew her close before she could escape.

His whisper at her ear was urgent. "I've spoken with Harrow. He's agreed, but you must come with me now."

"Agreed to what?"

He didn't answer but instead pulled her out onto the ballroom floor and into position for the waltz.

Though she knew nothing of any agreement between him and Harrow, something in his eyes drew her and wouldn't allow her to refuse. If this was a torment she must withstand to lend fuel to the fire when Harrow cast her out, then so be it.

At least I'll have one last dance with the man I love…

The orchestra struck up the tune, and they swung into motion. She could only look into Lucas's eyes and hope he saw her love for him in hers. Learning that he'd stayed with her after her fall, hearing Harrow describe how he'd worried over her and refused to leave until he was certain of her safety, had told her all she needed to know.

He loved her, but she'd had no choice other than breaking his heart as well as her own. Fate was capricious and cruel to give her such love only to tear it away. She must savor these last moments and commit them to memory.

Halfway through the dance, the hammer fell as Harrow appeared and tore her from Lucas's arms, eliciting from her a very genuine squeak of alarm. "I took you in and gave you everything, including my heart!" he yelled down at her. "I thought I had yours in return. You swore to me you had no love for him, but I see you lied about *that*, too!"

Her flinch was involuntary. In all the time she'd known Harrow, she'd never seen him look so enraged. He'd always been so cool and reserved, even when facing down men who'd threatened to kill him in a duel. But this red-faced, trembling man before her was entirely believable, enough so that she felt the blood leave her head.

He shook her by the shoulders. "What *other* lies have you told me?"

That's my cue. Her voice, for all its inadvertent unsteadiness, dripped with scorn. "You talk of love after you've willingly shared me with other men?" It was so strange, acting this out. It was as if Diana was no more, as if someone else stood in her place, occupying her skin.

Now it was Harrow's turn to flinch back as though she'd struck him. "I assumed you'd have told me had you not been amenable to—"

A gasp erupted from her throat, cutting him off. "How was I to object to anything you suggested when my very survival depended upon satisfying your every whim?" She raised her voice a bit more. "*Your* desires dictated my actions!"

"*My* desires? And what of yours? You *wanted* Blackthorn—a blind fool could see that much!"

Real heat flooded her face, for this was truth, not pantomime. She shook off his arm and spoke through clenched teeth, pouring all her bitterness at how she'd been repeatedly robbed of happiness into her words. "I might not have done, had *you* not invited your friends into *our* bed!"

His lips tightened into a grim line for a moment before he answered. "Don't act as though you took no pleasure in it. I may have shared your favors, but until Blackthorn, it was always something we did together. I admit I made mistakes, but I've never *once* strayed from you on my own since the night I took your maidenhead, not even with my own wife. Does that not at least deserve your loyalty, if not your love?"

A great swell of affection tightened her chest, and she had to fight to prevent it showing on her face. In front of countless witnesses of import, he'd just refuted the claims that had brought about her initial downfall in such a way as to forever call into question the integrity of the man who'd made them. She spied Grenville, who'd come to the fore to gloat over her humiliation, as he blanched and tried to press backward into the crowd. But the fox had already run among the chickens, and people nearby were already whispering and glancing at him in evident speculation.

Gathering her courage, Diana pushed on. "I loved you well enough until you made me into what everyone else already thought I was," she flung at him. Despite knowing this was all a sham, she couldn't help the tears that welled in her eyes at this statement, which was so close to the truth. "You are to blame for this rift between us, not I. Had you allowed it, I would have remained faithful."

Harrow's face took on the familiar cool indifference she'd seen him adopt so many times. "I very much doubt it," he said dully. His gaze flicked to her left, and his eyes narrowed. "Ah, Blackthorn," he said smoothly. "Come to claim your prize? You need not concern yourself that I'll make any objection if you want to use her. She's all yours, if indeed you still want the little jade." Not waiting for a reply, he again directed his speech at her. "I want you gone from my house by this time tomorrow, and I wish never to see you again."

Lucas moved in between her and Harrow, his expression hard and defiant. "Then I fear you'll need to remove yourself from London," he growled. "Because I intend to make her my wife."

Gasps—including her own—erupted all around, rippling outward in a great susurration to the far corners of the room. The floor seemed to drop from beneath Diana's feet, a faint buzzing began in her ears, and a queer sort of numbness spread from her midsection to her extremities.

What is he doing?

Turning his back on Harrow, Lucas took up her frozen hands between his own, his touch acting as an anchor, drawing her back into the sharpness of *now*. "I've thought about this for quite some time, and I know it's what I want."

He dropped to his knees before her, eliciting another mass exhalation from those watching. "Marry me, Lady Diana Haversham, and make me the happiest of men."

Astonishment robbed her of both breath and speech for several long heartbeats. "You cannot marry me," she blurted. "I'm—I'm—"

"The only woman under heaven with whom I'm willing to spend the rest of my life," he cut in. Reaching into his jacket pocket with his free hand, he pulled out a piece of parchment and held it out so she could see what was written on it. It was a special license. "We can be married tonight."

"Why are you doing this?" she whispered, shaking so hard she was surprised her bones weren't rattling against one another loud enough for the entire assembly to hear them.

"Because I love you," he said loudly enough that all those around them heard it. "More than life itself." The smile he gave her then nearly smote her to the ground with its sweetness. "I...*adore* you, Diana. Say you will become my wife?"

She looked into his shining, rain-gray eyes and knew beyond any doubt that he meant it. This was no pantomime, no charade. It was real. His love was real.

Joy born from the very deepest part of her heart filled her to bursting. She'd thought love unreliable, that people would always fail her and break her heart. *I was wrong. I was wrong!* Never had she been so happy to be wrong in her life! "Yes," she answered, tears streaming down her cheeks even as she laughed. "I accept. I will marry you."

Rising, Lucas pulled her into his embrace and in front of God and what was likely the whole of the *Ton*, including Prinny himself, kissed her.

With all the love in her overflowing heart, she answered him back in kind.

When they broke at last, Lucas again faced Harrow. All

around them, wide eyes looked between the two men. "If you're going to call me out, I'll request at least one night with my wife before facing you on the field."

Harrow's face was like a stone. "Why bother risking my life over something of no worth? She's your concern now. I wish you all the luck with your fickle-hearted bride." Turning on his heel, he strode away, the flabbergasted crowd hastily parting before him.

Diana watched him go with deepest gratitude, knowing Lucas would tell her of his plans later in privacy. Her husband-to-be offered his arm. Taking it, she ran the gauntlet past their boggle-eyed audience with a smile—a smile that, almost impossibly, stretched just a little wider as they passed her aunt and uncle, who were, like everyone else, too stunned to do anything but stare.

Epilogue

Diana strolled beside her husband, enjoying their afternoon constitutional. It was beautiful here. The sun was warm on her back, the breeze cool on her cheeks, carrying with it a hint of the flowers blooming in the hedgerow.

Lucas laughed at the spectacle ahead of them as their almost four-year-old son, Jason, chased after his new puppy, which gamboled to and fro across the path. When the rambunctious duo trundled off to have a look at the pond and see if there were any frogs to catch, Lucas put his arm around her shoulders, pulling her close. "I meant to tell you, Westing and Charlotte will be visiting us next week."

She grinned in delight. "I can hardly wait to see them again!" The pair had brushed off Society's disapproval to become their closest friends. "I also have news. I received a letter today from Mr. Lambert."

"So *that's* why you wanted me to come along on your little jaunt," he teased, shooting her an amused sidelong glance. "And how is your dear cousin?"

Her "dear cousin" was actually Harrow, who'd written them faithfully over the years under an assumed name to share happy news of his travels with René.

"He's purchased a villa in Naples, and we've been invited to holiday with them this winter."

"Really? It *would* be a damned sight warmer there than it will be here that time of year," he muttered appreciatively. "I know my father would relish the idea of keeping his grandchildren for a month or two. We should go."

The idea of going someplace where nobody looked at them with accusing eyes appealed, but the thought of leaving behind her Jason and his two-year-old sister Daphne made her chest tight. "Perhaps," she said noncommittally. "It *would* be wonderful to see them again. It's only June, so we have plenty of time to consider it."

The last time she'd laid eyes on Harrow had been at the docks in Liverpool. A week after the wedding, she and Lucas had gone there to begin their honeymoon—a sail around the peninsula and a two-month-long tour of Greece. By no coincidence, Harrow had also been at the docks with René, preparing to board a ship bound for the East Indies. That was where they'd said their final goodbyes.

How their lives had all changed since that day!

Lucas's father, although wroth over his decision to marry her, had refused to punish him, citing his own poor example as the fault. Although absolved in the eyes of Society of the original reason for having been cast out, thanks to Harrow's comment about her virginity, he'd been unable to accept a "fallen woman" as his daughter-in-law and had refused to receive her. His enmity had finally abated, however, when she'd presented him with a grandson.

Her mother-in-law had received word of their marriage with even less equanimity than his father but had likewise thawed upon Jason's arrival. The lady had also taken a lover last year, an Italian painter she'd gotten to know while having her portrait made. Her mood had since, in general, improved considerably.

Bolingbroke had never gotten over his mortification and, along with her aunt, had withdrawn from London Society entirely and retired to the country—on the other side of England. They'd never attempted to contact her.

Grenville and his wife were still in London, but that gentleman's standing had been greatly diminished by the news that his allegations regarding Diana's immorality had been false.

All in all, everything had turned out well for her. She wasn't the Society darling a duke's daughter ought to have been, but she was more than happy here in Surrey, where she and Lucas had settled upon returning from Greece. She peered at her husband's profile, marking the healthy glow of his sun-kissed face. "Do you ever regret giving up the excitement of living in London for such a quiet life as we have here?"

Stopping, he took her face between his warm, dry palms and looked deep into her eyes. "Never. There is no regret when it comes to love, save for those who choose not to have it. I'd give it all up again without hesitation to have you, Lady Blackthorn."

As he pressed her lips in a tender kiss that quickly heated with the promise of passion later tonight, Diana thanked Fate for leading her, though the path hadn't been an easy one, to this place. This was her home now, where she belonged—in Lucas's arms. And this was her life, a life of love that had proven capable of weathering any storm.

She couldn't have asked for more.

Acknowledgments

My family, for encouraging me to achieve my dreams and supporting me throughout this incredible journey.

My fantastic agent, Lane Heymont of the Tobias Literary Agency.

Erin Molta, Senior Editor at Entangled Publishing, for being amazing and helping me bring Lucas and Diana to life.

My ARWA siblings, for their unfailing support and encouragement. I wouldn't be here without y'all!

About the Author

Liana LeFey delights in crafting incendiary tales that capture the heart and the imagination, taking the reader out of the now and into another world. Liana lives in Central Texas with her dashing husband/hero, their beautiful daughter, and one spoiled-rotten feline overlord.

Discover more Amara titles...

A PROTECTOR IN THE HIGHLANDS
a *Highland Roses School* novel by Heather McCollum

Scarlet Worthington flees her home in England to Scotland to help her sister run a school for ladies. There, Scarlet begins to rebuild her confidence by recruiting a fierce Campbell warrior to teach her and the students how to protect themselves. Burned in a fierce fire, Highland warrior, Aiden Campbell, has finally healed enough to take temporary command of his clan. That's where his focus should be instead of on the feisty, beautiful Sassenach.

TEMPTING THE HIGHLAND SPY
a *Highland Hearts* novel by Tara Kingston

It had been one glorious night, and Harrison MacMasters, Highland spy, never thought to see jewel thief Grace Winters again. Now he's forced to protect her as they join together to catch a killer, even though he can't trust her with anything, especially his heart. Grace will do anything to keep her family from the poorhouse, including a pretend marriage to the one man who tempts her to make it real.

HARDEST FALL
a *Dominion* novel by Juliette Cross

Even though Bone refuses to take sides in the apocalypse, there's one job she's not willing to do for a certain demon prince. If she doesn't, her head will end up on a spike. Of course, there's a good chance we're all going to die anyway, but I will do anything to protect this fierce woman—and not just because she saved my life.